Jane Wenham-Jones is a journalist and presenter and the author of ten books. She has written for a wide range of magazines and national newspapers, including a monthly advice column for *Writing Magazine*. She is also a regular contributor to the *Isle of Thanet News*, for which she has won 'Kent Columnist of the Year', and *Kent Life*.

As a presenter, she has hosted the Romantic Novel of the Year Awards since 2011, and often pops up on radio and TV. A regular interviewer on the literary festival circuit, she has been "in conversation with" hundreds of top authors and celebrities and is a founder member of BroadstairsLit – literary events throughout the year – in the seaside town of Broadstairs, where four of her novels are set. But her major claim to fame is being the one to first coin the term "Writer's Bottom"! Strange but true…

www.janewenham-jones.com

facebook.com/JaneWenhamJonesAuthor
twitter.com/JaneWenhamJones
instagram.com/jwenhamjones
youtube.com/janewenhamjones

Also by Jane Wenham-Jones

Mum in the Middle
The Big Five O

OLD ENOUGH TO KNOW BETTER

JANE WENHAM-JONES

One More Chapter
a division of HarperCollins*Publishers* Ltd
1 London Bridge Street
London SE1 9GF
www.harpercollins.co.uk

HarperCollins*Publishers*
1st Floor, Watermarque Building, Ringsend Road
Dublin 4, Ireland

This paperback edition 2021
First published in Great Britain in ebook format
by HarperCollins*Publishers* 2021

A catalogue record of this book is available from the British Library

ISBN: 978-0-00-847549-9

Printed and bound in Great Britain by
CPI Group (UK) Ltd, Croydon CR0 4YY

Chapter One

I t has happened at last and I'm so bloody happy I can't breathe.
Every time I think about when, eventually, he leant across
the table and took my hand, I am touched with tiny shivers of joy.

All those romantic books I used to read ... so many that Mum
was worried about me. "Life's not like that really, you know..."
Yeah, yeah, yeah – she can be such a sour old bag sometimes. All
those books where women were swept off their feet by tall, strong,
handsome men, I did know they were only stories. I didn't really
think it would ever be like that for me. But oh, dear diary (that I
usually feel so stupid talking to), it is!

After all those weeks of me gazing at him and wanting him so
much, and hurting with how desperate I felt for him to respond ...
and now it turns out he feels the same! He wants to wake with me
every morning and still be there to kiss me goodnight. The women
before don't matter. This time, he knows it is absolutely right and
we are made to be together. He says he wants to love me and
cherish me and make me feel special. All he longs for – and these
were his exact words – is for me to be his. For ever...

"Well hell's bells and fancy that! Congrats, darling!"

Simon took Ellie's face in his hands and kissed her flamboyantly on both cheeks. Then he grasped her left hand and held it up to display it to the rest of their colleagues.

"After a week grappling with those noisy little bastards from Casablanca, we could do with some good news!" He raised his oversized G&T high into the air. "Here's to the forthcoming nuptials of Ellie and Tom! May he be just as gorgeous in the flesh as he looks in that photo." He looked at Ellie through lowered lashes before tossing back his dark waves of hair. "You must bring him to meet me, darling," he murmured. "Looks adorable. I rather like a bit of experience myself."

Ellie laughed, half-thrilled, half-embarrassed. She had thought she would burst if she didn't tell someone her news, but of course Simon had immediately thrown it out around the whole table and now everyone was clapping. She glanced around, glad the bar was not yet too crowded. She could feel herself blushing.

"It's so quick!" said Janine, sitting opposite and sounding envious. "You haven't even moved in yet, have you?"

Ellie shook her head. "No, but I'm going to over the bank holiday. I thought I'd wait for that three-day stretch to sort out all my stuff."

"Because you won't get another day off till October," put in Simon. "Did you know we're already at record numbers for August?"

"Yep! Lots of head-banging available!" Their boss spoke from the end of the table. Blake was the Director of Studies at the Margate Academy – a centre of excellence in the teaching of English as a Foreign Language at all levels, as it said in the brochure – where they all worked. Groans and laughter rippled around the table. Head-banging was their nickname for working what was effectively a double teaching shift during their busiest times, which many of them, needing the extra money, jumped at.

"So, when are you getting hitched?" Janine leant forward, pushing her long, dark hair back behind her ears. "Has Tom been married before? Is your mum pleased or does she—?"

"No," interrupted Ellie firmly. "And of course!" She took a mouthful of her Peroni. It was a staff tradition to go for drinks on a Friday night – it was when they all caught up on the personal stuff after five days of waving to each other as they whizzed from staffroom to classroom, clutching folders and student registers. Ellie felt as though she was always running against the clock at work – her timekeeping had never been a strong point – and she always looked forward to sitting back with Simon and Janine, Lisa and Andy, and the others, sharing how wrung-out and exhausted they all felt, swapping their worst student moments, and moaning about school trips and whatever they had lined up for the following week.

Today though, she wasn't tired at all. Energy hummed beneath her skin; flickers of pleasure danced through her as she glanced at the little diamond catching the light. "It's not much," Tom had said, "but it's a symbol. We'll get you a bigger one later." He had smiled at her in that way that made her want to hug herself.

"We probably won't actually get married for ages," Ellie said to Janine now. "But Tom wanted me to have a ring so I'd know he was there for the long haul, he said—"

Janine nodded longingly. "You're lucky."

"Yes, I am." Ellie tried not to sound smug as she smiled sympathetically at her friend. At twenty-seven, Janine was four years older than Ellie and hadn't had a boyfriend in all the time Ellie had been teaching at the school. There was an older Turkish student she used to spend time with (even though personal relationships with the customers were frowned upon from a great height) and Ellie had found her in tears when he left, but there'd been nobody permanent.

"I know we haven't been together that long," Ellie went on. "But it just feels right to move in with him. And, well, I didn't expect this before we were even living together but" – she stopped and turned the ring again so she could see it glitter – "I've never felt more sure of anything. Everything about Tom is … just perfect. Now I know why I've never really clicked with partners my own age…"

On the other side of Janine, Anna Ward, the Accommodation Manager, gave her a small smile. She looked tired. "What does Tom do?" she asked, taking a sip of her water.

Ellie smiled back at the older woman. Anna was in her fifties and had worked at the school longer than anyone. She was in charge of finding host families to accommodate the hundreds of students who came to the academy, and was known for her ability to remain unflappable, even when students went missing, got arrested, or managed to comprehensively flood the house where they were lodging, all of which had happened in the last six months.

Anna was also the one to whom they turned to bring her own brand of calm to the situation when Aaron, the eccentric owner, was kicking off. She was tall and elegant and could sound almost haughty when she spoke on the phone, but Ellie liked her a lot, finding her kind and motherly. She would sit back and smile, looking almost bemused, while the rest of them got louder and more raucous. They were all fond of her.

"Tom has his own business," Ellie told her proudly. "Waste disposal, skips, that sort of thing. And some property development," she added, as she saw Janine's nose wrinkle. "He's doing really well," she added defensively. "You should see his flat."

She thought about the stripped wooden floors and white walls of the large, airy rooms overlooking Turner Contemporary; the brushed concrete and steel kitchen, the modern black sofas, the huge, masculine bed…

Usually on a Friday Ellie was one of the last to leave. Sometimes, she and Simon and Janine and a couple of the others would go for a curry and make a night of it. But today she wanted to get away. She was meeting Tom at 8 p.m. and her heart thudded with anticipation. She nudged the bag of clothes at her feet, checking it was still there, remembering the way she'd casually asked Tom if she could leave her toothbrush and moisturiser in his bathroom cabinet. It was after he'd said he wanted her to stay again – he was going to take her to a new restaurant that had opened in Ramsgate. "Meet me here and leave the car," he'd said. "You can go to work from here in the morning."

But still her heart had been in her mouth, in case she was pushing it too quickly. She wanted it to work out so badly that her nerves jangled.

Now she'd added cleanser and deodorant, perfume, and the conditioner she liked. She'd been careful to keep her portion of the shelf tidy. When she'd left her silky robe on the back of the bathroom door, she'd pretended she'd forgotten it.

"You're practically living here anyway," he'd said, when he told her, laughing, that she may as well move in. She hadn't said anything at home yet. She had seen her mother, Clare's, lips fold in when she'd said she wouldn't be home again tonight. But she hadn't commented. Nor looked particularly pleased when Ellie announced she'd be at home all weekend as Tom was going on a stag-do to Benidorm.

Ellie shook back her blonde hair. Her mum could hardly object, could she? And it would give her more time to fuss over her beloved Josh. Ellie inwardly rolled her eyes. She loved her brother, but God he could be annoying...

"Oh dear, we *are* lovesick..." Beside her, Simon gave her a small, disapproving poke. "You're miles away, darling... I was just saying, are we going for a third?" He held a ten-pound note between his fingers. "Who's in for the next one?" They always ran a kitty – it was the only fair way to

6

do it and there were still a couple of fivers and a heap of change in the middle of the table.

Ellie shook her head. "I'm going. I'll see you Monday." She stood up and blew kisses around the table. "Have a good one!"

"Can you be in by eight?" Blake reminded her. "New intake, tests to do…"

"Yep!" Ellie nodded. "I know!" They were lucky with Blake. He was good to work for, understanding when students were difficult, and fair about the way he allocated classes. He didn't always come for a drink with them on a Friday – sometimes he was ensconced with Aaron until all hours – but when he did, he was easy company, unlike your usual sort of boss. Not that Ellie had had many to compare him with. She really mustn't be late on Monday.

As she picked up her bag, Anna got up too. She'd been unusually silent during the drinks, only speaking to ask Ellie the question about Tom's work, saying little to anyone else. Ellie had heard Nick, a teacher new to the school, ask her if she was OK. But now Anna waited for Ellie to finish her goodbyes and walked alongside her to the door.

As they reached the pavement, Ellie smiled at her. "See you next week." But Anna suddenly laid a hand on her arm.

She looked flushed, and for a moment Ellie wondered if she was drunk, before remembering the older woman had barely touched her glass of Prosecco and had asked for a glass of water when the second round was ordered.

"Are you all right?" Ellie asked, frowning.

Anna appeared to take a deep breath. "I was listening to you talking," she said. "About your new chap. About Tom."

Ellie waited.

"The one you're going to move in with," said Anna, as though it needed defining. "And it seems" – she looked at Ellie's finger where the little diamond glinted in the light from the windows behind them – "marry."

There was a pause and Ellie felt a frisson of alarm. What was Anna going to tell her? She knew so many people – all the hundreds of families who took in students from the school. Ellie had walked through Margate with her and she was always being greeted or was stopping to say hello to someone. Now she was looking so serious. For a horrible moment Ellie thought Anna was going to tell her that Tom was already married, or was a convicted criminal. But Anna didn't know Tom. Did she? Or was that why she'd asked about his job? To check if it was the same man she was thinking of…

"Well, one day," said Ellie uncertainly. "Not now…"

"I know how exciting it is," Anna went on, in her cultured tones. "Believe me, I do. And I'm not saying this to be cruel, but because you are such an exceptionally bright and beautiful young woman."

She stopped and Ellie frowned again. Anna again briefly touched her arm. "I know you won't listen to my advice – and you'll probably be angry or upset. After all, it's none of my business. But if you were my daughter…"

She stopped again, then seemed to gather herself to continue. Ellie wasn't sure in the dim light of the bar doorway if perhaps there were tears in her eyes.

"I do think of you as my friend," Anna said, pausing as Ellie nodded in agreement. "So I will take the risk and give you the only advice that in all conscience I can."

Anna stopped again and gave a small, sad smile.

"Oh, Ellie. Don't do it!"

Chapter Two

"Why are you doing it?"

Ellie's mother shoved a lump of parmesan into the grater she was holding. She knew she sounded too sharp and tried to soften her tone. "It's a big thing," she said, pushing down the metal cover. "It's not a game. He's so much older than you and—"

She stopped as her daughter gave a loud hiss of annoyance. Ellie stood in the doorway of their kitchen in cut-off jeans and a T-shirt, her feet bare, her long blonde hair loose on her shoulders. She looked, thought Clare, with something that felt strangely like rage, astonishingly beautiful, her green eyes wide with indignation, her skin glowing, her full lips enhanced by a slick of pink gloss. She was shaking her head at her mother.

"I cannot believe you," she said, her voice rising. "Are you listening to yourself? What kind of hypocrite are you?"

Clare began to turn the handle of the grater, watching as soft slivers of cheese fell like snowflakes into the bowl in

11

front of her. She kept her breathing even. When she glanced back, Ellie was glaring at her.

"You were only a year older than me when you met Dad, and he was nearly forty-four which, unless counting has changed dramatically in the ensuing years, makes him twenty years older than you." Ellie glared some more. "Tom is only forty-two, so our age difference is only nineteen years. So, what is the fucking problem?"

"Don't swear at me," said Clare, more for something to reply with than because she cared about Ellie's language.

"Well?" Her daughter had folded her arms. "How can you criticise me?"

Clare kept grating. It was a good question. It shouldn't make a difference how old Ellie's boyfriend was but somehow it did. "You've only known him five minutes. What's the rush to move in? And as for getting—"

"Uh, *hello*? You moved in together within months! You told me you did. As soon as you'd got shot of Claudia," Ellie added with an edge.

"There were problems already," said Clare. "Their break-up was nothing to do with me."

"Whatever." Ellie moved in closer and leant her hands on the end of the kitchen island as Clare adjusted the diminishing lump of cheese and turned the handle once more. "But as soon as they'd sold, you got another place together."

"We didn't get married."

"You had a *baby*!"

"That was later." Clare put the grater down as Ellie leant forward.

"You were pregnant with me before his divorce even came through," her daughter said menacingly. "You didn't hang about."

"This isn't about me."

"Well it should be. You married someone with a bigger age gap than we've got and you're being completely horrible because I want to do the same."

"I'm just concerned." Clare tried to keep her voice even but she wanted to explode. *You're never here now*, she wanted to cry. *Nothing is how it used to be. I'm worried about you getting stuck in a mistake, about your brother being unhappy, about your father and...*

She leant down and pulled a large earthenware dish from the cupboard next to the hob.

"Why?" Ellie's voice was still hard. "You did it and you're still together. However many..." She stopped to do the maths. "Twenty-six years, isn't it?"

Exactly!

"Not quite," Clare said briskly. "It was different then," she went on inadequately, unable to scream as she wanted to: *and maybe I don't want that for you!*

"Well, Daddy doesn't care how old he is—"

He absolutely does.

"Or about the age gap."

But I do. Now.

Ellie suddenly smiled. "Do you remember when that awful woman asked him? Dad was brilliant, wasn't he?"

"He was quite rude."

"Are you talking about me?" Rupe appeared in the doorway, large and imposing, with his shock of iron-grey

13

hair and defined features. He stood and surveyed his wife and daughter for a moment and then strode forward and put an arm around Ellie's shoulders. "Who have I been abusive to this time?" He picked up the last small nugget of parmesan and popped it into his mouth.

Ellie giggled. "That woman who came round with Auntie Ange – the one you didn't like. She asked whether you'd been conscious of the age gap, being married to a much younger woman and you said, 'Yes, I think about it every day. It's wonderful. Women of my own age have such scraggy necks...'" Ellie went off into peals of laughter.

"She was dreadful." Rupe looked pleased. "I don't know where your sister finds them..." He grinned at his wife. "And you do still have a very fine neck."

"Well, that's the main thing," said Clare tightly. She picked up the bowl of cheese and dropped a handful of it into the béchamel sauce that was simmering on the hob, reaching out for a wooden spoon and beginning to stir.

Rupe took a bottle of red from the floor-to-ceiling wine rack in the corner, and opened a drawer for a corkscrew. Clare looked pointedly at the clock but both Rupe and Ellie affected not to notice. "Want one, poppet?" said Rupe to his daughter, as he took his favourite glass from the cupboard. "Sun is damn near over the yardarm."

Ellie shook her head. "I'll have one with dinner. What time are we eating, Mum?"

"After 7.30," Clare said shortly. "When Josh gets home from work."

Rupe gave a bark of laughter. "Work!"

"He's spending all day driving and delivering, and

14

getting paid for it," snapped Clare. "What would you call it?"

"I'd call it time he got a proper job!" said Rupe triumphantly. "Why are you in such a bad mood?"

Ellie immediately jumped in. "She's being all sanctimonious about the fact that Tom is older than me and I'm going to move in with him." She looked at her father defiantly. "And then we will probably get married."

"Show Dad your ring then," said Clare. "If it's only *probably*, why are you wearing one?"

"He bought it for me as a symbol of his commitment," said Ellie, enunciating slowly, as if her mother might need to lip-read. "When we're ready to set a date, he says I can choose a bigger one."

"This the one with the scrap business?"

"Yes, Dad, Tom. Tom, who I have been seeing for seven weeks… You know it is. It's not scrap exactly. He hires out skips."

"Lot of money in that."

"Which is all that matters," put in Clare drily. Rupe, sipping at his wine, appeared not to hear her.

"And he has rental property." The pride in Ellie's voice was unmistakable. "He started off with just one flat that he got really cheap because it was damp, and now he's got nine…"

"All sounds very capitalist and elitist," put in Clare, looking at her daughter meaningfully, remembering a time when Ellie would have dismissed anyone fitting that description out of hand.

"It's called being an entrepreneur," said Rupe. "And you've not done so badly out of it!"

Ellie flushed. "Tom's not like that. He's very compassionate… He's just lost thousands of pounds, after these awful tenants ran up arrears and wouldn't move out. Tom says he let them move in, even though they were on housing benefit and didn't have the full deposit."

"Only got himself to blame then." Rupe was filling his glass.

"The flat was empty – the letting agent said not to take them, but Tom felt sorry for them. And he needed the rent. He says he's had some really good tenants on benefits before."

"Fancy that," said Clare. She knew she sounded waspish and felt unreasonably annoyed with Ellie for making her like that.

"You're always going on about other people being judgemental," said Ellie hotly now. "But you are the worst of them all. You haven't even met Tom. He's really kind. He says he won't discriminate!"

Rupe stepped across the room and put his arm round Ellie again. "Bring him round, poppet," he said soothingly as Clare said nothing. "Does he like a drink?"

Ellie nodded, throwing a disparaging glance at her mother before smiling at Rupe. "Yes. He drinks. Not as much as you, of course."

Rupe gave a roar of laughter and stretched out an arm to include his wife in his embrace. "Nobody," he said, with satisfaction, "drinks as much as I do!"

That was true, thought Clare sourly, allowing him to

squeeze her shoulder briefly before she slid away. Or it was, at least, among their circle of family and friends. Rupe had always drunk an astonishing amount and since he rarely seemed to suffer any ill-effects – he'd certainly never admitted to a hangover in nearly three decades – she had long given up remonstrating with him.

The last time he'd been called into the surgery for a well-man appointment, he'd reported with glee that the nurse had looked visibly shaken at the number of units he was consuming and had insisted he go home with the number of an addiction service, but Rupe remained unrepentant. "Nothing wrong with my liver,' he had declared – a fact that was borne out by the blood-test results a week later. "And I could stop if I wanted to. But I don't want to!" he'd added. And that was that.

"As long as you're nice," Clare used to say, but his mood no longer seemed to be affected. He would ramble a bit if he had too much Côte du Rhône, might get sentimental, make occasional grand gestures of generosity, or reminisce in a way that had more than a dash of fantasy, but since he'd sold his disaster recovery business and retired, he was no longer so tightly wired or quick to irritation. He no longer rapped out instructions as though Clare was his secretary, but then he no longer needed to.

She no longer kept his diary or made the travel arrangements. There were no more clients for them to entertain, and she did not have to spend her days thinking up menus, or booking the latest restaurants, bracing herself for long evenings making small talk with clients' wives with whom she had nothing in common. Or far more rarely, clients' husbands...

She had counted down the days to when the sale of the company had gone through and, after an initial handover period, they had been able to walk away. She had wondered how Rupe would cope with the sudden end of it all, but it had been she who had seemed to feel the most restless and ... uneasy. She couldn't get used to his constant presence in the house. The way he would stand in the door of the kitchen and watch her cooking, or worse, spend all afternoon using every pot they owned and cook himself.

If only he would take up golf or do the garden, but Rupert had little interest in anything horticultural apart from his annual foray into growing runner beans. He would occasionally cut the grass with bad grace, but she and the gardener did the bulk of it. At least he'd started going out walking each day since retiring, which gave her an hour or two of space. But still she felt stifled; they had developed a strange awkwardness with each other – or was it just her? Ellie had already told her off for being "horrible" to him.

When Rupe came into the kitchen, she felt her insides tense. At times, it was all she could do not to screech at him to go away. Rupe was drinking more than ever because he had all day to do it in, and when he drank he became expansive and wanted to discuss the issues of the day with her. Once they had congratulated themselves on never running out of things to say. When had she started longing for him to shut the fuck up?

She was jolted from her thoughts by Ellie speaking directly to her.

"I thought we could have a Sunday lunch..." Her daughter's voice had softened and suddenly Ellie looked young and vulnerable. "Maybe invite Figs and the gang." She turned and looked at her father appealingly. "I think you'll like Tom." She turned back to Clare. "Mum, why are you being like this?"

Clare felt a piercing pang of remorse. "Well, we could," she began carefully. "We've not had a proper family lunch for ages."

"Don't invite that other bloody sister," said Rupe.

"Of course I will." Clare began to brush the dish with olive oil. "I can't leave her out."

"We could have Gran too." Ellie was smiling.

"I think probably—" Clare began, but Ellie's phone was ringing and she grabbed it and disappeared from the room. "Hello!" they heard her crying joyfully as her feet pounded up the stairs.

"What *have* you got against him?" Rupe took a gulp of his wine. "I'm the one who's the miserable bastard – you usually love everyone."

"I don't know." Clare concentrated on layering the dish with sheets of pasta. "I've just got a bad feeling."

"Well let's take a look at him and see. She's a sensible girl; if she thinks he's OK he probably is." Rupe drank a bit more. "And if he's not good enough for her, I'll tell him to sling his hook and not darken my precious little princess's doorstep ever again..."

Clare gave a wry smile. Rupe was only half-joking. Ellie could do little wrong in her father's eyes, while Josh, sadly, could do little right. Mainly because Ellie adored her father and would defend any amount of his bad behaviour and Josh had recently called him a bigot.

"OK, but not a big lunch. Just us first."

"Suits me – I'm not mad keen to see all your bloody relatives." Rupe gave her a wolfish grin. "You know I only do it for you…"

"Yes, you're all heart." Clare gave him a small shove to move him away from the hob. "I need to get at that."

When Ellie returned, Clare was spooning out the last layer of ragu. She put the final sheets of lasagne on top and turned to look at her daughter.

"Dad and I have just been saying, why don't you bring Tom round for a drink with just us first? Or supper," she continued, as Ellie said nothing. "And do the whole family lunch thing later." Clare kept her voice light. "We don't want to give him too much of a baptism of fire, do we?"

———————

Clare left Rupe shouting at the 10 o'clock news and went back to the kitchen. Josh was still sitting at the table at his laptop, a bowl of cold pasta and a cup of tea beside him. She heard him swear and then the lid of the computer came crashing down. "Fuck," he said again. "Fucking bastards."

Clare picked up the kettle and moved towards the tap. "What's happened?" she asked calmly.

"I've just spent *all* day, every time I've had a break, making up answers to their stupid questions," Josh said furiously. "And now I've been given a timed test and I've failed it. Why didn't they set the test *first*? Why do I have to spend my life saying when I've been part of a team, and when I've used my fucking initiative – which is all bollocks anyway – and then they turn me down in ten seconds flat?"

"Oh Josh. Was it Maths? English?"

"Neither. One of those what-would-you-do-if things. Like, if you were a manager and half your work force killed themselves, or the presentation you'd been preparing for weeks clashed with your granny's funeral, or your boss is consistently late. Would you a) shoot him, b) be late yourself c) report him to the chief executive, d) cut your own fucking throat…"

Clare smiled. "You'll get there," she said, as she always did.

"But I won't, will I? There's a job here that would be just brilliant – it's PR and marketing for all the big car manufacturers. You know how much I know about cars. But I won't even get an interview because I've got the wrong degree and I've no experience. But I can write about features and benefits. I could do it just as well as—"

"Get your hair cut, put on a suit, and go and see them." Rupe was in the doorway. He crossed to the bottle of red that stood open on the work surface.

Josh gave a long-drawn-out sigh. "See who? It's an online application – with hundreds of questions. It will all be sorted by computer. They'll see my degree is in accountancy and finance and reject me straightaway." He shot his father a look. "I should never have done it."

"It's the money men who run everything," said Rupe, refilling his glass.

21

"Oh really?" His son's voice was laced with sarcasm. "You've never said that before."

"It's a good degree to have," Rupe continued. "You should have finished your training."

"I hated it and I was crap at it too."

"Of course you weren't."

"I was useless. If I hadn't left, they would have sacked me."

"I'd sack you too with that attitude."

"*Stop!*" Clare glared at Rupe. "Josh wasn't cut out to be an accountant and we didn't want him to do something that would make him unhappy, did we?"

"No of course not, but—"

"Something will come along," Clare cut across Rupe and smiled at Josh. "Don't give up."

"You can easily find who's heading up that company online," said Rupe, "and then phone his secretary. When I was your age I banged on dozens of doors—"

"Yes, you've told me. And I've told you, that was back in the dark ages. The world doesn't work like that anymore!" Josh picked up the laptop and strode out of the room.

Behind him, Rupe pulled a face. "He's too negative," he told Clare. "He won't try. It might all be on computers these days, but when you get down to basics, business still operates the way it always has. Bosses need people with guts and determination, people who think around a problem instead of giving up at the first hurdle."

Clare sighed. "Yes, but he's right – he has to get past the software filters first…"

Rupe carried on as if she hadn't spoken. "He thinks I don't know anything because I got my jobs decades ago, but he forgets I've only just come out of the workplace. That I ran a team. They might be doing it all by algorithms but I am telling you, when you scratch below the surface, *people are still the same…*"

He looked at Clare as if challenging her to disagree.

She shrugged, a familiar frustration rising in her chest. "Maybe," she said shortly. Turning away from him as she added silently: *not all of us…*

Chapter Three

Anna clicked off the phone and walked back into the sitting room where her husband was sitting in his big wing armchair, his feet on a footstool, reading. He looked up expectantly.

"They can't come this weekend," she said, willing her voice to stay level, even though the disappointment was wrenching. "They're both exhausted. Stevie says they think Tay's teething and neither of them has had any sleep for days. He's got him now while Fen has a lie-down."

"Oh." Jeremy's voice was flat. "Are you upset?" His tone suggested he would rather she wasn't.

Anna shook her head, feeling the tears behind her eyes. "Can't be helped. They'll come another time. Stevie says they're looking forward to some sea air."

She busied herself picking up an empty coffee mug and a discarded newspaper. "Probably just as well," she said with forced brightness. "I need to go into school on Sunday

25

now – we've 240 students arriving." She sighed. "Aaron is predicting some drama or other."

"What?"

"I said," Anna raised her voice slightly, "there'll be things to sort out. They need me there." She paused. "You said you were going to phone up about a hearing test."

"You said you wouldn't mumble."

"I do not mumble. I speak in exactly the same way that I've been speaking for the last thirty-seven years." Anna looked at him in exasperation. "Since you first told me that if ever you became one of those annoying old people who cupped their ears and said *what?* I must make you get a hearing aid."

"Pah." Jeremy looked sceptical. "You worked last weekend too. Is that why you're home early?"

"I thought I'd get things ready for tomorrow..." She stopped and swallowed. She hadn't realised how much she had been hanging onto the thought of her son and daughter-in-law and baby grandson being here. She'd bought chicken and chorizo for Stevie's favourite dish, some gorgeous-smelling bath oil so Fen could have a long soak while Anna held six-month-old Tay, his little fingers wrapped tightly around hers...

"You usually go to the pub." Jeremy's voice had taken on a slightly querulous note.

"Well, I wanted to get home." Everything was done really; she could have gone for a drink as usual. She couldn't tell Jeremy that she felt awkward with one of her colleagues now. He wouldn't even remember who Ellie was. She'd tried to explain to the younger woman why she'd felt compelled to warn her, to make sure she really knew what she was getting into. Had told her the story of how she had been swept off her feet by Jeremy when she was even younger than Ellie.

Anna looked at her husband who seemed so small these days, in that great chair he'd had for years. His neck appeared to have shortened, gone in on itself. His cheeks had taken on a sunken look. She could still clearly visualise him when he'd been upright and strong – running and playing squash, priding himself on his ability to arm-wrestle. He had always seemed so invincible. As if old age wouldn't dare get him.

She'd described it all to Ellie: that she'd been nursing when Jeremy had first walked onto the ward, a group of student doctors crowding behind him. He'd been forty-nine, a divorced consultant cardiologist, who'd invited twenty-two-year-old Anna out to dinner to share his fiftieth birthday – and married her a year later. "I had never been more certain of anything in my whole life," she'd said to Ellie, and Ellie had nodded and smiled and thanked her for caring.

She had listened politely, but Anna could tell she didn't really want to hear about Jeremy in his seventies when the osteoarthritis had started to set in or how he was now, in his mid-eighties, his mobility so restricted that he barely left the house.

"It was wonderful when I was thirty, even forty – we never thought about it," she'd explained. "But gradually…"

Ellie had given her a brief, firm hug but Anna had noticed she hadn't stopped by Anna's office for a chat all week, and when Nick had asked Anna if she was coming for a drink, and she'd shaken her head, Ellie hadn't tried to persuade her...

"Will you stop it all when you're sixty?" Jeremy was speaking more loudly too. "Are you going to retire?"

"No – I've told you that already."

"We don't need the money."

"It comes in quite handy." Anna kept her voice mild. "And we might really be glad of it – if we get to a point when you need—"

"I'm not going anywhere. The only way I'm leaving this house is feet first, in my box."

"—people to come in."

He said it every time. His other favourite was to declare that when he'd had enough, he would finish himself off with pills and whisky. What pills, or where he would get them from, had never been specified. But he kept the whisky stocks plentiful. Just in case.

"And I enjoy going to work," Anna said.

"Hmm."

She felt guilty in the mornings sometimes, when she swung out of the front door as he hobbled painfully around the kitchen behind her, but as she drove her car slowly along the narrow road, glimpsing through the gaps in the houses the sea glistening beyond the shingle, she felt herself breathe out. On the half-hour drive from Whitstable to Margate, she became Anna again – a woman who still needed other people and intellectual stimulation, who was still capable of feeling energised and vibrant, of feeling somewhere, deep inside – despite the crow's feet and small aches and pains that went with her fifty-nine years – young.

She smiled to herself, recalling the look of surprise on her newest colleague's face when she'd said she was nearly sixty. "No way," Nick had said. He himself, he told her, was thirty-eight, though his floppy fair hair and rangy limbs gave him an almost boyish look and he could have been younger. He'd come home from two years of teaching in Bahrain, where he'd gone after his marriage broke up, and said he would have put Anna in her late forties. She knew this was flattery – but she also knew she was holding up quite well for her age. She was tall – almost as tall as Nick – and years of yoga and Pilates had had kept her spine straight and her limbs reasonably toned.

She took long walks at weekends and often on Fridays too when she left the car and walked to the station, and then further at the other end to get from the train to school, so she could have two or even three drinks instead of one. She enjoyed those times sitting around the long pub table with the teachers; they were all younger than her but accepted her into their circle with warmth and humour, often confiding their problems.

Perhaps it had been wrong of her to say anything to Ellie – it had felt like a moment of recklessness at the time – but she'd still been driven by a deep urge to point out the realities.

She recognised the glow in Ellie's eyes, but suppose, as he aged, her Tom also became insular and cranky? Suppose his conversation became more and more limited because he wouldn't see anyone or go anywhere, until they were reduced to discussing only their adult children and the front page of *The Times*, which, mercifully, he still read each morning.

Jeremy wasn't really interested in anything Anna did at work. Years ago he'd come to the Christmas party, but now he wouldn't even go for festive drinks next door. He said it was too difficult – they wouldn't want him clonking about on his Zimmer frame and taking up space – but really, he just didn't want to make the effort to converse anymore…

She couldn't remember the last time they'd gone anywhere that hadn't been a medical appointment or an election.

But of course, Ellie wouldn't want to visualise a world like that, just as Anna hadn't when she was young and they'd worked hard and socialised even harder. In the days when life had been a long round of dinners out and theatre dates and parties and – even when the children were small and Jeremy was at the hospital twelve hours a day – he still took them on wonderful holidays and would surprise her with a babysitter and a lavish London lunch. She tried to remember when it had started to fall apart.

Was it when they'd started sleeping in different rooms, after the kids had left home and Jeremy began to snore and get up in the night? Or when he'd finally retired from everything, even the research, and withdrawn into himself, looking pained if anyone came to the house.

She stood in front of him. "Are you hungry?"

"Not really."

She wasn't either. She'd had a sandwich at her desk at lunchtime and the last of the Quality Street that a grateful family had given her after she'd rehomed an awkward Russian and sent them an easy-going Spaniard instead.

There were salmon fillets in the fridge along with all the ingredients for the meals she'd planned for her visiting family, but she'd had a dull feeling in her stomach since the phone call.

"Shall we have cheese?" She tried to sound encouraging. Jeremy was thin and needed to eat.

"All right. Open a bottle of claret."

There didn't seem much point laying the table. Anna put cheddar and Stilton (for him) and Boursin and Manchego (for her) on a tray with crackers and the butter dish. Stevie loved cheese, and she'd got St Agur and Époisses de Bourgogne and Brie as well. She'd wandered around the new deli in Margate's old town, enjoying choosing a portion of this and that, piling her basket with packages, imagining her eldest son's appreciative grin as she brought out a huge board decorated with grapes (only she and Fen would eat them) plus celery for Jeremy who insisted on it and then barely ate two inches of a stem before leaving the rest to rot.

The compost bin at the end of the long, narrow garden was full almost entirely with browning celery that Jeremy always wanted in the house but never ate, and green sprouting potatoes.

Jeremy's contribution to the running of the household was internet shopping – he often missed off things she'd written on the list but he never failed to order endless potatoes as well as a glut of bacon. That sometimes went green too. He didn't eat much at all of anything anymore.

"Have we got pickled onions?"

"Of course."

Anna rose from the sofa and went down the long hallway to the kitchen, opening up the big cupboard and grabbing the pickled onions and the jar of Branston pickle.

As she went back into the room, Jeremy gave her a crooked smile. "You know me so well."

She smiled back. "I do."

They lapsed into silence, the low coffee table between them, as they both cut cheese and sipped at wine. It was not yet 8 p.m.

"We could watch something," Anna said. "Shall we look at the TV guide?"

"It's all rubbish, isn't it?"

"Not all of it. You liked that drama about the prison officer. We could look for a film on Netflix…"

But Jeremy was already shaking his head. "I'll finish my book until it's the news. Are they going to sack that idiot?"

Anna shrugged. "I've not caught up with anything today." Sometimes she read the papers in the staffroom at lunchtime – often the lunchtime news was on the TV screen in the corner – but today, with the huge intake looming, she'd not left her office.

"He's hopeless."

She knew he was talking about the current home secretary who was hanging onto his job by his fingernails after handling yet another post-Brexit immigration crisis with appalling crassness.

She nodded. "It's all a mess."

"Thatcher wouldn't have stood for it."

Anna didn't reply. She remembered when Margaret

Thatcher was Prime Minister. Jeremy referred to her as "that bloody woman" and disagreed with everything she did without exception. Recently, after reading a series of political memoirs from elder statesman, he had become almost misty-eyed about "when we had proper politicians" and had formed a deep attachment to both John Major and Michael Heseltine, both of whom he had once loathed.

"You'll be praising Ann Widdecombe next," she said eventually.

"Never!" said Jeremy. "Of all the blind fools who went for Brexit…"

Anna found herself drifting as Jeremy went into a well-worn diatribe. Her mind turned back to her son and his family, but the odd word – *Boris* and *bus* and *exchange rate* – punctuated her thoughts and she gave the occasional nod. She knew Jeremy neither expected nor wanted a response. He just liked to hear himself say it, and she was his only sounding board.

She thought about her son Stephen and his partner Fen, exhausted with her baby grandson, and wished, as she always did, that they could be here in Whitstable where she could help them, instead of two hours away. They talked about moving back to the coast sometime but Anna knew it wouldn't be for years. Both had demanding jobs in the capital and St Albans was only half an hour by train…

Jeremy had gone quiet as Anna rose to collect the plates. She stopped in front of him. "Do you want anything else?"

"Only a whisky."

Anna placed a small crystal tumbler in front of him and went back to the kitchen to slot cutlery into the dishwasher without resentment. She did more and more for him but she didn't really mind that. They'd always had a fairly traditional marriage where she did the washing and he put the bins out. Except that now, she had to lug the rubbish about as well. That in itself didn't matter.

When the boys were young, she'd occasionally shouted that she did everything around here – that they all treated her as a drudge. But now, those far-off days of noisy family meals and debates – Jeremy reading aloud from the newspaper, calling out crossword clues, and making jokes about her cooking before they all watched a TV drama or film, or even, like the decent, middle-class family they were, played Scrabble or Monopoly – felt like some sort of heaven.

Anna looked at the cat flap in the back door, wishing it would rattle open and Nigel, their large black cat, would shove his head through. Even if he had his latest prey clamped in his jaws. She hadn't seen him yet this evening but there'd been another mouse head in Jeremy's slipper this morning. Anna missed the cat when he didn't appear, as if, she thought wryly, he were one of her children.

She could go out with her friends more often, but it seemed mean, when she'd been away all day, to leave Jeremy on his own even longer.

She took a deep breath. "Brace up!" she told herself sternly. There was nothing stopping her finding something to put on the TV. She too had a stack of books waiting to be read. If she wanted to talk, Jeremy would have plenty to say once they'd watched *News at Ten*. There was no need to feel lonely. Jeremy was in the next room. Just metres away.

Anna sat down at the small kitchen table and felt in its drawer for the packet of cigarettes she'd sworn not to touch today.

The silence wrapped around her and squeezed at her heart.

Chapter Four

C lare took a long breath and drank in the stillness. The house was large enough to mean that you often couldn't hear the others in it, but you could always feel them. It was strange how the atmosphere changed so dramatically when everyone had gone out and it was just her, walking up the stairs in blissful silence.

The kids were at work and Rupe – after an infuriatingly long breakfast during which he'd decided to make porridge and had driven her insane with a running commentary on his methodology until she'd snapped, "It's fucking oats, Rupert, not Heston's foaming beetroot curd," at which he'd looked blank – had finally gone out for his daily constitutional.

She had an hour before she was due at the charity shop where she volunteered two afternoons a week, and really she should be prodding the chicken she was going to cook this evening – Tom was coming to supper and Ellie had been very particular about what she wanted Clare to make for him – but instead she was wandering from room to room, just relieved to be on her *own* at last. It felt as if she'd had no solitude for days.

She stopped in the doorway of the small upstairs room that had been her "office". It needed a dust. She could see the film across the computer screen from here, picked up by the sun coming through the single window.

In the beginning she'd worked here so she could be with the children. Later, Rupe had wanted her in the company's office in the mornings and she'd come back in the afternoons to be in position for after-school. But gradually, even when the kids were old enough not to need her here every minute of the day, she had settled back into a rhythm of doing her main work from home. It was easier to concentrate on the books and invoicing without Rupe's voice resounding in her ears – you could hear him wherever you went – or the distractions of their staff coming and going.

She could create her spreadsheets in peace here and manage the various logistics by email and phone. As the years went on, she only popped into their increasingly cramped offices behind a shop front near the station when she really had to. The new owner was planning on moving them to a unit on the new industrial estate behind Westwood Cross and if she were him, she would have done too.

It was fine when the team were out seeing clients but if they all ended up back at base at the same time, there wasn't room to swing a cat. But Rupe had resisted upgrading. He went to the clients' premises when meetings were required, or took them out to dinner. She looked at the old work phone lying on the desk that she really should get rid of now the contract had been cancelled. Josh had said she'd get fifty quid for it if she took it to the repair place in the high street.

She'd longed for this time when the business had gone and she could make the rest of her life whatever she wanted it to be. Why did she feel so empty now it had happened? Was she someone who needed to work? Rupe would say they didn't need the money now, but...

She'd looked around at jobs when the sale first completed. The only ones she saw that she could have done were a position as a bookkeeper – for which she had no formal qualifications even though she'd been doing it for decades – and a hotel receptionist. And wouldn't they want someone young and lovely for that – looking more like Ellie than her? Anyway, did she really want to kowtow to a load of weekend visitors? She'd liked the cut and thrust of growing their business – in the beginning at any rate. Handing out room keys wasn't really going to cut it...

She pulled the door of the room to behind her. If only they could think of a business Josh could run. Rupe had been disparaging when she'd suggested it. Said Josh wasn't "hungry" enough but she knew her son simply hadn't yet found what he could be passionate about. Or at least enjoy...

She peered through the open door into his bedroom. The desk was a mess of paper and cables. A Waitrose padded jacket was flung over the chair. His laptop was lying in the middle of the crumpled duvet, next to sheets of scribbled writing. Picking them up, Clare saw they were notes for a job application. Something about obstacles and challenges. Josh had crossed it all through in thick black pen, as if losing patience with his musings. As she turned the paper over in her hands, he'd written FUCK IT in bold letters to confirm it.

Clare automatically straightened the duvet and plumped up his pillows. She felt a sudden tug, like a physical pain, thinking of him aged about seven, lying on this bed, face screwed up in concentration over a games console that her sister Figs had brought him back from New York. His only problems then had been one of his cartoon figures exploding or losing one of his plimsolls at school – something he did with unfailing regularity, she recalled, remembering how exasperated she used to get. It seemed rather sweet now. She wanted to hold his small body tight against her, and make everything right for him as she'd always been able to do before. She'd hug his big body too, if only he'd let her!

And Ellie. When did she last cuddle her daughter? Ellie was still tactile with Rupe but Clare just seemed to irritate her. They used to be so much closer…

Clare crossed the landing and pushed open Ellie's door. The bed looked like sale time at Primark, lost under a colourful jumble of T-shirts and dresses. Of course it was time for Ellie to grow away from her mother, to forge her own life with a partner, even if Clare felt misgivings about it. And she'd always been a daddy's girl. Clare remembered her aged nine. Rupe had come home from the pub after a work gathering somewhat the worse for wear, and gone to bed without wanting the dinner Clare had saved him. Ellie had shaken her head sorrowfully at Clare's acid tones. "Don't be mean, Mummy. Daddy can't help being tired, can he?" So why did it hurt Clare so badly now, when Ellie always took his side? Because Clare might just have reason to feel—

Clare went quickly downstairs and picked up her jacket and keys before she could get overemotional. Things would shake down with Ellie and work out for Josh. And for her. Things always did – in the end.

Miraculously, she found a space just a few doors down from the shop on Northdown Road. It was two minutes to one as she locked the car and hurried to the Oasis charity's second-hand boutique.

"Hello, Tony." Clare stopped by the man sitting in the entrance of the empty electrical shop next door. "I thought you were at the hostel."

The young man shrugged. "Only two nights."

Clare frowned. "Did you go to the council like I said?"

"They won't help cos they say I made myself homeless." He shrugged again. He looked exhausted.

Clare felt a stab of anxiety for him. "I'll bring you a coffee in a bit."

Stepping past him and into the shop, Clare wondered what she could do. The shop raised funds for the victims of domestic abuse. All the literature was carefully worded to recognise the fact that these could be of any gender but Clare knew that all the inhabitants of the charity's refuge were women.

Tony had never said he'd suffered abuse but she had heard about his girlfriend's rages, her racist mother who didn't like her daughter having a child with a man of colour, his history – before he'd moved in with Kelly – of a childhood spent largely in care. He wasn't much older than Josh. It had been raining when Clare first saw him in a doorway further along the road and she'd given him £15 to stay in a B&B he said he knew. She'd shuddered at the thought of what it would be like for that money but at least he would be dry.

"He'll probably spend it on drink instead," her volunteer colleague Lyndsey had said briskly, adding darkly when Clare related how he had been forced out of his flat with no money and only a black bin liner of clothes, "You've only heard his side of the story."

But Tony had thanked her so movingly the next time she saw him. Said he'd been able to have a hot shower and how good it had been to sleep in a proper bed again. He'd slept in the park in a tent for four nights, until someone stole it. It had been doorways since.

Clare walked through the shop, raising her hand in greeting to the manager, Karen, who was talking to a customer at the till. Lyndsey was in the storeroom at the back, steam-cleaning a red velvet dress. Bulging bags of clothes were piled up behind her. As Clare hung up her jacket in the small kitchen area, Lyndsey put the dress on its hanger, hung it up on the long rack against the wall, and selected a wrinkled tartan shirt.

"What do you want me to do?" Clare peered into the basket of children's clothing in the corner. "Shall I sort this?"

Before Lyndsey could answer, Karen followed her in. "I thought we'd have a flash sale." She smiled at Clare. "See if we can clear the rest of the winter stuff before we put the spring stock out. Can you mark everything apart from the designer stuff down to a pound?" As Clare nodded, Karen continued: "Harriet's making a poster for the window."

"Harriet?"

"She's new," Lyndsey interjected, meeting Clare's eyes with a look that said she hadn't made a full and final assessment of her yet.

"I thought you could help show her the ropes," finished Karen kindly. "There are a few new bags to go through too." She wrinkled her nose slightly. "I'm not sure..." she trailed off. "Put the gloves on..."

There was the ring of the shop door opening and Karen went back to the till. Clare looked at her back fondly. Karen was lovely about everyone – grateful for every scrap of help, every last stained T-shirt that was pushed through the door. Lyndsey hung a denim skirt on a rack and adjusted a flowery shirt on a hanger before passing the steamer over the first sleeve.

"Do you want tea before I get started?" Clare asked her.

"Please. I've not stopped."

Clare went back into the main shop. The woman she'd thought was a shopper was sitting behind the till with

Karen, using coloured markers on a large sheet of card. Clare leant over for a look. The results were impressive. "Gosh, that looks very professional,' she said smiling. "You must be Harriet."

The woman nodded. She was about thirty-five, caramel-coloured hair in a shiny ponytail, beautifully made-up and wearing a lilac cashmere cardigan over close-fitting pale jeans. "I was a designer," she said.

"It shows!" said Clare, feeling frumpy and dowdy in her own saggy denims and loose sweater. "Are you new to the area?"

"No, not really." Harriet shook her head and smiled briefly but did not elaborate.

"I'm going to make some tea," said Clare. "Or you can have coffee. It's only instant, I'm afraid…"

"I've got a teabag." Harriet gave another fleeting smile before turning her attention back to her poster. "So just some hot water perhaps?"

"Sure." Clare went back through the storeroom to the small kitchen beyond, trying to shake off the feeling of being the waitress to a well-heeled customer.

Lyndsey spoke over the sound of the kettle boiling.

"Been in Margate two years. Husband's something mega in the city. She used to be a creative director at the advertising agency that did the annoying stuff for sanitary towels. That trapeze artist in the white leotard? 'Life's all yours with freedom from leaks'?" Lyndsey screwed up her face in disgust. "They bought a house in Dalby Square and have Farrow and Balled it to the eyeballs and she's given up work entirely to be a better mother to her daughter because

44

it wasn't as if they *needed* the money..." She intoned this with a well-bred accent that did sound wickedly like Harriet's. "And it was *so* much more important to be there after school..." Lyndsey turned the flowery summer dress she was steaming around on its hanger. "All right for some!"

Clare smiled. "How did you find all that out so quickly? She didn't seem very forthcoming to me."

"I was with her all day yesterday. She'll be leaving at three so she can pick up the kid. So she comes in at eleven. Not sure she was quite up for sorting out some of the stinking offerings we had in. Some lowlife had hidden his rubbish under an old pair of curtains. But..."

"It's good of her to do it," finished Clare.

"She did find this!" Lyndsey swung round to a rack behind her. "Spotted immediately it was genuine Vivienne Westwood. What I would give to be a size eight..."

The afternoon passed quickly. As Clare clipped new price labels to the stock, making up rails of sale items, Harriet worked quietly beside her, removing the old tags, quietly arranging items in groups by colour, and making the whole effect, Clare had to admit, a lot more stylish.

From time to time she tried to engage the younger woman in conversation. But Harriet, apart from speaking with enthusiasm about her seven-year-old daughter whom she was taking to ballet after school this evening, did not seem keen to be drawn into anything deeper. Yes, she was enjoying living by the sea, and it was a very different lifestyle from the one they'd had in London.

"I've never regretted giving up work – I want to be there

for Millie," she said eventually, when Clare asked outright whether she ever missed the bustle of the city.

"When you first stopped," Clare ventured, not really understanding why she wanted the opinion of someone she'd only just met, but strangely compelled to ask, "did you ever feel sort of…" Clare hesitated. "Non-useful?"

Harriet's well-shaped brows bent into a V of surprise. "I have never felt that," she said.

They lapsed into silence till Harriet left to get Millie, and Clare carried on alone, occasionally serving a customer when they got busy and finding time to empty out a large bin bag of shawls and shoes that had a pair of green Jimmy Choos nestling at the bottom.

"I'd have bought those if they'd been a size bigger," she said, regretfully.

Lyndsey rolled her eyes. "Story of my life."

Clare had already got her jacket on and was preparing to leave when her phone beeped. Tony had disappeared but had left his mug and the small plate Clare had piled biscuits on, just outside the Oasis shop door. Clare picked them up and carried them back through the shop to the kitchen, glancing at the message as she went. It was Ange, wanting to know where they were going for a drink; she couldn't remember if she was coming to the shop, or Clare was picking her up…

"Shit!" In all her agitation about Tom, Clare had completely forgotten she'd arranged to see her elder sister. She should have cancelled yesterday. She walked rapidly to her car, got in, and put the phone on speaker. "Ange, I'm so sorry – I've cocked up. I've got this new bloke of Ellie's coming for supper and I've got to go home and cook. I didn't get anything ready before I came to the shop..." She heard her sibling's sharp intake of breath and started the engine as she hurried on. "Look, let's do it tomorrow. I'm not doing anything – we could have lunch..."

"No." Her sister's tone was abrupt. "I'm working through tomorrow to make up my flexi hours. What time's he coming?"

"Er, seven." Clare felt the warning signs as she indicated and pulled out behind a bus. "I really need to get home now and get the food going. Ellie wants me to do this chicken with coriander thing..."

"Oh well, I'll just come back with you." Angie was decisive. "I can drink wine while you cook." She laughed. "We can have a catch up and I'll go before he arrives. I'm still at work. I'll wait outside..."

Clare's nerves immediately began to jangle. That was the last thing she wanted. She knew very well that Ange, once settled on a stool at Clare's breakfast bar with a couple of wines down her, would not leave until forced to. And then probably there'd be no cabs and she'd angle to stay and they'd end up having to invite her to eat with them. Which was absolutely not in the plan. Rupe would make no effort to hide his disgust and Clare would be terribly uptight. It was not a route to the relaxed evening Ellie wanted and Clare felt wound up enough about it already. She cursed herself for not remembering earlier and dealing with this then.

She slowed down as the bus stopped, then overtook it, putting her foot down as the road ahead cleared, as if by driving smartly in the opposite direction to Angie's offices, she could put her sister off.

"I really don't think that's a good idea this time." She raised her voice and spoke firmly. "I've got a lot to do. I won't be able to talk."

"You can just listen then," said Ange. "I've had another run-in with that bitch, and I want to get your take on it."

"I won't be able to concentrate. I've got the whole dinner to do…" As she said it, Clare realised this was true. Why hadn't she started things before she'd left this morning? The knot in Clare's middle tightened. "I'll meet you after work tomorrow."

"Hmm." Angie was silent for a moment, but Clare knew that sound.

Her sister gave a loud and theatrical sigh. "The thing is…" she began, with a slight note of whine entering her tone, "I'm psyched up to tell you now."

Clare gave a hiss of annoyance. Ange was pathologically incapable of putting anybody else's feelings before her own. "Well I'm sorry," she said. "But I'm quite stressed too. I just need to get home and focus on what I have to do to get dinner ready before Ellie and Tom arrive."

Angie didn't speak. The silence filled the car and drowned out the noise of the engine.

"So, I'm sorry," continued Clare determinedly. "I'm sorry I've messed up the arrangements, but we can't meet now."

"I can always make the salad or something," said Angie, sounding wounded now. "I wouldn't overstay my welcome."

That would be a first. Clare turned down a side road towards the seafront, deliberately not replying until she'd reached the end and swung the car towards home, suddenly noticing how hard she was gripping the wheel. She took a deep breath, flinching at herself as her voice came out more loudly than she'd intended. "NO!"

Chapter Five

"What are you doing here?" Rupe looked at Angie with displeasure. "Drinking all my wine again? I bet you didn't bring any, did you?"

Angie, sitting at the kitchen table with a glass in front of her, pulled a face at him.

"He's only joking," said Clare automatically, crushing coriander seeds hard with a pestle and glancing anxiously at the clock.

"No, I'm not," said Rupe. He picked up the open bottle of chianti that was on the kitchen counter and looked at the label. "On the good stuff, then? What disaster are we recovering from this week? Who've you been upsetting?"

"Ignore him." Clare turned to stir the onions that were caramelising in a big pan on the hob.

"I was already," said Angie. "Have you got any peanuts?"

"Perhaps I could make you a sandwich?" Rupe pulled a

51

face back. "Or some egg on toast? I mean, you don't want to go to the trouble of cooking for yourself, do you...?"

"Shut up!" Clare glared at him. "Can you lay the table, Rupe?"

"Of course I can, my sweet." Rupe opened the cutlery drawer and began to noisily gather spoons and forks. Angie sat very still, eyebrows raised, until he had gone through into the adjoining room.

"Anyway," she continued, with exaggerated patience, "she's clearly just trying to make her mark – be the new broom and all that. But I said to her, raising your voice is not the way to get the best out of me—".

"Josh!" Clare felt a rush of pleasure and relief at the sight of her son coming through the back door. "You're back early."

"Yeah, I was done. Hi, Auntie Ange." He peered into the pan. "What are we eating?"

"A chicken thing," said Clare vaguely. "Have you remembered Ellie's bringing Tom round?"

"No." Josh shook his head. "Do I have to eat with you all?"

"I think Ellie would like it if you did." Clare had no idea if her daughter would care about Josh being there, but she could do with the extra company to dilute things. "I mean, it's a bit weird if you say hello and then don't join us, and it will look very anti-social if you don't appear at all. Ellie will think—"

"Not that I've been invited, of course," put in Angie.

"No, you haven't." Rupe poked his head through the

opening that led through into the dining room. "What else do you want on this table?"

"Yes, OK." Josh nodded at Clare, without looking at his father. "I'm going upstairs after the meal though. I'll say I've got job applications to do."

"And have you?" Clare asked lightly, handing napkins to Rupe and waving him back towards the long oak table.

"No. What's the point?"

"Oh, Joshie." Angie put out a hand and squeezed his arm. "Something will come up."

Josh gave her a strained smile that was more a grimace. "Yeah. Probably."

"Oh, bless him," Angie said as Josh went upstairs. She drank the last of her wine. "I remember that feeling when I'd left uni. It's awful. Remember I worked in that bookshop... God, that awful man..."

Clare let Angie's voice wash over her as her sister reminisced about past slights, grateful that at least she was saved any more vitriol about the new line manager who had committed the twin sins of daring to question one of Angie's working methods and being both younger and thinner than Angie.

Clare breathed deeply as she chopped and stirred, trying to analyse why she felt so wound up about this evening. She had cooked a thousand dinners like this, for hundreds of different people. She'd either like Tom or she wouldn't. It would make bugger all difference to what her daughter did next, and why should it? And she was not so unaware, Clare thought crossly, that she didn't realise her anxiety about her daughter rushing headlong into a relationship was mostly about her own strange, perplexing dissatisfactions...

"We're going to have a Sunday lunch," Clare said placatingly to her sister, when Ange had made another side-swipe about not being included. "Tom can meet everyone else then. We don't want to overwhelm the poor chap first time." She always felt she had to mollify Angie in a way she never bothered about with her younger sister, Figs. But then Figs was so much easier all round...

Clare gave the chicken another stir and swirled a bit more yoghurt into the sauce. She wiped her hands on a tea towel and took a deep breath. But Rupe got there first.

"If you want a cab," he said to Angie, as he extracted the cork from a bottle of rioja, "you'd better phone one. It can get very busy round here on a Wednesday night."

"Really?" Angie looked at him suspiciously.

"Absolutely," said Rupe, pouring himself a glass of the wine but not offering Angie any more. "My lovely wife will call you one, I'm sure..."

Clare nodded, half-irritated, half-grateful for his bluntness. She picked up the handset on the counter. 'Yes, I can do that..."

Angie gave a long sigh and picked up her handbag. "It's OK! I can see when I'm not wanted!"

"I know when I'm not wanted!" A mile away, their sister Figs tried to keep her voice light. But she was aware it had a plaintive note to it as she looked at a close-up of her husband's nose looming out of her phone screen. She'd seen he still had a shirt and tie on, and she suspected from the way his head was lurching about that he was answering emails while pretending to be fascinated by her day.

"Don't be like that, love." She could definitely hear the tapping of keys. "You're coming out with the kids as soon as Til's done her exams, aren't you? We'll have a really great time then. There's a new champagne bar on the roof of The Majestic – you're going to love it…"

"That's four weeks away yet!" Figs looked crossly at the slightly thinner patch on the top of his head as he leant forward to attend to something more gripping than her. "I do get a bit lonely, you know. I thought a long weekend would be—"

"Yes, it would have been, normally. But we've got this conference in Abu Dhabi and it's not like you can even come with me. Honestly, it's going to be so full-on. And doesn't Tilda need you around?"

"It would only be for three nights; they can both stay with Clare—"

"We'll sort out another time. When I'm not so busy."

"Like that's going to happen."

"Well, it's only for a few more months, isn't it?" Don suddenly grinned at the camera, showing a lot of teeth. "Think of the money!"

"Nine to be precise," Figs said shortly. "And I do!"

She knew she was lucky to have this house and her car, and a lifestyle where she didn't have to work unless she wanted to. She had been all for Don taking the job in Dubai and they'd both agreed she should stay here so the kids could stay at the same schools and not have their exams disrupted. But in the beginning she went out there a lot and Don came home for long weekends regularly. Now the job appeared to be all-consuming and there was always some reason why it was better if she delayed a trip there herself. Even if he claimed to miss her.

"I really want to see you too…" Don was saying. He was now gazing straight at the camera. "All of you…" he added, still smiling widely.

Figs carried the phone across to her bedroom window and looked down at the circular paved driveway below. The magnolia tree by the gate was covered in small tight buds. In a week or two it would be glorious. She pulled open a drawer stuffed full of red and black satin and pulled out a camisole, running the luxury silk between her fingers. There was no point trying to tell Don how she felt by using words like *isolated*. He really didn't get it. She made herself grin back instead, dangling his most recent gift in front of the camera and leaning down to blow him a kiss. "Eat your bloody heart out…"

Angie crossed with them on the path. Clare, standing in the doorway and waving to her sister, saw Ellie stop to kiss her and the tall man beside her shake Angie's hand. Ellie and Tom made a striking couple. They were both tall – Ellie so long-limbed and blonde, Tom dark with suitably chiselled good looks. As they turned to come towards Clare, Ellie saw her daughter determinedly take Tom's hand and push her chin up, meeting her mother's eyes with the challenging stare she'd perfected as a toddler. Clare put on a big welcoming smile.

"Hello, darling!" Her voice sounded strange, even to her. "Nice to meet you, Tom."

She thought for a ghastly moment he was going to try to kiss her already, but he was holding out his hand and smiling back warmly. She could see why Ellie would be attracted to him – he had a slightly Mediterranean look, tanned skin, thick, curling hair, enviable lashes…

"I've been hearing all about you," he said, with a small laugh. "Of course!"

"Ditto." Clare pulled a face and rolled her eyes, feeling self-conscious under Ellie's scrutiny.

"So let's go in then," said her daughter briskly, "and you can see if it was all true…"

———

Clare looked down the table to Rupe who was sitting at the other end. He had gone into salesman mode and was showing great interest in Tom's business, listening intently to how he had got started, with the one second-hand skip he had spray-painted himself, to the difficulties of negotiating the increasingly stringent regulations on waste management.

Tom was also playing the perfect guest: answering Rupe's questions with easy smiles – showing an equal interest in the company Rupe had owned, and making sure to include Clare in both the conversation and his beams.

"What are you going to do next?" he asked her, when Rupe had finished extolling the benefits of his retirement in terms that Clare barely recognised. Listening to her husband, you would have thought he cooked daily, was entirely responsible for the state of the garden (Jim the gardener didn't even get a mention) and was a burgeoning and committed artist (even though the box of water colours she had bought him was still in its cellophane).

She wished Tom had cross-examined him over his chuckling assertion that he'd "still got fingers in a few pies", as she'd have been interested in that answer herself. She wondered where Rupe, who after the initial handover had no connection to the business now at all, thought these pies were!

She liked Tom's question to her. So many people had assumed that just because Rupe, at nearly seventy, had finished paid work, she would be following suit. "I don't know yet!" she said firmly. "I do a bit of voluntary work but that only takes up a couple of afternoons…"

Ellie looked bored at this. Clare ignored her and gave a brief résumé of the work Oasis did, to which Tom nodded gravely. "Would you like some more rice?" she finished. She sat back as Tom politely declined and turned his attention to Josh. "Ellie tells me you're in between things?"

"Yeah," said Josh, without enthusiasm. "Driving a delivery van!" Tom waited. Clare realised she was holding her breath. Josh gave a mirthless laugh. "Trying to find something meaningful to do. Having spectacularly failed as an accountant…"

"You didn't fail," put in Clare. "You didn't like it. It's not the same. It just wasn't for you—"

Rupe rolled his eyes and Clare frowned at him.

"You've got to enjoy what you do," said Tom evenly, and Ellie nodded, looking up at him, Clare noted, with adoration.

"Are you keen to stay around here?" Tom was asking.

Josh shrugged "It all depends. My girlfriend lives in London so I'm looking at jobs there, but…"

"Her parents don't approve," put in Ellie.

Clare waited for Josh to snap at her but he was still looking at Tom, who said sympathetically, "Oh that's tough."

"Yeah," Josh nodded. "It's nothing personal – they haven't even met me. They're Hindu and they want her to marry one of their community. Her dad was hoping she'd fall for some fourth cousin he'd got lined up for her, but she's told them no." Josh gave a rueful smile. "She said they might have eventually come around if I were still going to be an accountant – or a doctor or a lawyer." Josh gave a brief, tight smile. "But a delivery driver isn't quite going to cut it. So," he sighed, "I'm not sure what we're going to do."

Clare tried to keep her face neutral. This was more than Josh had ever said to her on the subject. She'd tried to discuss it just the other evening, asking how Nikhita was and if she was enjoying her master's, wondering if they'd made any plans… Josh had given her one-syllable answers and then said: "Leave it, Mum."

Tom was nodding. "Something will come up. What sort of thing do you want to do…?"

He was clever – Clare had to give him that. He was all things to all of them, siding with Josh as Rupe trotted out his speech about job-hunting, by agreeing calmly how difficult it was to get in front of the right people these days, while bonding with Rupe over the state of the country, the lack of appreciation of the role of the entrepreneur, and the common misapprehension that they were the feckless rich busily avoiding their taxes instead of the backbone of job creation...

Clare was determined not to be drawn, but when Ellie started nodding away like a dog in the back of a Ford Fiesta, she could contain herself no longer. "I thought property was theft?" she said acidly. "It only seems five minutes since you were singing, 'Oh, Jeremy Corbyn'."

"And you disagreed with me!" said Ellie immediately. "You said he'd ruin the economy and he wouldn't make a good prime minister."

"I did!" countered Clare. "But I'd still never vote Tory..."

Ellie gave an exaggerated yawn. "Well Dad has, several times, and it didn't stop you marrying *him*."

"Nobody else to vote for," said Rupe. "Did you hear that idiot the shadow chancellor, whatever his name is, the other morning? Hasn't even got a basic grasp of maths—"

"I'm in favour of a mixed economy," said Tom mildly.

"So is Mum!" said Ellie triumphantly. "She always bangs on about that, don't you?"

"If you say so," said Clare, pulling the empty dishes towards her. "Have you finished, Tom?"

"I certainly have." There was a beat where he met her eyes with amusement. "And it was all delicious."

"So...?" Out in the kitchen, Ellie still had that challenging look. "What's the verdict?"

Clare bent to put a bowl in the dishwasher. "He's very charming."

"Coming from you, that isn't a compliment."

Clare straightened and looked directly at her daughter. "It was. He seems very nice. Very friendly" – she was floundering under Ellie's gaze – "good company, and I can see he adores you."

Her daughter's face softened.

"He's not as right-wing as Dad."

"Well, it really doesn't matter. You're the one who has to be happy about that."

"He only voted Conservative the same year that you did – to keep Nigel Farage out of Thanet South."

Clare nodded.

"But he says his natural home is in the middle," Ellie went on. "He wishes the Lib Dems were a viable alternative."

Clare looked at her suspiciously. Why did she feel Tom was being carefully packaged so she had to endorse him?

As if in answer, Ellie said, "So, you approve? I want you to like him, Mum."

Clare made her voice bright as she opened the fridge. "I do."

As her daughter took plates in for the lemon tart Clare had bought – and the cheeses she'd hastily assembled – Clare tried to analyse what she did feel.

There was nothing wrong with Tom – he was bright and polite and good-looking and apparently solvent and he was sympathetic to her son and he loved her daughter. But there was something that rankled. His easy confidence, his sense of self, the way he *expected* to be liked by her, so sure of his charm…

Why did she feel, she thought as she switched on the coffee machine in case he wanted one, almost as if she needed *his* approval? Why was she fussing over him with desserts and hot beverages in a way she probably wouldn't have if it had been any old boyfriend of Ellie's own age? Why was she so bloody *unsettled?*

Because, she realised with a sudden clarity that hit her in her middle, it made her remember when she was in her twenties and caught up in the heady first months of a relationship. Ellie's boyfriend made her think of how her husband had been when she met him and he, too, was youthful and hungry for success, oozing his good-looking magnetism, unflagging and optimistic. Funny and generous. And in his virile forties.

Clare grasped the seldom-used cheese knife she'd dug from the back of the drawer.

There was something about Tom that reminded Clare of a much younger Rupe…

Chapter Six

"So, the basic problem is" – Anna looked at the notes on the desk in front of her – "he doesn't like baked beans!"

Nick, their newest teacher, leaned back in Anna's other office chair and smiled at her. "There does seem to be rather a surfeit of them being served. If he is to be believed..." he added. "It could, of course, be exaggeration. He also says his room is very small and the host family's youngest son goes in there and moves his things."

"Well, the room would have been inspected when I took them on," said Anna briskly, "so it must be an acceptable size. The other boy going in there isn't on. I'll give them a ring on that one," she continued, "and bring up the subject of menus while I'm talking. Can you ask Asif to pop in and see me in the afternoon break? Let me get a few more details..."

"Sure." Nick smiled again. "He does complain quite a lot so—"

63

"I'll have a word with him. It's a fairly new host family to the school, so it might be that I do need to talk to them."

Nick nodded. "Thanks."

Anna looked at him for a moment. "Is everything else OK? Are you settling in all right?"

"Yes, great." He stretched out his long legs. "The staff are really nice, aren't they? And the students. No problems really."

"Glad to be back in England?"

Nick nodded. "I think so. Bahrain was fine, but you know I went there to get away from all the problems I was having here, and it was time to come back and start getting a life together again. My wife … my *ex*-wife," he corrected, "she's sold the house now and we can finalise everything. I'm going to try to buy a flat."

"Oh, good."

"Not sure where. I do like Whitstable actually, but it's really expensive now, isn't it? Someone said Margate was still the place to get a bargain, but I'm rather liking Ramsgate. Although if I was here, I could walk to work…"

"Where did you live before?"

"Hemel Hempstead."

"Really? One of my sons is in St Albans."

She felt a little twist inside her. She still hadn't seen Stevie. "I'm hoping he'll come down for the weekend soon," she said, surprising herself. "We haven't seen him for ages. They work such long hours—"

"My wife did." Nick turned the plastic coffee cup in his hands. "We lived in Hemel so she could get to the city. She was a lawyer. Married to a lowly EFL teacher who only clocked up a quarter of her working week." He gave a rueful smile. "It didn't help."

"No, I suppose…"

"What does your husband do?" he interrupted her, before she could sympathise.

"He's retired. He's much older than me," she added in a sudden burst, "so he doesn't do much at all these days, I have to say." Why did she? She couldn't seem to help herself rushing on. "He has osteoarthritis and he rarely goes out now."

Now Nick was looking at her with such sympathy in his grey eyes that she felt emotional and made her voice brisk.

"But you know, he tries to keep himself busy…" (Why had she said that when it was so palpably untrue?)

"How old is he?"

"Eighty-six."

Nick did not attempt to control his surprise. "Oh wow. That really is an age difference."

"Approaching twenty-seven years."

"You still look much younger than that to me!"

She laughed. "Flattery will get you absolutely everywhere."

"There was this woman my wife knew, who was married to a man about forty years older," Nick said conversationally. "She made no bones about the fact that she was there for the money. They had a huge place outside Berkhamsted with a tennis court and she was always talking about what she'd do when he'd died. They'd married when she was thirtysomething and he was in his seventies and he had endless health problems – a heart complaint and high blood pressure, and he'd been a smoker and his father had died at fifty – you know the sort of thing." Nick took a swallow of his coffee. "And they both assumed he wouldn't last long. She was just waiting. She came round to see Emma once and was talking about restyling the house, 'once John has gone'. But he didn't go. When he was eighty-two, she got cancer and died – he was devastated. Last I heard he was over ninety…"

He pulled a face and Anna felt strangely defensive. "Is there a moral to this story?" she enquired.

He shrugged. "Only marry for love, I suppose."

"I did." Her voice had gone tight. She tried to smile and couldn't.

"Well, yes, of course. I wasn't—" His hands came up in a gesture of apology.

"No, I know. It's just—"

"It was a crass story to tell. Sorry." He gave her a brief smile and went straight on. "Are you coming out for a drink tomorrow? You haven't been for ages."

"It's not been that long. But yes, maybe I will."

"Fantastic." He looked genuinely pleased and for a moment Anna felt flustered. He raised his eyebrows. "Although I guess it's not so much fun when you have to drive home?"

"Perhaps I'll come on the train," she said. "I do sometimes. Then I can have more than one!"

"So your husband doesn't mind you going out enjoying yourself without him?"

"No, of course not."

Anna knew this wasn't strictly true either. Jeremy would

never openly complain, but the reproach was clear in his eyes when he asked her what time she would be home. When she told him she would be later than usual because she was getting the train, he would simply nod and say in a neutral tone: "OK, I'll get my own food then." And she would feel guilty because that meant he would take a Waitrose ready-meal from the freezer when once upon a time he would have cooked something elaborate from scratch.

He had always been a better chef than she was. He took it more seriously – planning his dishes in detail, gathering the ingredients, going on a special shopping trip to get lemongrass or shiitake mushrooms if that's what the recipe required, rather than chucking in something else instead, as Anna would have done. But then, if he was still cooking, he might be coming with her. In the old days, Jeremy would have loved to have been at the drinks too – making the younger women laugh, being the one to suggest champagne, and probably paying for it as well...

"My wife was a bit older than me too," Nick was saying. "Five years. She used to get furious about me going to the pub or out to see friends while she was working. Wanted me to be at home waiting. It was one of the problems."

"Doesn't sound ever so reasonable," said Anna lightly.

"She's a control freak – she admits it." He smiled. "Brilliant lawyer but wants to direct everything else too. We get on much better now she doesn't feel she has to be in charge of me. Sadly..." He shrugged again. "My own fault for tying the knot. The writing was on the wall in the beginning..."

He looked at Anna expectantly, as if he were waiting for her to spill some similar beans – perhaps to admit she should never have married a man old enough to be her father. She just nodded but didn't speak. She still felt rattled by his earlier tale.

These days she seemed to spend an unseemly amount of time thinking about how it would be when Jeremy died. When making plans, sorting financial things, they too had always assumed he would go first. But he might not. When she thought of Jeremy dead, she was shot through with a mixture of adrenaline and dread. As if she were about to jump out of an aeroplane – galvanised and terrified in equal measure – in a stunt for which she'd been training for a long, long time but for which she could never be quite ready...

"I'd better get back to class," Nick said. "I'll send Asif up later."

"Yes," Anna snapped back to the present, and addressed Nick coolly. "You do that."

Chapter Seven

He was already in the bar when she got there the next evening. They all were. Anna was relieved to see Ellie look up and give her a big smile as she approached the long table. The evening sun was shining in through the back window and Anna had to squint to see Nick's face. He had got to his feet. "What are you having?"

Ellie pointed to her glass. "We've got a bottle of cava on the go, if you want a glass of that?"

Anna nodded. "Lovely."

Nick had picked up a chair from another table and they were all shuffling sideways. He put it between him and Ellie. Simon was blowing her a kiss from his place opposite. As Anna took her first mouthful, she felt a rush of gratitude wash over her. She liked being with these friendly young people who wanted to include her. She didn't want to retire in August just because her age suddenly had a zero on it. Not that they could do without her then, anyway. Even if she wanted to give up work, she'd have to wait till their quieter winter months and it would still take weeks to train up a replacement…

"You OK, Anna?" Blake broke into her thoughts. He already looked tired and they hadn't started their *really* busy period yet. "Did you sort out the Spanish group?'

"Eventually…"

She went on chatting to him across the table, talking shop about the two hundred teenagers due in mid-July, the impossible agent in Madrid who had demanded changes to the students' activities programme three times so far and the twenty-six new host families she still needed to visit before the season really took off. Beside her, she was aware of Nick listening and nodding. "Sounds like a nightmare," he said at one point.

"It is, but Anna is amazing," said Blake. "Everything would fall apart without her."

"Hardly." Anna laughed self-consciously, pleased with the compliment. Ellie topped up her glass. "I don't know how you do it either," she said. "Remember when Luca let the family's hamsters escape?"

"Oh, I loved Luca," Janine joined in. "He was so naughty but he kept us all entertained, didn't he?"

Simon rolled his eyes, "Not when he'd been to that hideous joke shop, he didn't." Simon affected an expression of terror. "Nearly gave me a breakdown, darling." They all laughed.

"He was in there every weekend," Ellie told Nick. "He was thirteen, from Pisa. Looked totally angelic but he used to come into school with whoopee cushions and pretend dog poo. He put that on the floor by my desk and I screamed. His poor parents – he had this huge bulging carrier bag of stuff to take home. Plastic spiders, stink bombs, all sorts. I asked him what his mother would say. He just said, 'She know me.'" Ellie laughed merrily. She was glowing.

"How are things with you?" Anna asked carefully, when the conversation had moved on and Nick was talking to the others. "Is Tom well?"

"Oh yes, brilliant," Ellie said happily. "He's coming to my parents' for lunch on Sunday – he's met Mum and Dad already but now he's going to meet the whole bloody clan!"

"You haven't moved in yet, then?" Anna asked.

"Well. Yes, I have really. I mean, I'm there all the time. I just haven't cleared my room at home cos I can't face going through all the junk and Tom's flat is quite minimalist, you know? So, I go back at weekends to get more clothes, and see Mum and Dad. Sometimes I sleep there if Tom is out late but..." Ellie shrugged. She looked very young.

Anna wondered if perhaps Ellie was not as sure as she had been. Still clinging onto the safety of her teenage nest, just in case. Anna's younger son Marcus still had cupboards full of clobber in her house, even though he'd never come home after university. She liked it being there, especially while he was so far away...

She smiled at Ellie. "Does your mother like cooking for lots of people?"

Anna remembered the Sunday lunches they used to

hold when Jeremy was just retired. He would get a huge rib of beef and do it with all the trimmings. She would be in charge of dessert. There'd often be twelve of them crammed around the table in the dining room; they seldom used it now. Lots of shouting and laughter. Buckets of red wine. Jeremy at the head of the table, in his blue and white striped apron, carving with a flourish…

Ellie was answering. "She doesn't mind really. She just pretends to make a fuss. Mum said last week that as I was the one who wanted the whole gang there, I could cook it all then, but she'll do most of it when the time comes. She won't be able to resist…" Ellie laughed. "And I'm fairly crap at cooking so just as well…"

"More drinks, darlings?" Simon was waving a twenty-pound note around the table. Andy and Lisa were nodding, Blake put his hands up as if he were helpless. "Why not?" They all laughed.

Nick got up to help Simon, and Anna finished what was in her glass. She felt mellow and relaxed. She was glad she had come.

"What are you doing this weekend?" she asked Nick when he sat back down beside her.

"I've got a couple of flats to see. Just out of interest. Thought I'd start to look at what's out there. One here and one in Broadstairs."

"Where's the one here?" Simon was handing round glasses. "You need to run the locations past us, darling, so we can warn you off the dodgy ones. It feels like I've been here for ever, but there are still roads I wouldn't go down in the dark, dark night…"

"It's not that bad," said Lisa, who, Anna knew, had lived in Margate all her life. "Simon's a drama queen."

Simon pulled a face and everyone laughed again.

Nick grinned at him. "I'll be sure to ask your advice," he said. "The one in Broadstairs is in Chandos Square?"

There were murmurs around the table: "Oh, nice," and "Lovely!"

"And the one here is in the tower block up by the station. Is it Arlington House?"

Several people spoke at once.

"Really?"

"They're usually like hen's teeth."

"I'm surprised! They sell the moment they're on the market – if they ever are…"

"What's it like in there these days? It was considered a bit grim when I was young," Lisa said. "My dad wouldn't let me babysit there."

"Oh, it's great." Another teacher, Beth, spoke up from further down the table. "I used to rent a place there. The views are amazing," she told Nick. "Sunset or sunrise?"

"Oh, I dunno." Nick frowned.

"That's what they ask you when you've just moved in. On one side you can see Turner Contemporary; on the other you get to see Turner's sunsets… I really loved it there. The people were great. I only moved out because I needed another bedroom…"

Nick looked across at Janine, who wasn't speaking, and Anna thought how kind and thoughtful he was. "Where do you live?" he was asking her warmly.

"Westgate," she said, colouring slightly. "Still at home,"

she added ruefully. "Can't afford to do anything else... I don't really want to share," she went on, as Nick nodded, "and anything nice is too expensive."

Anna saw Simon frown and start to speak, and gave him a small warning shake of her head as Janine continued. "And my mum sort of needs me there. She's disabled." Nick nodded again. "I bet she's so glad of the help," he said, as Janine flushed again.

"I've got quite a few friends who still live at home," Ellie said. "I wouldn't have been moving out, if I hadn't met Tom." She laughed. "All that salary going on rent when I live somewhere really nice."

"Yeah." Janine gave a weak smile and Anna's heart went out to her. She had been to the flat Janine shared with her mother. She knew Ellie didn't mean to rub her nose in their differing circumstances but she somehow always did. Anna was sure Janine must envy Ellie the looks, the boyfriend, the affluent upbringing. Anna wished Janine could find someone nice, and from the way she was now gazing at Nick – who seemed oblivious – she guessed Janine did too...

She looked at her watch as she sipped the last of her drink. There was a train that would take her home in half an hour. "I'd better be off." She smiled down the table. "Have a good weekend, everyone!"

"I'm going to make a move too," Nick stood up. "I'll walk to the station with you."

"Oh!" Anna felt a little rush of pleasure. "Lovely."

The evening air was soft. They walked down to the end

of the High Street and onto the seafront, where couples were having dinner in the plaza, and families queued for fish and chips. Knots of people stood outside bars or leant against the railings overlooking the sea. The light was beginning to fade, the mauve sky punctured by the setting sun. The lights of the harbour arm shone across the water – glowing from the row of tiny bars and cafés beyond the Turner Contemporary, which rose up pale and stark against the darkening sky.

As they made their way along the parade, the last of the seagulls lingered on the wide steps down to the sea, taking short flights to avoid the occasional swing of a leg or charge of a toddler. They passed a series of bars, skirting those drinking craft beer on the pavement, hearing the voices and chink of glasses floating down from the balcony of the Sands Hotel.

Between the gelato shop and pizza bar, a shopkeeper pulled in her display stand of sunglasses and postcards.

"Pizza with pear and ricotta?" read Nick. "What's wrong with good old pepperoni?"

"I quite like goat's cheese on a pizza," said Anna.

"Nah," said Nick, smiling. "It's got to have chillies…"

Closer to the sea, beachgoers were packing up Bluetooth speakers, while teenagers cuddled and giggled and smoked. Anna pointed out the silhouette of Reculver, twelve miles down the coast, defined against the horizon like a giant's binoculars. It was what she and the boys used to say when they were small.

"We used to walk there along the Saxon Shore Way," she

told him. "It's a really interesting place. Lots of birds to watch." She stopped, touched by a sudden sadness at the thought of Jeremy striding along, binoculars slung around his neck, rucksack on his back packed with beers and cheese. They'd walked hundreds of miles together when they were both fit. Some of their best evenings had been spent in small pubs along the routes of various trails, comparing sore muscles and blisters.

"I'll have to take a look," said Nick.

The sun had almost gone, but the sky was ablaze. They found a space to cross between the cars queued around the mini roundabout, beneath the pearly face of the clocktower lit up in shimmering orange. Nick paused on the other side of the road, taking in the view. "Turner knew what he was talking about."

They walked on, past the bingo halls and candy floss stall and the open doors to The Mechanical Elephant – the Margate branch of Wetherspoons – where a burst of noise and warm beer fumes hit them.

"Having fun in there," said Nick, as they edged round a group of young girls in perilous heels and tiny skirts, laughing outside.

"Not my sort of fun," said Anna. "Not these days."

"Yes, I quite like to be able to hold a conversation myself." Nick gave her arm a soft nudge. "We're getting old, darlin'."

"Well, I am…" Anna smiled at him, trying to keep her voice even, although the unexpected touch had startled and electrified her.

As the huge, dark mass of Arlington House loomed

above them, studded with the lights from the flats' windows, Nick stopped and looked up at the tower block. The street light caught his hair, making it look blonder than usual.

"I rather like it," he said.

Anna nodded. "I do too. People tend to love it or hate it."

"Isn't it what they call Brutalist?" Nick said

"Yes," Anna nodded, used to explaining it to students. "A lot of these went up in the Fifties and Sixties."

"When was this built?"

"I think it was 1964. It was pretty cutting edge at the time. Quite posh – there were shops around it, and all sorts of facilities. Later it got very run down, but you heard what Beth said…"

"It would certainly be handy to live here – a ten-minute walk to work." Nick continued to gaze upwards. "And right by the station."

Anna looked at her watch. "Talking of which…"

"Oh right, sorry. What time's your train?"

They walked briskly past the block and up the slight incline to reach the classic brown-brick station. Anna stopped as they went through the barrier onto platform one, where Nick looked up at the board. There was a train to Ramsgate in seven minutes.

"I need to go over there," Anna indicated the platform opposite and nodded towards the underpass. "So … I'll see you on Monday."

Nick beamed at her. "You will!" he said. "And you have a lovely weekend till then." He put his hand lightly on her arm. "I'm glad you came for the drink. It's been really great to spend time with you."

"Oh!" Anna shook her head, smiling and embarrassed, as he leant in and kissed her on the cheek.

She heard her own voice sounding prim and formal as she repeated. "It was very nice to see you too…"

Chapter Eight

"**G**ood morning!" Rupe's voice boomed up the hall as he swung open the front door. "How's my favourite mother-in-law in the whole world?"

As Meg swung her mammoth handbag through the doorway and dumped it inconveniently in the middle of the rug, Rupe gave her a smacking kiss on both cheeks followed by an extravagant hug that all but engulfed her.

"Get off," Meg said, giving him a small shove as she emerged. "I can't breathe."

Clare, waiting in the kitchen doorway, gave a wry smile.

"What's the matter with you?" Meg surveyed her. "Face that would stop a mangle."

"Clock," corrected Clare. "Stop a clock. Start a mangle."

"Your bloody expressions," said Rupe. "Nobody else says that."

Meg snorted. "My mother did!" She jerked her head towards her daughter. "And she looks a misery anyway."

Meg burst into her big, raspy laugh that ended in a cough, and Rupe joined in with gusto.

"Cup of tea?" Clare turned on her heel and went back to the kettle. It was lovely that Rupe adored her mother the way he did, but she did wish they didn't invariably make her feel ganged up on, and, even more, that Rupe, if she ever mentioned it, wouldn't make her feel the problem was entirely her failure to see the joke. It would be nice if her mother was on her side, just for once. The way she, Clare, would have been on Josh's...

"Gran!" Ellie had come down the stairs and was also hugging her grandmother, who stood stock still as if waiting patiently for it to be over.

"How did you get here?" Clare asked her mother when Ellie had let her go and Meg had followed her into the kitchen.

"Drove, of course!"

"You're not going to have a glass of champagne when they all get here?"

"Might have a mouthful. Can't be doing with too much, as you well know. And when you lot have all got red faces at four o'clock and are talking rubbish, I'll be glad about that." Meg turned to Ellie. "Where's this new fella of yours, then?"

Ellie adjusted the comb that was pinning up her long hair. "Gone to look at a house he might buy. The owner's doing it as a private sale and he phoned to say he was down here for the weekend, so Tom's gone round there now. He can probably convert it into three flats." Ellie looked at her grandmother expectantly.

Meg raised her eyebrows. "Thought he was scrap metal?"

"Skips. And he has rental property too."

"Where there's muck there's brass, my father used to say," said Meg. "His grandad grew up in a slum, started a scrap business, and was the first man in the street to own a car. All the neighbours came out to have a look."

Ellie nodded patiently at this often told story. "Tom is doing really well," she said proudly.

Meg grinned at her. "I'll let you know what I think when I've had a good look at him."

Ellie grinned back. "I'm sure you will."

"So, what are we doing?" Meg had stowed her bag and was inspecting the various foodstuffs laid out on the central island in the kitchen. Ellie had disappeared again – so much for her doing the cooking!

"A rolled sirloin. I'm going to cook it fast when everything else is almost done." Clare watched her mother poke at the potatoes she had parboiled. She waited.

"You want to get some flour and mustard powder on those," Meg said. "And give them a good shake."

"I was about to…"

"What *is* the matter?" Meg frowned. "His Lordship being tricky?"

Clare considered if it was worth it. "He's driving me mad," she tried. "Being here all day."

Her mother brightened. "Oh, tell me about it!" Meg felt

in the pockets of her cardigan and pulled out a packet of cigarettes. "Your father drove me to distraction when he retired. I used to complain when he went to the pub, just to keep us in a routine, but the truth was, I lived for those two hours."

"I thought it was one hour. Five forty-five p.m. to six forty-five p.m. before dinner." And woe betide the poor old bugger, thought Clare, if he was five minutes late. Dishing up waited for no man.

"He went lunchtimes too, didn't he? Used to go out to 'post a letter' every day at noon. Took that same letter with him for about three years. Never posted it – went straight round the corner into The Half Moon. Thought I didn't know. Damn envelope was still in his jacket when he died."

"What was in it?"

"A coupon for free seeds."

"How old were you when you met Grandad?" Ellie had reappeared. She had tied her blonde hair back into a ponytail now and was putting on one of Clare's aprons.

Clare felt a flash of irritation. Ellie knew the answer perfectly well. She was just making a point.

"Twenty-one," said Meg triumphantly. "And he was thirty-three."

"See?" Ellie flashed her mother a look. "It's in the genes. We're all attracted to older men."

"I wasn't," said Meg immediately. "You had to take what was going. You were expected to get a husband as soon as you could back then. And there was a shortage because of the war."

"The war had ended nearly twenty years before," said Clare. "Weren't you all running around in miniskirts by then?" She opened a cupboard and picked out a jar of horseradish.

"It took a while to get the stocks back up," said Meg. "What would you know about it? You weren't there. We were all in Coventry during the blitz. My mother had three of us under five."

"You've never told us that before, Gran!" Josh came into the room and laughed. Clare shook her head in resignation. She had long given up bothering to contradict her mother on this one. Clare's grandmother had been in Coventry in 1940 maybe, but Meg hadn't been born until three years later. Half her mother's stories weren't true.

"Cheeky!" Meg extended a cheek towards her grandson. Josh dutifully pecked it, as she dug in the other pocket for her lighter. "I'll just have a quick cig and then I'll help you with the veg."

Ellie took the jar from her mother and unscrewed it. "Gran! You're supposed to have given up."

"Says who? Doctor said it would be too much of a shock to the system after all these years. I told him I started when I was sixteen and worked in Boots. They all did then. I said, I've been doing it for sixty-two years and it hasn't killed me. And he said, that doesn't mean it won't." Meg snorted. "And I said – well, at seventy-eight I've had a fair innings already, don't you think? And he gave up then and said see the nurse about your flu jab."

She pushed open the back door and stood with one foot across the threshold to light up. "And I didn't bother with one of them, either." She took a long drag, and blew the smoke out in satisfaction.

"Go outside and shut the door!" yelled Rupert from the hallway. "I can smell your bloody fag from here."

Meg gave a delighted throaty cackle. "Go and stand somewhere else then!"

Clare smiled. This was a well-worn exchange that took place whenever her mother came to visit and which slowly rose in intensity as the seasons progressed, with Rupe going through the motions of complaint in the summer months and reaching a furious crescendo, during which he bellowed ferociously, in February, when she was letting in blasts of ice.

"Four years now," Clare said, as Meg, still in the doorway, sucked on her cigarette as if her life depended on it. "Do you not miss him at all?"

"Never! I get better conversation out of Melvin." Melvin was a cockatoo that Meg had taught to say *bugger off* – something she firmly denied. He had the run of her house and Meg, so particular about all other forms of household order, happily trailed after him with kitchen roll.

"I do," said Clare firmly. "I think about Dad every day." There was a small silence. Ellie, she noted, was spooning the horseradish into a small glass bowl. We were really pushing the boat out today.

Meg snorted. "So do I," she said matter-of-factly. "What's that got to do with anything?"

There was another silence until Meg ground her cigarette out on the paving slabs. She was wearing leather lace-up boots with narrow black trousers and some sort of tunic top under her trademark long cardigan. She was tinier than ever, Clare thought, underneath the loose layers. She looked at her mother's small bony hands covered in rings as she stooped to pick up her butt, then the cropped silver hair as she straightened again. "I lit a candle," Clare continued, "last Tuesday."

"He wanted to go," said Meg. "He said to me the night before, when his breathing was bad, 'It's time to go soon. You could do with a break.' And he kissed me on the cheek when he went to bed and we'd stopped all that sort of thing a long time before, but I let him do it and I squeezed his hand and I said, 'You'll be all right'. And in the morning, he was cold."

Meg stepped back into the kitchen, opened the cupboard beneath the sink, and flicked her cigarette end into the bin.

Clare swallowed. She'd heard the story a hundred times but it still got her every time. "It's what he wanted," her mother repeated. "He'd had enough."

She'd said it at the funeral, adding, "We always knew I'd be left on my own one day." Which was the only time she had ever referred to anything that could possibly be construed as loss.

"Rupe will complain about that bin later," Clare said now. "He hates the smell of cigarettes."

Meg kicked the door shut, unperturbed. "No prude like a reformed tart."

The three of them worked together for the next forty minutes. Meg made her famous gravy – thick enough to stand a spoon up in – that Rupe would eulogise over. Clare wondered if other women her age would think how lovely this was – three generations preparing vegetables side by side, the rhythmic sound of chopping and stirring, the latter rather more carried out by her and Meg than by Ellie, it was true, but side by side nonetheless. Josh had gone to ground again while Rupe was apparently "doing the garden". Clare had seen him on the bench with *The Sunday Times*.

But there was peace. Meg had told them a long tale about Melvin and what the window cleaner had said, and Ellie's eyes weren't flashing. It was as good as it was going to get. The potatoes were in, together with the cauliflower cheese. The beef was prepared, the frozen Yorkshires laid out on a tray. Angie's unappealing-looking nut-and-lentil bake was in its own dish with some onions, and Ellie had mixed up some vegan packet sauce so there'd be no dramas about gelatine this time.

Clare had asked her sisters to come at midday. It was bright and warm – they could maybe have drinks in the garden. She put nuts and olives into dishes. But when the doorbell rang at two minutes past twelve, Clare still did not feel ready.

"Where's the new man then? Hello, Mum." Angie did not attempt to kiss her mother but thrust a bottle of red at Clare. "There you are – that should stop him moaning."

"Gone to see a house he might buy," Ellie was explaining. "He'll be here in half an hour."

"Ah, I know. He wants to make an entrance," said Angie.

Because that's what you would do, thought Clare sourly.

But Figs was late as always and Tom arrived first. He had brought Clare roses, creamy white ones, their petals tinged with pink – the sort she loved. He had also brought two bottles of Châteauneuf-du-Pape, which went down very well with Rupe. "Marvellous choice!" he cried, clapping Tom on the shoulder. "You can come again!"

Clare watched them all through the kitchen window, sitting out on the patio, glasses in hand. Figs was wearing a beautiful linen dress with bright, chunky beads. It wasn't yet June, but she already had a deep tan. Clare had seen Tom's eyes widen slightly as she'd shrugged off her jacket and come towards him. At forty-eight, her sister turned heads just as much as she had in her twenties. Figs was vibrant and beautiful and both men and women would take a second look at those glossy black waves and dark, smoky eyes. On someone else the make-up would be too much, but on Figs it was arresting.

Beside her, Ange looked drab by comparison, with her mid-brown hair and blouse. There were only five years between them but it could have been more than a decade. Figs was flamboyant, whereas Ange's style could best be described as safe. Figs's fourteen-year-old son Alex was sitting on the low wall by the barbecue, looking at his phone. Her daughter, Tilda, had stayed at home, ostensibly to revise for her imminent AS Levels about which she said she was panicking, but probably, as Figs explained, so she could spend the afternoon Facetiming her boyfriend. "Or getting him round for the full grope," she added. "All right for some!"

Rupe had enveloped Figs in a big hug too, before they exchanged their customary greetings.

"How you doing, SIL?"

"Pretty OK, BIL. You?"

"Champagne or gin? My old MIL has snaffled all the scotch."

Meg had snorted. "Wouldn't touch it with a bargepole! I'll have a very small sherry if you're asking…"

Knowing Rupe's feelings about his various in-laws, Clare had spent time on the seating plan. Rupe was, as always, presiding from the end, with Ellie next to him and Tom beside her. Figs was on his other side, next to Meg.

When all the dishes had circulated, Clare sat back from the other end of the table and watched Tom watching them. He looked relaxed and cheerful, laughing at something Meg was telling him, swapping tales about Dubai with Figs – she'd told him about Don's job and Tom apparently had a friend who'd made a fortune importing wine when the licenses were first being given out – while his arm lay casually along the back of Ellie's chair, his fingers occasionally resting on her shoulder. Ellie appeared to have a hand on his knee under the table.

Clare looked at her expression. Her daughter was happy. It was all that mattered. And for God's sake, Tom was forty-two; Ellie probably had thirty years before she'd start to feel the gap. Anything could happen by then. This whole relationship could all be over in a year's time. She caught Ellie's eye and gave her a big, encouraging smile. For a second Ellie looked startled. Then she shone her mother a beam back, flicking her eyes back at Tom and mouthing, "Thank you." Clare nodded, a lump in her throat.

"He seems very nice," Angie said from beside her, where Clare had sat her to keep her away from Rupe. "Quite a catch." She sounded suspicious.

"Yes," Clare nodded firmly. "He's great."

Rupe was looking around the table too. "Why isn't your girlfriend here?" he boomed down to Josh.

Clare glanced anxiously at her son, but he was meeting his father's gaze. "Didn't want to subject her to you lot!"

"How is she?" Tom asked pleasantly, as Rupe guffawed.

Josh nodded diffidently. "Yeah, she's good, thanks."

"We were in The Lifeboat last night," Ellie told him. "And these two absolute arses were trying to chat up one of the girls serving. One gave up after a bit, but the other one really tried it on when she was collecting glasses. Tom had to step in. Tell him to leave her alone."

Angie's eyes had widened. "God – what was he doing?"

"Oh, you know, can I buy you a drink, do you want to go somewhere after? Just kept on and on, and following her around the bar. And she was so not interested."

"He was quite drunk," said Tom.

"Nikhita hates that," Josh told Ellie. "She says she and her friends really don't like it when blokes come over and say, can we buy you one."

Angie was nodding gravely, but Figs shrugged. "That's how it always used to work. We ancients didn't have Tinder. You looked around a bar for someone attractive and hoped he'd smile at you, and then when you smiled back you hoped he'd come and offer you a drink… There wasn't any other way to do it."

"What's Tinder anyway?" Meg had begun clearing the empty plates. Clare hoped no one had wanted any more. Alex got up. "I'm just going to…" he said to Clare, trailing off. He'd hardly said a word the whole meal but then that was teenage boys, she supposed. She nodded, smiling at him.

"It's a phone app, Gran," Ellie was explaining. "You can choose people you like the look of and if you both like each other, you send a message."

Meg wrinkled her nose. "Sounds very involved. When I was young, it was something you used to light the fire."

"Anyway," Figs continued. "Sometimes people must meet in the flesh in an ordinary way. How did you meet Nikhita, Josh?"

"At university."

"And what about you two?" She smiled from Tom to Ellie.

Ellie giggled. "In a bar actually. Tom bought me a drink!"

Tom laughed. "I smiled at her first," he told Figs.

"There you go!" she said. She glanced at Alex's empty seat. "I was in a hotel bar quite recently and a guy did all the eye-contact things and then asked if he could buy me a drink. I wasn't at all offended. We had quite a nice chat."

Ellie squealed. "Auntie Figs!" she said. "You're married."

"I didn't have wild, unbridled sex with him," said Figs, unruffled. "I had a gin and slimline. You young people are so bloody moral. Marriage doesn't preclude the need to have the odd conversation!"

"What would Dad say?" Alex was standing in the doorway, looking, Clare thought, faintly anxious.

Figs made a dismissive gesture with her hand. "Oh, he wouldn't care. It was in full view of about a hundred people!" She laughed. "And I'm quite sure he has plenty of drinks with women he meets on *his* business trips…"

As Alex continued to frown, she added brightly. "I think I told him. In fact, I did. Because the chap and his wife had a place in Marbella and he said it was really warm all year round and Dad always maintains it's not hot enough to go to Spain in the winter."

Alex nodded, apparently satisfied.

As he sat down, looking away, Figs rolled her eyes at Clare and mouthed "phew", mock-fanning herself.

Clare knew very well she hadn't told Don. She could always tell when Figs was being creative. Angie called it lying.

"You're not up to anything are you? Clare asked her younger sister when they'd finished clearing the first course. Beyond them, through the opening into the dining room, everyone was talking, but Clare had still lowered her voice.

"Of course I'm not," Figs said loudly. "I have drinks with all sorts of people. Don't be such a stiff." She bent to put the last of the dinner plates into the dishwasher. "And I could do with a bit of a social life right now I'm going stir crazy stuck at home."

Clare raised her eyebrows. "Come off it!"

Figs was always doing something. It was Pilates or lunch or shopping or her art class, massage or beauty treatments. Now she looked theatrically, downcast. "I haven't had a job for months."

Figs did freelance event management. They didn't need the money – Don was earning shedloads in Dubai – but she liked the buzz. From time to time, Clare would feed her niece and nephew while Figs presided over a corporate golf day at Sunningdale, or have them both to stay for a few days so Figs could fly off to Bali to organise a conference.

"Something will come along," Clare said, in the same tone she used to Josh. "Every time you say that, something exotic suddenly appears." She smiled fondly at her sister.

"Hmmm. Maybe," Figs conceded. "I probably need to put out some feelers."

"How's the pottery?"

Figs, bored with "just painting" at her art group, had signed up for a pottery course and, after the first session, had bought a potter's wheel. She had set it up in her vast garage, positioned at a careful distance from Don's prized Maserati which spent nine months of the year shrouded in its dust covers, and which Figs rolled her eyes about at every opportunity. But also mentioned. Quite a lot.

"Oh my God, I forgot!" Figs rushed into the hall, rummaged in a bag, and came back holding something encased in bubble wrap. She thrust it at Clare. "For you."

Clare unpicked the tape. Inside was a plant holder. It

was very slightly wonky but that only added to its charm. It was bright yellow and painted with white daisies, their centres the same colour as the rest of the pot. Clare was startled to feel tears at the back of her eyes.

"Oh, Figs, that's—"

"It's a bit bonkers, I know, but it's the first one I've finished."

"—beautiful. I love it. Really." Clare hugged her sister.

"Hey!" Figs scrutinised her as they parted again. "It's only a pot. What's the matter?"

Clare shook her head. "I don't know."

Chapter Nine

W hen they brought in dessert, Angie had moved into Figs's seat, next to Rupe, the better, Clare surmised, to get into conversation with Tom, who was now almost opposite. He had clearly asked what she did for a living. Or, knowing Angie, she had told him, because Meg was halfway through another familiar speech.

"Your dad used to go on and on about the civil service. Said it was the scourge of society. Too many layers of bureaucracy. All that money wasted. I don't know how he knew. Do you remember? Too many people doing nothing—"

"Well, I don't do nothing," said Angie. "It's all very busy and stressful. But I'm beginning to think Dad had a point!"

"Busy and stressful eh?" echoed Rupe. Angie ignored him.

"I've got a new line manager," she told Tom. "She's done literally nothing yet apart from strut about."

Clare saw the rising gleam in Rupe's eyes and shook her head at him. He grinned.

"Giving me grief," added Angie

"She probably can't cope," Rupe said to Angie.

Angie frowned. "No, you're probably right," she said, sounding mollified. "She's only been doing it for six years. I've been there for twenty-nine!"

"How come she's your manager then?"

"Oh, she's come up another way." Angie shook her head as if the question were an annoying fly.

"Old Frank did have a point, then," continued Rupe. "I mean do you *need* a line manager, Angela? Aren't you perfectly capable of running that office yourself?"

"Well, yes, I am, as it happens!" Angie was watching him, waiting for the sting.

"I bet you could cut the manpower in that place by half and nobody would notice the difference."

"Well, no, we would—"

"None of you would get a job in the real world!"

"You don't get much more real than Health and Social Care," said Angie hotly.

"But you're not actually doing it," said Rupe. "You're just filling in the forms – you told me. You work nine to five and have three months a year off sick. They'd never stand for it in the private sector. If you left now, you'd never get employed again."

"And neither would you have been!" said Figs, as Angie turned puce. "So stop winding her up. I'd say if you hadn't run your own business – with Clare keeping you organised – you would have been totally unemployable."

Tom had been witnessing these exchanges with an amused expression. Now Clare watched his eyebrows go up; he was looking at Rupe, waiting to see how he would respond.

But, typically, Rupe seemed pleased with this. "That's right!" he said. "When I was selling photocopiers, one of my references said I was a maverick. I had to look it up."

"You wouldn't be allowed to say that these days," said Angie, crossly. "References have to be—"

"A maverick but gets results." Rupert spoke over her. "I should think I bloody did – I turned over half a million quid for them." He took a swallow of red wine. "That's why they couldn't fire me."

He grinned at Angie. "And they can't fire you either," he said good-naturedly. "Don't you have to do something really terrible to get kicked out of the Civil Service? Shoot someone or refuse to stand up for the Queen? And then you get about thirty warnings and six months' gardening leave before you go. You don't get sacked just for being a bit shit, do you?"

"Rupert!" Clare frowned towards Alex, who was grinning.

"So if I were you, next time she gives you a hard time, just tell her to eff off!" He looked at Clare, as if waiting for her praise for curbing his language. He poured more wine into Angie's glass. She smiled.

Figs rolled her eyes. "You are incorrigible," she said, holding out her glass. "Don't I get a top-up too?"

Quiet fell as they ate dessert. Tom broke the silence. "This is wonderful," he said. "I've not had summer pudding for years." He looked down the table at Clare.

"Figs brought it," she said. "It's good, isn't it?"

"I didn't make it, of course," Figs put in. "I got it from this wonderful woman down the road who does home-catering. She has a weekly menu and you just phone up and she delivers. I'll give Ellie her number. Or you can find her on Instagram. The chicken pie is to die for."

"Well, it's great." Tom smiled at her.

"It's very easy to make," said Meg reprovingly to Figs. "I don't know why you spend all this money on other people doing you food. You can cook!"

"She really can't," Alex put in. They all laughed, Figs included.

"I actually can't be arsed," she told Tom. "I cook Don a mean steak when he comes home and I'm very good at colourful salads, but that's about it." She laughed again. "Thank God for Waitrose Easy-to-Cook! And takeaways!"

Meg shook her head. "It's not how they were brought up," she said. "I cooked everything from scratch and I still do." She nodded at Ellie. "I hope you can peel a potato."

Ellie rolled her eyes. "You know I can. I've cooked for you lots of times."

"Twice," said Clare. "I can still remember the washing-up."

Angie put her spoon down into her empty bowl. "A friend of mine is going to pick me up here at half-past four," she announced.

"Supposed we wanted you gone before then?" Rupe said.

Angie looked pointedly away from him. "We're going for tea…"

"Tea? After all this? No wonder you're—"

"That's fine." Clare cut across him, loudly.

"To drink." Angie turned back and pulled a face at Rupe. "A cup of tea. And hark at Mr Sylph-like!"

"You tell him," said Meg.

Clare saw Tom trying not to laugh. "Who is it?" she asked Angie.

"You don't know her," said Angie airily. "Her name is Chrissy. She's quite a new friend…"

Clare saw Figs give a small smile, while Rupe adopted a sceptical expression. Angie had a lot of "new friends". They were flavour of the month for a while – much praised and quoted – and then usually disappeared quite abruptly, never to be mentioned again.

Rupe was fond of making oblique Orwellian references to "The Ministry of Truth" whenever another favourite bit the dust, which Angie either did not, or chose not to, pick up on.

"We met on the KAALE demo," Angie volunteered. "She helps out at TAG."

Tom raised his eyebrows in query. "They are…?"

"Kent Action Against Live Exports and Thanet Animal Group," Angie rapped out at him firmly. "I support both," she added, as if daring anyone to question it. "Next time," she said to Clare, "you need to get me something, walnut burgers are good – you can buy those from Waitrose."

"I'll be sure to make a mental note," said Clare.

Figs gave a tiny yawn. "We'd better order a cab too," she said, making no effort to do so.

Clare brought out cheese and picked at a piece of stilton while around her they chatted on. She moved places so she could ask her nephew about school, making herself a jasmine tea first, beginning to feel heavy and a bit dozy from all the wine. The rest of them, apart from Josh and Alex and Meg – who had been drinking tea for at least an hour – were made of sterner stuff. Rupe was getting a bit red and voluble but everyone was laughing so Clare shrugged to herself. She felt more mellow and relaxed than she had for a while. Her mind drifted to homeless Tony, as Alex told her about his Geography field trip. She wondered what he was doing this afternoon, while she was surrounded by her family.

When the doorbell rang, Angie jumped up to answer it, almost knocking her wine glass over. Clare liked the look of Chrissy. She was about thirty-five with short bleached hair and a nose stud, dressed in a red skirt and blue Doc Martens. "Hi, all," she said firmly, looking around the table. Angie began introducing them.

"Are you another servant of Her Majesty?" enquired Rupe, when she got to him. "Also known by my late father-in-law as 'another bloody parasite'?"

"Dad!" Ellie shook her head. "Ignore him, Chrissy. He thinks he's being funny. This is Tom," she went on, "my fiancé," she added, not able to resist a small glance at her ring. "And I'm Angie's niece, Ellie. My brother Josh has disappeared with my cousin Alex."

"This is my other sister, Figs – Felicity," put in Angie, looking slightly peeved to have had her flow interrupted. Chrissy nodded around, smiling, and then addressed Rupe. "I don't work with Angie, no. I'm a cat behaviourist."

Figs burst out into peals of laughter. "Your face," she said, jabbing a finger at her brother-in-law, "is a picture."

Clare smiled. "Weren't expecting that, were you?" she asked her husband.

"I want another cat," Ellie sounded very young as she put her head on Tom's shoulder. "Can we?" Clare thought he looked uneasy.

"You can't have cats in flats, can you?" he said lightly.

"Well, people do," said Chrissy. "But personally, I think they should have a decent garden to roam in."

Clare watched a familiar pout fleet across her daughter's face, before she adjusted her features again. "When we get a house then," Ellie said.

"Can I get you a drink?" Clare turned her attention back to Chrissy. But Angie shook her head. "I think we'll get going, shall we?" she said, before her friend could answer.

"Sure," Chrissy nodded, looking, Clare thought, a tad disappointed. Rupe looked sorry too. Clare knew he'd been gearing up to make a lot of cat jokes.

Tom joined her in the kitchen as soon as she'd closed the front door behind them both. "Please let me do something," he said, looking at the dishes on the table. "That beef was quite something," he went on. "It all was."

Clare looked at the stub end of sirloin remaining on the big platter. "Rupe loves an excuse to buy an enormous chunk of meat."

"Well, I must return the compliment very soon. But I shall probably get a takeaway – I can't compete with that. Do you like curry? There's a fantastic new Indian opened in the old town. In fact, let me take you both there. We can have drinks in the flat first."

Clare nodded, feeling a sudden curiosity. She'd closed her mind to it before, but now she did want to see where her daughter was living, wanted to see them as a couple in their own setting. Before she could reply, Ellie wandered in and leant against Tom. He put an arm around her. "I'm just saying your mum and dad should come round to the flat one night."

"OK," Ellie agreed, not looking overly ecstatic but not pulling a face either.

"Sounds good to me," Clare said lightly.

"I'm just going to look for some teaching materials I need," Ellie said to Tom. "Do you want to come upstairs?"

"I'm going to give Clare a hand."

"There is really no need; I'll do the rest later," Clare said, as Ellie's feet pounded up the stairs. "Come and sit down. Do you want fresh coffee, or another drink?"

But Tom didn't move. "I've really had the best time today," he said. He grinned at her. "Ellie told me you were both rather straight – especially you – but I don't know what she was talking about." He clapped a hand to his mouth. "Sorry – I really shouldn't have said that. I blame your husband. He kept pouring me red wine."

"Yes, he's good at that," said Clare drily. "And both my children think we were born in the dark ages. Especially me, where Ellie is concerned," she added ruefully.

"I know – I did point out you were only eight years older than I am." For a moment his eyes seemed to pierce hers. Clare looked away.

"Anyhow, we will make a date for you to come to me as soon as possible," Tom continued. "And I, for one, will look forward to it very much."

Clare smiled at him. "So will I," she said.

———

Alex disappeared to his bedroom as soon as they got home. As Figs went upstairs after him to find Tilda, she heard the roar of the crowd on his FIFA game.

Tilda was in her room too, sitting in the middle of her bed, legs crossed, tapping at her phone. She looked up and smiled at her mother. "How did it go?"

"It was fine. The usual. Clare was a bit uptight at first, I thought. Though she was quite happy by the time we left. Angie was Angie. Rupe was Rupe. Nanna was on form…"

"What did you eat?" Tilda looked wistful.

"Roast beef. What have you had?"

"A sandwich."

Figs surveyed her. "And what else did you get up to?"

Tilda sighed. "The unification of Italy—" but she looked away as she said it and coloured slightly.

Figs smiled. "And how are things with Ryan?"

Tilda smiled back self-consciously. "All right, thanks."

Figs sat down on the end of the bed. "You are revising too though, aren't you? The exams are only two weeks away and—"

"I know! I saw Ryan for about an hour and the rest of the time I've been looking at my history notes, I promise. He's got to revise too. He's got his first one even sooner."

"OK, but it's essential you do well, isn't it? You said yourself that the AS levels were really important if you wanted to get good final grades for a top university. If you don't, you'll—"

"Yes, Mum!" Tilda's voice rose. "I told *you* all this. I *am* revising. But we have to have breaks too. Mr Matthews said we should revise in small chunks and have rests in between. Forty-five minutes four times a day."

"It doesn't seem like very much…"

"Well, that's what he said. Check if you don't believe me."

"OK! OK." There was a pause. Figs said in a calmer tone, "Clare loved her pot."

"Oh, good."

"She cried."

"It wasn't that bad." Tilda laughed. Then looked concerned. "Is she OK?"

"Bit menopausal, but…" Figs shrugged.

"Did you like Tom?"

Figs nodded. "I thought you'd ask about him first!"

"I've seen him all over Ellie's Facebook. She's got videos up and everything. There's loads of it."

"Yes, he seemed very nice. Very successful-looking." Figs paused. "Which reminds me, we're going to Facetime with Dad after supper. Not that I can eat another thing. But I'll make you something and no doubt Alex will soon be starving again."

"I just want salad."

"And some protein. Cheese omelette? Tuna mayo?"

"Yeah, either. Thanks, Mum." Tilda pulled her laptop towards her. "I'll do a bit more first."

Figs stood up, leaning across to briefly stroke her daughter's dark hair. "Well done."

Shredding lettuce in the kitchen downstairs, she tried to push down her unease. In her one short meeting with Ryan, the eighteen-year-old had seemed perfectly pleasant, but she worried about how deeply attached Tilda seemed to be. Ryan would be off to university in October if he got his grades and then what would happen? Tilda was talking as if it wouldn't make a difference, as if they'd carry on and she'd join him at the same place – his first choice was Bristol – a year later, but how could it survive when they were so very young? And Tilda should choose the best university for *her*... Suppose she got there and then he dumped her?

Figs shook herself. There was no point worrying; it could all be over before then. But she'd seen the way her daughter looked at him...

She thought about her older sister. Clare had been getting herself in a right tizzy about Ellie living with an older man – for reasons she couldn't even explain – but Tilda's situation was more of a worry. As she'd said to Clare, her daughter wasn't putting her whole future in the balance. She was just moving into a very nice flat in Margate! If it didn't work out, she could simply come home again. But when you were only seventeen, the decisions you made could affect everything...

Almost as if on cue, Figs's phone beeped. She wiped her

hands and picked it up from the counter. A WhatsApp notification. She felt her heart quicken a little as she opened it up. She realised she was holding her breath as she scanned the words in front of her. She'd had a feeling it would be, she thought, as she began to smile. It was another message from *him*…

Chapter Ten

"I am sitting on the bus no!" repeated Khalid with another beam. "No bus," he added helpfully, making an extravagant arm gesture. "No bus London me sitting."

Anna looked at the smiling Saudi sitting across the desk from her, and smiled back as enlightenment struck. "Ah!" she said. "You don't want to go on the coach trip to London tomorrow?"

Khalid nodded. "Yes, London. No, sitting on bus."

Anna tried again. "You want to go to London but you don't want to go on the bus? Well, that's the travel arrangement—"

"Yes bus London." Khalid held up one finger. "No bus London." Now he held up two fingers.

Anna frowned, as Nick came into her office, carrying a mug. "How's your Arabic?" she asked him. "Judy's gone home sick and I'm having to sort the weekend activities as well."

She spoke calmly but inside she was getting increasingly

harassed. It had been one thing after another since she had got into work this morning, with their boss, Aaron, in overdrive about the schedules for August when she was still struggling to get through all the preparation for July...

Nick turned to Khalid and said a few words Anna didn't understand. Khalid grinned widely and responded in a rapid stream of Arabic. Nick nodded. "Again," he said in English. "Slowly."

Khalid appeared to repeat it just as fast, but Nick was nodding again.

"OK," he said, turning back to Anna. "Khalid is meeting his uncle in London tomorrow evening and staying in a hotel with him. So, he wants to go to London on the bus with everyone and do the sightseeing tour, but he won't be coming back on the coach. He will get a train on Sunday."

"All right." Anna pulled a sheet of paper towards her. "Ellie is the teacher going. I'll write her a note. But tell Khalid to please remind Ellie when he gets off the coach that he's not coming back, and also to tell his group leader. We don't want any panics when they think he's lost."

When Khalid had left, still grinning, Anna glanced at the clock behind her.

"I hadn't realised the time."

Nick was now sitting in the chair Khalid had vacated. He'd taken to coming in here most days during his coffee break and she had begun to look forward to it.

"How's it going?" she asked.

"Yeah, fine." He hesitated. "I, um... What are you doing this weekend? I know you said you can't come for drinks later but..."

"I've got to sit down with Aaron and go through things. And then I need to go home. I've already worked late twice this week and…" She shrugged. She'd already told Nick her situation at home. How she didn't like to leave Jeremy alone for too long, too often. "Why do you ask?" she said, aware of her heart beating a little harder.

"I wondered if you'd come and look at a couple of flats with me?"

"Oh. I don't know," she said feeling flustered. "Why? Do you—?"

"I've seen two that I like. That one in Arlington House that I told you about? The agent's got a load of viewings lined up and says it won't be around long, and the other is in Broadstairs. I'd just really value another opinion. In case there's a snag or downside I've missed." He went on quickly. "My landlord isn't going to be able to renew my contract at the end of the six months because his daughter wants the place or something, and so I thought I'd better get moving." He gave a short laugh. "Literally!"

Anna could see he was ill at ease, waiting for her response, looking self-consciously at his hands as he waited. "I'll ply you with wine after," he added, with a half-smile.

She felt flattered and pleased to be asked, slightly awkward at the thought of doing something so … intimate … together, then shook herself mentally. He just wanted a bit of local knowledge, someone else to bounce his thoughts off. She still felt pleased he had chosen her.

"Sure!" She said it more briskly than she had intended. "What time?"

She left early the next day, allowing double the time needed for the twenty-minute walk to the station, wanting to be able to stroll in the sunshine, with time to take in the flowers in the gardens of the terraced houses along the route. She stopped to smell the roses in front of a large bungalow on Nelson Road and lingered to look at the street art on the side wall of the tattoo shop.

The warmth on her face felt good as she wandered past the Turkish barber's, vegan café, and funeral parlour, idly glancing in the windows of the florist and a shop selling vintage clothes. She stopped and looked at her reflection in a free-standing full-length mirror in the window of the antique shop.

She'd dressed carefully, feeling guilty as she'd chosen the pale cotton trousers and soft shirt, winding the emerald silk scarf around her neck, choosing beads and earrings, trying to look casual yet stylish, and fussing over the right amount of understated make-up to highlight her eyes without going for the full mutton.

It wasn't unusual to want to look one's best, she told herself – she always paid attention to her appearance. Ellie had commented, sweetly, on how elegant Anna was only the other day.

But as she applied lipstick and perfume, Anna knew what she was doing. Nick was only a friend, she repeated silently, caught between excitement and shame. She hadn't lied to Jeremy about who she was meeting today but when he had assumed that the younger colleague in need of advice was female, she hadn't corrected him either.

Much younger, she reminded herself, as she crossed the road by the library and turned towards the station. Twenty-odd years. He needed her opinion, that was all. But still she felt that small thrill as she remembered the way he'd kissed her cheek again the afternoon before, his hand lingering on her shoulder, his smile as he said he was looking forward to today.

Anna looked up and smiled at a woman sitting on her balcony, who gave her a small wave back. That woman would see another sensible-looking older female heading for the station. She would think she was going out for lunch with friends or to see her daughter perhaps. Anna knew she didn't look like the sort of person who was going to meet a man she hadn't told her husband about.

She paused to admire a huge cherry tree set back in the garden of one of the bungalows, and to take a deep breath. She wasn't doing anything wrong. Not by helping a colleague she'd become sociable with.

She had leant down and kissed Jeremy before she left, had said, "Love you," the way they'd always said it, once upon a time. He hadn't really looked up; had replied, "And you," as if he were thinking about something else entirely. For a split second, she'd wanted to cry, *Hug me!* like he used to before, when he would hold her as if he never wanted to let her go…

But she'd just said, "See you later," adding as she opened the front door, "have a good day." She'd thought she heard him give a small snort at that.

Anna walked on. Minutes later, she turned into Railway Avenue and headed purposefully for the station. She was off to meet her friend.

———

"Oh!" Clare surveyed Tom, standing on her doorstep, in surprise. "Is everything OK?"

He looked stylishly casual in chinos and an open-necked shirt. He was smiling. "Yes, of course. I've come to pick up something for Ellie. She said she'd text you?"

Clare stood back to let him come in. "Never rely on my daughter to remember to do anything." She smiled back. "But it's fine. What does she want? And where is she?"

"She's on a trip to London with the students. But she wants a dress for this evening – we're going out with some friends of mine. She said you'd get it for me," he added apologetically. "I don't know what it's like. She was supposed to…"

"Text me," finished Clare, as Tom pulled his phone from his pocket and began to tap at it. "She's probably forgotten already."

"I'll let her know I'm here," he said.

"Would you like a coffee or something?" Clare walked ahead of him to the kitchen. She didn't really want him here – it was her precious *me* hour. Rupe had gone on his "daily constitutional" and Josh was working. But Ellie might take ages to reply and she couldn't just leave Tom standing there.

He sounded distracted as he continued to send the message. "Yes, great. Thanks."

"Pick your poison." She pointed to a wire bowl piled high with colourful Nespresso capsules. "There's a card there to tell you what they all are."

"I've got one myself." He held out an orange foil dome. "This is perfect."

He perched himself on a stool as she pressed the button on the machine. "I never tire of the smell of coffee," he said, as the aroma drifted towards them. "And I could certainly do with one." He shook his head and pulled a face.

"Bad morning?" she asked lightly, adding silently, *Yippee. Now you're going to tell me about it...*

"Oh, you know, tenants..."

"I don't really." Clare knew her voice sounded clipped. "Rupe used to want us to buy a property to rent out but we never have. I always thought I had enough to do already."

"The figures don't stack up the way they used to," said Tom. "When I bought my first, it was easy, but now..." He shook his head again.

"I thought you were just in the process of buying another one?" Clare raised her eyebrows.

"That's a bit of a special case. I'm getting it for a really good price because the place is falling apart and the bloke needs a quick sale."

"Milk?" Clare handed him a small mug and reached into the fridge.

"It's going to cost a fortune to bring it up to standard," Tom continued. "The media loves to demonise the private landlord – as if we're all lining our pockets and not bothering with repairs but—"

"Well, in fairness," interrupted Clare, pushing the milk towards him, "some landlords *are* like that. Josh's student accommodation was absolutely shocking. It was damp and the heating was always breaking down. I went down there and there was black mould in the bathroom and they hadn't had any hot water for a week. I went straight to the agents and kicked up merry hell, I can tell you."

"I bet you did." Tom grinned. "But I'm a good landlord. When they tell me there's water dripping through the ceiling I send round a plumber. But unfortunately, sometimes they don't bother to tell me until the drip is a trickle, or even a downright gush and the ceiling is about to come down. My letting agent just did a six-month inspection on one of my flats and the tenant said the storage heater in the bedroom hadn't worked since he moved in. Well, why the hell didn't he say so?"

Tom took the spoon from Clare and began to stir. "And he complained about mould in the bathroom too. So, I went round there and guess what? He'd disconnected the extractor fan because it was noisy! Probably around the same time as he took the batteries out of the smoke alarm because he wanted them for something else. But if he burned to death it would all be my fault!"

Tom threw her a challenging look. Clare returned it. "Hmm, well, they must be old-style alarms if he could get the batteries out, and why is the extractor noisy?"

"It isn't, particularly. He's just making a fuss. But complaints about mould are the bane of my life. It forms because they don't open windows." He grinned at her, although the challenge was still there. "And I bet Josh and his mates didn't. A previous tenant in another flat complained endlessly about her bathroom. Dried all her washing in there and never opened a window once. She'd actually painted the frame shut – in purple! We freed it up when we were redecorating for the next one to move in. She ventilates the place properly. And there's never been a problem! How often does your heating break down?"

Clare shook her head. "I don't know. It doesn't. Oh once, a few winters ago," she added, recalling Ellie's wails when she couldn't wash her hair.

"Exactly!" said Tom. "Mine neither. Tenants' heating? All the time!"

"There must be a reason for that," said Clare, warming to the debate. "Perhaps you're putting in the wrong boilers. Or they're ancient. The one in Josh's house looked pre-war!"

"I put in good boilers!" Tom said, with equal spirit. "You might want to think I skimp because that suits the all-landlords-are-grasping-bastards narrative but the truth is—"

"I didn't say *all*. But Josh's one was a shyster. All his accommodation was substandard – I talked to another parent and her daughter's house had rats!"

"But that might have had more to do with the standard of cleaning and how often they took the rubbish out?"

Clare smiled. "Possibly. Josh's kitchen was a bit of a health hazard, I must admit. But that landlord—"

"I agree," Tom interrupted her now, "that some of them are irresponsible. But some tenants are too. You may not like to hear this, but it is a fact that when people get their rent paid entirely for them through housing benefit, they don't have the same sense of responsibility – there's no feeling of ownership…"

Clare gave him a hard look. "That's very sweeping."

"It's what I've observed," he said calmly. "Not always," he added quickly. "I've got one tenant I've had for five years and she's on benefits – she's on her own with a couple of kids. She's brilliant. The place is always immaculate; the kids are polite…"

He gave her what he clearly thought was a winning smile. Clare continued to hold his gaze. "Gosh, single mother brings up kids well!" she said drily. "How amazing. Perhaps some tenants don't take pride in their accommodation because they don't feel secure in it," she swept on. "Because life is a struggle, always being short of money. Because they have low self-esteem, because they feel there is no hope of anything improving?"

"Yes, maybe," Tom conceded, mildly. "I can see that. But I think things always can improve if you really put your mind to it."

"Which, again, is hard to do if you're dragged down and depressed," Clare said doggedly. "Not everyone has your get-up-and-go."

"Indeed." Tom put his coffee mug back on the breakfast bar. "And that's why I try not to be too much of a bastard!" There was a gleam in his eye. "And quite often let arrears slide and spend more money clearing up after them than I should have to. And this bloody government doesn't help.

The new wiring regulations are going to cost me thousands."

"But will keep your tenants safe, presumably," said Clare sweetly. "You can always think about how much rent you'll be raking in."

"A very paltry sum by the time you've paid the bank loan and the letting agent's fees and the endless maintenance." Tom grinned at her.

Clare gave a wry smile back. "You look OK on it to me." She nodded at his empty cup. "Do you want another one?

Before he could reply, his phone gave a loud beep. "Ah, Ellie!" He read from the screen:

Tell Mum is on the right of my wardrobe. Red Mango with bow on back.

Clare got off her stool. "I know the one."

She ran up the stairs, positively cheered by the altercation. Once she had argued like that with Rupe. They would spend hours wrangling enjoyably over politics – him calling her naïve and idealistic, her shouting that he was a diehard reactionary who needed to open his eyes to the way the world had changed – and sometimes the kids would join in and they'd all be yelling. Clare remembered the table-thumping fondly.

But these days, Rupe would become increasingly repetitive and didactic whenever she tried to discuss the news. Especially if it was post-wine. He would simply ignore all her points and trot out the same old tropes until, far from finding it stimulating, Clare just wanted to throttle him.

At least Tom listened.

She picked her way across Ellie's room – which looked as if its owner had been searching for several items before leaving in a hurry – making a mental note to collect the coffee cups before they grew enough mould to rival any of Tom's bathrooms. Clare stepped over a pair of ankle boots and threw a couple of cushions back on the bed, before rummaging through her daughter's still-stuffed wardrobe. As she came back down with the dress in her arms, she heard the front door open and Rupe's voice raised in greeting.

She pushed down the slight flare of resentment. Surely he'd not been gone that long!

"You don't need to tell me!" he was saying loudly as Clare went back into the kitchen. "I'd sack the bloody lot of them."

Clare handed Tom the dress. "I've suggested Rupe runs for the local council," she said. "He's got so many ideas about how things should be done…" *And he'd have to go to all those meetings…*

"Rather eat my own leg," said Rupe cheerfully. "Bunch of idiots! Would you like a drink? I've got rather a nice Bordeaux needs opening. It is the weekend after all…"

"No, I can't, but thank you." Tom was moving towards the doorway. "Need to get back. Lots to do before I pick Ellie up." He smiled at Rupe warmly. "But it would be great to share a bottle or two with you soon." He looked at Clare. "Let's go for that curry? I'd love to take you both out."

"Excellent!" Rupe nodded vigorously. "Always up for a good madras…"

He pulled a bottle from the wine rack, leaving Clare, as usual, to fix a date. She wrote it on the family calendar.

"Give my love to Ellie," she said, as she walked with Tom to the front door. "I hope you have a nice evening."

"I'm sure we shall. And we certainly will next weekend!" He gave her a brief, firm hug. "I'll look forward to that."

"So will I," said Clare, realising, as she closed the door after him, that, strangely, it was true.

Chapter Eleven

"So, what's the verdict?"

Nick came back to the table with a bottle of rosé in a cooler in one hand and two wine glasses in the other. He put them down in front of Anna. "Start pouring," he instructed, as he disappeared again. Moments later he returned with dishes of olives and nuts. "Hope you like these?"

"Yes, lovely."

It was. They were sitting outside a small Italian restaurant and bar up on the Westcliff Arcade, overlooking Ramsgate harbour. The sun was warm. It bounced off the rows of boats moored below them, catching the water and making it sparkle.

They'd got a train from Margate to Broadstairs but then Nick had called them a cab back here, so he could both take her to his favourite bar, he told her, and consider the two flats they'd seen from a distance. He didn't want to discuss either of them until they were sitting down over a drink.

"Which one would you buy?" he asked her now, when they'd both taken the first mouthfuls of the cold wine.

"That is really nice," she said first, indicating the bottle. "Thank you. This is a treat."

He nodded, smiling. "Which one?" he repeated. "I think I know the one you liked best, but you tell me."

"I can give you my views on both," she said. "But it's not about what I think – *you* have to decide."

"I'm interested in what you feel," he insisted. "And you know the area."

"OK." Anna took another sip of wine and a breath. "The view from Arlington House is amazing – I really loved that. And the people in the lift seemed friendly and it appeared to be pretty well-organised. The flat needs some work, but the agent said they sell like hot cakes so if you needed to move again, you'd get your money back and some..." She paused. He was watching her intently.

"But the position in Broadstairs is good too," she continued. "The flat was a bit darker of course, but I think it only seemed that by comparison. And the kitchen's bigger. You've also got a view of the sea – even if it's a smaller one. I love York Street, which is a moment away. It's only a short walk up the high street to the bus or the station. Though the bus stops right outside the school, so if I were you—" She stopped. "That's probably not the sort of thing you meant, is it?" She laughed and took another sip of wine.

"What did you think of the feel of them?" Nick asked seriously. "The atmosphere? Which one could *you* most imagine living in?"

Anna frowned. "It doesn't really matter what I—"

"It does," Nick insisted. "It does to me. I trust your judgement. And I want you to like whatever flat I buy because I hope you'll be visiting."

She looked at her glass, his serious tone making her self-conscious. When she raised her eyes, he was still gazing at her.

"Well, of course I will," she said brightly. "If I'm invited."

"You'll be the first."

Anna couldn't think of anything to say. She smiled and ate an olive, slightly thrown by his apparent intensity. She felt as if she should mention something about Jeremy, but Nick was still talking.

"I'm so happy that I've got to know you. It's been a big factor in deciding to lay down some roots. I thought it would just be a summer job. I didn't know if I'd be here beyond that but..." He took an olive himself and looked thoughtful. "Blake thinks he'll have enough work for me all winter, but even if he doesn't, I still think I want to stay in Thanet. Lots of things feel right about it. I need to buy a property before prices go up too much and around here" – he indicated the harbour in front of them – "there's a lot to like."

She nodded, feeling on safer ground. "Yes, Thanet has an awful lot going for it, and I believe it's a good place to invest in," she said, aware of her teacher-ish tone. "Lots of Londoners are moving down here. I think it's very wise to buy now. As you say, prices will only go up."

"But it's not just about money," he said earnestly. "I want to feel at home. I've felt" – he paused to search for a word – "temporary for too long. Renting in Hemel after my marriage ended, then being in Dubai. I want to feel settled now." He laughed. "Boring, eh?"

"Natural," said Anna.

"Since I came here," he went on, "I've begun to have a proper sense of who I am. For the first time in a long time." He was looking at her very intensely now. "You've really helped with that."

"Really? I don't know how; I haven't done anything." She picked up her glass, embarrassed, her other hand fiddling with her sunglasses on the table in front of her.

"You've listened. Been interested." He topped up her glass. "Just being able to chat about what happened with Emma has helped me process it. I hadn't really done that before. And it's lifted a lot of the sadness because now I realise it was never going to work. How could it? It wasn't her fault at all… It's me. I need to be true to myself about the sort of person I want to spend my life with. And since coming to Margate, I've begun to realise… I know I haven't put this into words before, but…"

Anna felt a sudden panic. She didn't know what he was going to say but felt as though she had to stop it. "I'm glad it helped," she babbled. "I sometimes think we do need to reflect to others in order to get clarity. I should probably do it more myself…"

She took a swallow of wine, realising her hand was shaking.

"Hey, are you OK?" Nick was looking at her with concern. "I'm so sorry – going on about myself. How are things with you? Is Jeremy all right?"

"Oh, yes, he's fine…"

Anna took some nuts. She realised she needed to eat. She wasn't good at wine on an empty stomach these days.

Nick seemed to read her mind. "Shall we have dinner here? Can you stay out?"

Anna looked at her watch. It was after six. She hadn't realised. Even if she left now, she'd be home after the time they usually ate together.

"I'll have to call Jeremy."

"Of course."

He got up, murmuring something about getting some water. Anna pulled out her phone, grateful for his tact.

There was a Waitrose fish pie in the freezer and the rest of a salad from last night. Tomorrow, she'd be home all day. She'd roast a chicken, do it all properly…

Jeremy no longer bothered with a mobile, but answered the landline after a couple of rings. "It's all gone on later than I thought," she said. "Would you mind if…"

———

"That's fine," she said moments later, when Nick came back to the table with a water jug and two tumblers.

"Great!" His face lit up. "I'll go get menus."

When he came back, he'd brought a second bottle of wine. He grinned at her. "So Jeremy's happy with you staying out? He sounds like a good bloke."

She nodded. Jeremy had been kind. Told her not to worry about him – to have a nice time with her friend. It made it all feel much worse. Part of Anna wanted to go to the station now. "I said I wouldn't be late."

"I'll get you a cab to the station when the time comes," Nick said. "It's a trek from here." He opened the menu in front of him. Anna picked up her own and was washed over by misgiving. When had she last eaten out with a man – just the two of them – who was not either her husband or one of her sons? Probably never – not since before that first dinner for Jeremy's fiftieth birthday…

"The linguini is very good here," Nick was saying. "But have whatever you like. I'm getting it!" he added firmly. "I am so grateful for today." He poured her more rosé.

"So," she said lightly. "Have you made a decision?"

"I keep thinking about that view."

"Yes, it was quite something, wasn't it? And I think you'd like the sense of community? On the other hand, the flat in Broadstairs doesn't need anything doing to it. Well, actually, the one in Arlington House only needs some paint, really, doesn't it? And new flooring."

Suddenly she was gabbling. It must be the wine making her suddenly so free with her opinions.

Nick nodded. "And a new shower room?"

"I know a great plumber."

Nick laughed. "I'll put an offer in on Arlington House and see if I get it," he said decisively. "If I do, it will be meant to be. If I don't, I will offer on Broadstairs."

"A bit further to travel to work?"

"Yeah, but I quite like the idea of home being in a different town from work. A bit of demarcation. Oh, Anna!" He looked at her happily. "I can't believe I'm going to move here – I thought this job would only be a stop-gap, but I really like the way things are turning out…"

And half an hour later, so did Anna. The combination of the creamy homemade pasta and the fragrant wine had relaxed her. She felt mellow and light. She looked at the table – the perfectly dressed green salad in its wooden bowl, the warm rosemary-infused focaccia, the dish of crispy calamari Nick had ordered on the side because it was among the best he'd tasted. This was good. It was what she missed.

Tomorrow would be all about Jeremy but for tonight she was glad to be here. Why shouldn't she have some fun? It wasn't as if there was anything going on between her and Nick. They were having a lovely evening, chatting like old friends…

"So, who else is in your life?" asked Nick. "You said you had sons?"

She'd already told him a little about Stevie and baby Tay. "My younger son, Marcus, is in Vancouver at the moment. His husband is Canadian – they may come back here later…"

She watched the unnaturally bright interest on Nick's face. It was a look she was familiar with – people falling over themselves to say how lovely that was, in case they should be thought homophobic – while searching her face to see how she *really* felt about it…

Anna felt a stab of disappointment. But at least Nick took it head on.

"How did you feel when he first told you he was gay?" he asked.

"I'd always known," she said. "Or for a very long time anyway. It was no surprise. I was worried about what Jeremy would say. He can be" – she paused, trying to find a word that was fair – "rather straight," she offered with a smile. "Traditional."

"And?"

"He was fine. He told me later that he was worried that some people might treat Marcus badly, but at the time he did everything right. He hugged him and told him he loved him. He wasn't sure about Rudi at first, but we both love him now. He's very different to Marcus but they're good together."

"My mother said something like that to me once," said Nick. "There was a boy at school I was very close to and my mother said, 'I wouldn't mind you being homosexual, Nicholas, not for myself.'" He had put on an educated mock-female voice. "'But I would be concerned that life would be much harder for you. It's always difficult to be in a minority.'" Nick rolled his eyes. "As if being gay was a decision I could make after weighing up the pros and cons." He gave a rueful smile. "She looked most concerned when I bought a pink silk shirt. And was over the bloody moon when I got married."

Anna smiled. "Is she still around?"

"Yes, she and my dad still live in Peterborough where I grew up. My father finds me 'soft'. Always wanted me to go into the Army. Doesn't think teaching English is a proper job."

"What does he do?"

"Retired policeman."

"Ah."

"Your parents?"

"Both dead."

"I'm sorry."

"It was some years ago now. My mother was the same age as Jeremy." She pulled a face. "Which could be a bit odd."

"Did they approve?"

"Oh yes! Marrying a doctor? Very commendable. Even if he was old enough to be my father. And some!"

Anna hoped he'd not noticed the slight tone of resentment that seemed to have entered her voice. She gave a wide smile to show it was all of no consequence.

"Is it … difficult, now he's got older?" Nick's voice was gentle.

She would usually have been brisk and positive but today, sitting here in the dipping evening sun, Anna felt compelled to be honest. "Sometimes," she admitted. "He gets grumpy. He's frustrated by his lack of mobility, his physical frailty. He was such a strong, fit man."

Nick didn't speak. His eyes stayed on hers. She looked down.

"I think we both find the role reversal hard," she went on. "I don't mind what I have to do now, but I hate the feeling of being his carer. Not that I could ever use that word to him. He always looked after *me*, you know? It's how it worked for us."

She took a sip of wine. Now she had started saying it, she didn't seem able to stop.

"I miss our old life together, but it all crept up so slowly

I didn't notice it had gone, until it had. I can't remember now when he stopped going out or..." Anna shook her head. "I'm not complaining..."

"I know you're not."

"But I sometimes wish," she burst out, "sometimes I wish I had a crystal ball. If I could just know... Because if he only had six months or a year left, I would throw everything into it and try to make him as happy as I could. Because I love him and he deserves that. But if he's going to be here for another five years – or ten even – I don't know if I can live this half-life. I want to visit Marcus in Canada, but I can't leave Jeremy that long. He wouldn't hear of anyone coming in. I still want to have fun, but he doesn't want to go out. I don't know how much more..." she said disjointedly. "I feel things at home getting smaller and smaller. As he moves further away and I can feel myself shrivelling up inside—"

She put a hand to her mouth. "I'm sorry. I never talk like this. I have never said that to anyone before. And I shouldn't..."

He leant across and put a hand over hers. "It's OK. You're only telling me."

"I dread him dying," Anna said bleakly. "But I think about it all the time. I just wish I could know," she said again.

"Why don't you live as if you do?"

She looked at him.

"Why not live your life as if you do know," Nick continued, "and make it the best it can possibly be? Because none of us know how short it might be. We could both be run over on the way to the taxi rank." He shrugged. "Why don't you try to have the finest, most fun-filled life you can, Anna? Because you can go back to shrivelling up, any time." He smiled.

"I must sound so awful—"

"You don't at all. You sound as if you're grieving. But maybe you're doing it too soon."

———

They wandered past the other bars and restaurants and down the steps to the harbour. Groups of young people were spilling out of the Royal on the corner, filling the pavement. Many of the boats and yachts were now lit up, colourful lights strung along their decks, the reflections bobbing on the dark oily water. Along Harbour Parade, the tables outside the bars were full, and the sounds of music and voices rolled towards them.

Nick stopped at a bench near the taxi rank. "Shall we just sit here for five minutes before you go? Do you mind if I have a cigarette?"

She shook her head. "Not at all. If I can have one too." She laughed at his surprised expression. "Smoking is my guilty secret. Literally nobody knows I do it. At home, I sneak out to the garden and pretend I'm taking in the night air."

"I suppose your husband would be against it, being a medical man?"

"Oh God, no." Anna laughed again. "He smoked like a chimney when I first met him. In bed and everything! Oh, sorry." She clapped a hand to her mouth. "Too much information."

Nick laughed too. "You look wonderful when you're laughing."

"I'm probably a bit drunk."

"Let's go along here if we're both going to indulge." Nick led her on past the two cabs waiting, and turned onto the pier. "We'll sit here where we can look at the lights." He sat down on a long, low seat, facing the boats, feeling in his jacket pocket. He pulled out a packet of Rothmans.

"Ooh, Clickers! I thought they'd been banned."

"Still got a stash from Bahrain."

"I like them." Anna took the cigarette, crushing the filter between her fingers to release the menthol flavour. She leant forward to take a light from him, inhaling deeply behind his cupped hand, aware of their physical closeness.

"So you're a covert nicotine addict?"

"We both gave up when I was pregnant with Stevie, and as far as Jeremy is concerned that was that. But a few of the younger ones do at school, and one night when we were all in the yard, I just had this sudden impulse. It felt rather thrilling to light up again after all those years. Sort of illicit," she said, feeling that same frisson now. "A packet lasts me ages," she added quickly. "I really only have the odd one..." She trailed off.

"You don't have to justify yourself to me! I've tried lots of times to stop and can't. But I've cut down loads."

They both went quiet. Anna felt calm. The air was still warm and soft against her face. She could hear the water lapping against the wall of the harbour. She looked over at the clock face set in the old Clock House, as she blew out a fragrant stream of smoke. "I must go to the station after this, but thank you so much, it's been really nice.'

Nick leant back and took another drag on his cigarette. "It's been wonderful. I felt quite lonely when I started here. Not knowing anyone. Making friends with you has made all the difference."

She felt comfortable now. "I'm glad."

"And Ellie has been really kind to me too. She's invited me along with Simon for a Chinese next week, with her and Tom. I was really touched."

"That's nice. She's a lovely girl. She and Simon are very good friends."

"Yeah, he said." Nick exhaled. "I went to see *Judy* with him last night. It was a sort of film-club thing at the Palace in Broadstairs. Whoever he was supposed to be going with pulled out and I leapt at it. I never got to see it at the time."

"I haven't seen it either. I gather it's good."

"It was really great. I love Renée Zellweger."

"Yes, me too."

"My wife hated *Bridget Jones*. We were very mismatched on films too. She wanted to see things like *Legend* or *Dragged Across Concrete* – she liked anything with a good punch-up in it – and all I wanted was to curl up in front of *Love Actually*. My lack of masculinity was a constant source of tension."

Anna turned and smiled at him. "Nothing wrong with being in touch with your feminine side."

She felt his hand lightly cover hers. "Yes, you'd think women would like a bit of sensitivity, wouldn't you?"

"I do." She immediately felt her insides go into a cringe. Why had she said that? "Well, what I mean is…" she began, embarrassed, but he spoke over her.

"That's why I love you!" He said it easily, smiling at her, giving her arm a brief squeeze and nodding back towards the row of bars. "You don't want to have one more before you go?"

Her heart was thumping as if something alarming had happened. He was joking. He'd had lots to drink too.

"I really can't."

"No, I know. I'm sorry. I shouldn't have suggested it. I've hogged you long enough. Tell Jeremy thank you."

She looked back at him. He looked serious now and sincere.

"I told him I was viewing properties with a colleague," she said. "I think he assumed it was a woman."

Nick shrugged. "Oh well, we've just established my credentials as an honorary girl. Come on." He ground out his cigarette and sprang to his feet before she could say anything further. "Let's get you to that station!"

She stood up too. "We'll have an extra drink next time," he said, swinging an arm around her shoulders and squeezing her towards him for a brief, warm moment. "There will be lots of next times, won't there?"

She looked at the smiling grey eyes and fair hair of the man young enough to be her son and something she couldn't define went through her.

She nodded. "I hope so."

Chapter Twelve

"So," said Figs, spearing a cube of feta cheese and adding it to a slice of beetroot. "Are you sleeping with Chrissy?"

Angie looked annoyed. "No, I am not."

"Would you like to?" Figs enquired.

Clare gave her younger sister a warning look which Figs ignored. They were in Quixote, Margate's newest café-bar, eating salads and flatbreads in Angie's lunch-hour. Figs had ordered wine and was becoming expansive.

"Don't look so appalled," she told Angie. "You do swing both ways – we all know that."

"You mean I'm pansexual," said Angie. "In other words, I'm not stuck in a state of pre-conditioned stereotype like you two. Which you can afford to be all judgemental about, because you're both married and have sex on tap."

"I wasn't judging," said Figs. "I don't give a fuck who you go to bed with. And how have I got it on tap when Don spends most of the year four thousand bloody miles away?"

She snorted. "Everyone knows married people are the ones who never get any, eh, Clare?"

Clare looked at her sharply. "Why are you saying that?"

Figs shrugged. "No reason. God, you two are a bundle of bloody laughs today. I'm going to have another glass of wine. Do either of you want anything?"

Clare nodded at her mineral water. "Got enough, thanks. I can't go to the shop smelling of booze."

"I don't know why you don't work with one of the animal charities instead," said Angie. "They're crying out for help."

"Why don't you then?"

"I've got a full-time job already," Angie said smugly. "And I sell raffle tickets for Cats in Crisis."

"Is that how you met Chrissy?" asked Figs, sounding bored.

"No! You never listen. We were—"

"I thought she was really nice," said Clare quickly. "I think it would be lovely if you and she—"

"If you must know," Angie said loudly, "I'm back with Zach."

Clare sighed. "Oh, Ange. You know what he's like."

Figs was waving to the young man behind the scrubbed wooden counter. "You're not 'with' him," she said, eyes still fixed on the back of the room. "You mean he's been round for a shag."

"He's never going to change," said Clare. "He's too—"

Angie glared. "Oh, so it's fine for your husband to be twenty years older and Ellie can have a sugar daddy, but just because it's the other way round—"

"It's not the age," said Clare emphatically. "It's the fact that he messes you around. But he is only twenty-bloody-eight—"

"Twenty-nine."

"And he has a purely sexual relationship with you, when there's nobody else around, which would be OK if that's what you wanted too. I'm sorry, I don't mean to be cruel." Clare put a hand on her sister's arm. "I'm just remembering how upset you got last time."

"He was having some problems then."

"He's one big problem, if you ask me," said Clare.

"Men under thirty are not going to be long-term with a woman of nearly fifty-four," said Figs firmly. "He'll want to get married to some bird of twenty-two with legs and tits, and he'll want kids. You're better off with Chrissy, if you ask me."

"Hmm." Angie appeared to think about this, before she abruptly changed the subject. "Chrissy thought it was weird the way we were all still in Thanet but I explained that it wasn't so much 'still' but gravitating back. I said Figs came back when Don found out he could buy a mansion down here for the price of his flat in London, and Clare followed Rupe."

"That's not quite right, is it?" Clare broke off a piece of flatbread and wiped up her salad dressing with it. "We both decided this would be a good place to set up home, for the schools and by the sea and everything, and Dad had had his heart attack. I wanted to be close to help out."

"You're the one who never really went away," said Figs. She took the new glass of wine from the young man she'd signalled and handed him her empty one. "Apart from going to university,"

"And I stayed there for a year after," said Angie. "I'd probably still be in Nottingham if it wasn't for that bloody Trevor..."

"Anyway, when are you seeing Chrissy again?" Clare exchanged glances with Figs as she deliberately interrupted. "As a friend, or whatever."

"She's coming to visit at the weekend," said Angie, sounding sulky. "We're going to look through the procedure for me pursuing a case against an employer for historical sex abuse."

"What?" Clare heard the shrill note in her own voice. "Against who?"

"Granville."

Both sisters looked blankly at her.

"Granville who owned the diner! Where I was a waitress. Surely you remember?"

"I remember you being a waitress," said Clare. "You used to boast about all your tips. I was really jealous."

"Well, it was him."

"Oh, come off it," said Figs. "Why've you never said anything before?"

"What you should be asking is why was I allowed to go and work there? I was only sixteen. The place should have been checked out. It's typical of this family. Mum was so neglectful—"

"Don't start that," said Figs. "Or you're really going to piss me off."

"He put his hand up my T-shirt."

"You never told us," said Clare.

"And when a group of businessmen said they'd pay an extra tenner if I, exclusively, looked after them all night, he said, 'Go for it, stick your chest out'..."

"And he gave you the money after," said Clare. "We've heard *that* story lots of times. You were really pleased."

"It was still abuse. I was being groomed. Not that our mother ever noticed."

Clare frowned. "But you worked there right up until you went to uni. And in all the holidays, if I remember rightly. You always seemed to really enjoy it. You were coining it in."

Figs narrowed her eyes at Angie. "I always thought you quite liked him – didn't you go out for a drink with him later?"

"I slept with him but that's not the point."

As Clare drew her breath in sharply, Angie carried on. "Chrissy says if it's eating me up, I should do something about it."

"Well, Chrissy doesn't really know you yet, does she?" said Clare crossly. "It's not a good idea at all. They probably won't believe you after all this time and that will eat you up even more. You know what a state you get in when—" She stopped and went on more kindly: "I expect you're only thinking about it now because you're stressed about work. You really can't go through a court case."

"Well, I can if I choose to," said Angie stubbornly, while Figs openly rolled her eyes.

"It would be awful," said Clare. "I'm only thinking of you."

"You always are – you're so bloody sanctimonious."

"Bloody hell, Ange!" Figs gave a brittle laugh. "Pots and kettles." She took a swallow of wine and shook her head disbelievingly. "Anyway," she went on, "if you never told Mum anything was wrong, you can't blame her."

"I can and I do. She never took any interest in what I was doing. Too busy doting on you."

"That's not true," said Figs.

"We both know you've always been her favourite."

"I'm just the one who's nice to her. Mum's great," continued Figs.

"She was horrible to Dad," put in Clare.

"That's cos he was a pain in the arse!"

"He could barely breathe!"

"I'm talking about when we were growing up," said Angie, putting her tea glass back on its saucer with a rattle. "I said it to Chrissy. She was never warm, was she?"

"I think she was," persisted Figs. "You've got to remember how difficult it all was when we were young. They didn't have any money. She'd taken a long time to get pregnant and then suddenly there were three of us, all young, with Dad always working. She was taken up with looking after us in a practical way – she didn't have time for all the touchy-feely stuff we've done with our kids. And she says herself it was all different then – says she didn't always get it right."

"Come off it. She's never admitted to that in her entire life." Clare laughed, realising too late she sounded bitter. She stood up abruptly. "I must get going." As she walked towards the loo, she wondered why they did it. She could manage both sisters one to one – but when the three of them got together, it was never long before the battle lines were drawn. Figs would always support Meg, Clare stuck up for their father, and Angie never failed to bring to the table a fresh story of negligence and dysfunction that had invariably passed the other two by.

Figs shrugged it off with a "you know what Ange is like," but it made Clare uneasy. She hoped Chrissy wouldn't encourage Angie in any more delvings into the past than was necessary. Clare had no doubt that this Granville most likely had shoved his hand up Angie's ample front, but she was also pretty sure that Angie hadn't much minded at the time – especially if she went out for drinks with him when it suited her – or they'd have all heard about it with bells on. She'd said some pretty awful things about Zach six months ago, and look at that now…

As she washed her hands, Clare felt overcome with weariness. Usually she looked forward to going to Oasis but today she felt restless, as if she needed a long, bracing walk, while at the same time, also drawn to climbing into bed and pulling the duvet over her head.

When she got back to the table, Angie was holding forth about her boss. Again. Clare pulled out her purse out and handed Figs a twenty-pound note. "I need to go."

Figs waved the money away. "I'll get it," she said. "I drank all the wine." She looked at Ange. "Do you want a coffee?"

To Clare's surprise Ange nodded. "I'm deliberately going to be five minutes late. She said I've got to take a lunch break so I'll take a bit of time over, and see how she likes that!"

Figs shook her head again. "Why do you *care*?"

Clare spoke at the same time. "Why do you have to antagonise her?"

It was to Clare that Angie answered. "I'm not the one antagonising. I've always worked through lunch if I needed to leave early. Roger never cared. Roger let me get on with it. He was a good boss."

"You complained about him at the time," said Figs.

"Just my luck to get a By-the-book Barbara this time," said Angie, ignoring her. "She had the cheek to threaten me with 'taking it further'. As if I were some wayward teenager. I told her I do not appreciate being intimidated."

Clare smiled at her to save sounding confrontational. "You don't sound very cowed to me."

"Maybe not, but I'm suffering from anxiety about it," said Angie darkly. "And I'm not sleeping. I'll come out in a rash next, you wait and see."

Clare felt as if she could be going down with hives herself. She walked briskly down Northdown Road, holding her head high, flexing her stiff neck, as if shaking her sisters out of her hair.

Tony wasn't in any of the doorways near Oasis. She hoped he'd found some proper accommodation now. She'd ask Karen if she'd seen him lately when she got into the shop. But before she could cross the threshold, her phone gave out a beep. Ellie was on WhatsApp saying she thought she'd come round to eat and have "a catch up". Clare raised her eyebrows. She paused on the pavement and called.

"Is everything OK?"

"Of course!" Her daughter's tone was sharp. "Does there have to be a problem for me to come and see my own mother?"

"No, but I thought you'd be—"

"Tom's in a stress about one of his flats." Ellie gave a long sigh. "He needs to meet a builder there. That awful woman's left it in a shocking state. Her boyfriend left her or something, I don't know." Ellie sounded as if she didn't much care either. "Anyway, he's not going to be home till later so I thought I could come for supper and see you, and we could talk about Dad's birthday."

"Really? It's not till—"

"September, which is no time at all. We need to make a plan. I thought you'd be pleased to see me."

"Yes, it will be lovely. I haven't given supper a thought but—"

"Oh, we'll get something out of the freezer," Ellie said breezily. "Or do you want me to pop into the Co-op on the way over?"

"Yeah maybe. I've got to go in the shop now. I'll think about food while I'm in there."

"Fabbo. I've got to go too. Byeee!"

Well, her daughter sounded bright enough anyway. Clare hoped Josh would be feeling better by this evening too. He'd seemed very downhearted when she'd seen him briefly at seven this morning. She'd stopped asking about the job-hunting, only responding if he mentioned it, but she could see how he was losing his confidence.

Karen hadn't seen Tony for several days. She'd given him some socks that had been donated and a pair of shoes, as his were falling apart. "He said he had some sort of appointment with someone about getting a room," she said. "Fingers crossed."

Lyndsey was off with a throat infection, but Harriet was in the back with the steam cleaner. She was as beautifully made-up as always, wearing a flowing smock top over white jeans, but Clare thought she seemed anxious.

"Are you OK?" Clare asked tentatively after she'd sorted through a couple of large boxes of baby clothes.

"Yes, thank you." There was a small silence until Harriet said, "Millie's been having some trouble at school."

"Oh really?" Clare was sympathetic. "Is it getting resolved?"

"I hope so." Harriet frowned. "A couple of the other girls are being awful to her. I've spoken to her teacher – and the head. They said they're on it, but..." She stopped and bit her lip. "It's terrible when you know your child is unhappy and you can't make it right, isn't it?'

Clare nodded.

Harriet put the steamer to one side and breathed deeply. "It gets you right here," she said, putting a hand to her middle.

Clare put a brief hand on the other woman's arm. "I know."

"How old are yours?"

"Ellie's twenty-three, and Josh is twenty-two."

"You had them close together."

"Fifteen months between them. I didn't plan on another baby quite so quickly but…" Clare smiled and shrugged.

"I can't imagine what it feels like to have an adult child," said Harriet. "I feel so protective of Millie; I can't bear anything to be horrible for her. It breaks my heart when she's upset. But when they're in their twenties, making all their own decisions, and you no longer have any control…" She tailed off and looked questioningly at Clare.

"It feels the exactly the same," Clare said.

Chapter Thirteen

"**H**addock! Excellent!" Rupe raised a thumb in approval and grinned at Ellie. "I think this calls for one of my special bottles of Muscadet. That's the thing for fish and chips." He walked past his wife and daughter to the utility room at the end of the kitchen, which housed the washing machine, tumbler dryer, and an extra-large second fridge for Rupe's white-wine stash. They heard the heavy door open and the clink of bottles.

"It was a great idea," said Clare, as they opened the various fragrant boxes. "The oven's hot – we'll pop it in there and just wait for Josh, yes?"

Ellie nodded. "I want to talk to you about him, while he's in the shower. You need to help him out with Nikhita."

As Clare raised her eyebrows in surprise, Ellie went on. "Her parents behave as though she's about sixteen – or younger. So, you need to respond to that. Phone the mother and ask if Niki could come to stay for the weekend. With us all here. As a family. Make it clear you'll be around the whole time. Don't mention I live with Tom."

Clare frowned at her daughter's slightly accusatory tone. "Well, yes, I can do that. But only if Josh asks me to. He hasn't said anything like this to me."

"Well, offer," said Ellie. "They need to see each other more. That's why he's such a pain."

"I thought he was upset about not getting a job."

"That as well."

"When did you speak to him about all this then?' asked Clare curiously.

Ellie shook her head, impatiently. "It's obvious, isn't it?"

"OK, I'll talk to him," said Clare, since it was clear that Ellie wasn't going to be any more forthcoming. "I mean, of course she can come and stay..."

"I think it should happen before Dad's birthday," said Ellie. "So she's already a bit used to everyone." She grinned at her mother. "You know what us lot are like. It's a bit much to throw her straight into a great big party."

"We don't even know we're having a party. I thought maybe just a family dinner out somewhere..."

"Of course we're having a party!" Ellie frowned. "He pulled out all the stops for your fiftieth, didn't he? It's the least you can do."

"He might not want—"

Clare stopped as Rupe reappeared and put two bottles on the kitchen island. "Are you talking about me?" he enquired with interest.

"Your birthday," said Ellie. "You want a party, don't you?"

"I don't know." Rupe shook his head. "When is it anyway?"

"You know very well," said Ellie crisply. "And it's only a couple of months away, really. I think we should be making a plan. There'll be all of us, and your friends and Danny of course."

"Of course," said Clare.

"I'm going to water the beans," said Rupe, opening the back door. "There's one of your mother's bloody fag ends here," he called over his shoulder.

"She picks hers up," Clare called back. "It will be the window cleaner's," she said to Ellie. "He's always doing it."

"We haven't seen Danny for ages," Ellie went on doggedly as if neither of her parents had spoken. "Is he OK? I keep meaning to text him."

"Dad spoke to him," said Clare. "He's fine – he and Mia are looking for a bigger flat." Clare smiled. "I think they're thinking babies."

"Cool," said Ellie, pulling knives and forks from a drawer. "You'll be a step-granny."

Clare tried to look pleased at the prospect. She loved her stepson and his wife, and a baby in the family would be a joy, but she was only just getting used to being fifty, without a granny tag to conjure with too…

"Just as well, really," continued Ellie, "because I won't be making you a real one any time soon."

"I should think not," said Clare, before she could stop herself.

Ellie glared at her. "What does that mean? Most normal

149

mothers are thrilled beyond belief when their daughters get pregnant!"

"And so would I be. I just meant you haven't known Tom very long. It's maybe a bit soon to be having—"

"We weren't going to anyway."

Clare busied herself putting salt and vinegar and mayonnaise on the breakfast bar, ignoring the unnecessary clatter her daughter was making arranging the cutlery. She liked Tom – she did – but the thought of him starting a family with Ellie brought up all those strange feelings of unease and doom again.

She gave her daughter a little nudge as she passed her with the tomato sauce. "Love you."

Ellie gave her a lopsided smile. "And you," she said grudgingly.

"Hey, Daddy," she said in an altogether brighter tone, as Rupe came back in. "How's Danny? I must text him."

"I've left the hose on," Rupe said to Clare. "Can you remind me?"

"We're not at the office now," said Clare.

Rupe kissed her cheek and picked up the corkscrew. "Shall we?" "Danny seems pretty good," he told Ellie. "Got a pay rise."

"Which is the most important thing." Josh spoke from the doorway. He was dressed in shorts and a T-shirt, his hair still damp. "And is my brother happy and fulfilled, Dad? Is he healthy?"

Josh walked through to the utility room without waiting for an answer. They heard the clunk of the fridge door before he returned with a can of beer. "Yes, you awkward little sod," said Rupe without rancour. "He was well and happy and enjoying life. Which is what you ought to be doing!"

Rupe poured a glass of wine and handed it to Clare.

"I'm trying," said Josh.

"You can say that again."

"Don't start, you two." Ellie held her hand out for the second glass. "We've been talking about Dad's big birthday," she told Josh. "And what sort of party to have."

"I don't want to think about that," said Rupe dismissively. "I don't know how it happened but seventy feels a bit old…"

"Better than being dead," said Clare tartly.

Rupe tipped up the bottle and filled his own glass. "I'll drink to that, my darling. I'll drink to that…"

The fish and chips were good – the white flesh firm and fresh, the batter light and crunchy. Ellie had driven to Ramsgate for them, where their favourite Newington Fish Bar won awards for the quality of its fat, floury yet crispy chips. "They're just the best," said Ellie, dipping one in mayonnaise. "I must get this for Tom; he's never tried it."

Clare nodded. She felt good. She didn't usually drink during the week, but the cold, dry Muscadet went beautifully with the salty potato, and it felt wonderful to be sitting around in the kitchen, just the four of them again.

She looked fondly at her family. They'd been laughing and joking like old times. Before Ellie was always off with Tom and Josh had stopped talking to her about anything important. Her eyes rested on her son. He looked happier too. She smiled at him. "Any news?" she said lightly.

He nodded. "Nothing to get too excited about but I've got a Skype interview. That financial PR company."

"Oh, brilliant!"

"Well done!" Rupe leant across and clapped his son on the shoulder. "Knew you could do it!"

"It's only the third round after the application and all the tests. Long way to go yet."

"It's great news," said Clare firmly.

Ellie raised her glass towards her brother. "Go for it."

Josh rolled his eyes. "Got to think up all that bollocks about when I've been part of a team, and met a challenge, and overcome a stressful situation..."

"Just tell them about living with Dad." Ellie grinned.

"Or coping with Leftovers Surprise." They both laughed.

"You can mock," said Clare. "There was never much left in the morning if you'd been to the pub."

It was an old joke. Once, upon hearing that Clare was preparing to be creative with everything still in the fridge, Josh had launched a pre-emptive strike and brought home KFC rather than face his mother's traybake – "pasta and bits" – extravaganza. Then he'd devoured every last mouthful of it when he'd rolled home with the midnight munchies.

"I have to eat it all on my own these days," said Rupe.

Clare looked at the last remnants of fish and batter strewn across the four plates. "I suppose I could knock up haddock fritters."

"Yuck!" Ellie pulled a face.

"If only I could be sure you were joking." Josh grinned at her.

"Put it all in one box," said Rupe. "We'll give it to the gulls in the morning."

"You'll be in trouble," said Ellie. "When Mrs P sees."

"The old witch," said Rupe, with spirit. "Bring it on."

"No, please don't,' said Clare. 'Peace has reigned for some time now…'

Mrs P was their forceful next-door neighbour with whom Rupe had a running battle over everything from the ivy that grew over from her side, to his massive winter bonfires, to his insistence on feeding scraps to the herring gulls – the same avian family had been coming for years and the latest generation would take food from Rupe's hand – to his loud playing of Dire Straits in the garden on a summer's evening.

He always referred to Mrs P as "old" even though she was two years younger than he was, and would rant for days whenever they'd had a run-in, but Clare knew he rather enjoyed the encounters. Mrs P was always pleasant to her, referring to Rupe as "him indoors", and had never been anything but kind to the children.

"I took out a chicken carcass a couple of Sundays ago, and it was like a scene from Hitchcock," said Rupe with satisfaction. "She popped her wizened old head over the hedge and started banging on about the acid in gull shit damaging her Ford Fiesta. I said, 'Don't live by the sea then, madam!'"

Ellie rolled her eyes.

"She's OK," said Josh. "She always used to give me barley sugars."

"Well, that was nice," said Clare, changing the subject as Josh began to clear up around her. "Thanks for bringing it, darling." She smiled at her daughter. "It was a lovely treat."

"Yes, thank you, poppet." Rupert looked pleased. "Fancy a drop of red with some cheese?"

Ellie put a hand on her stomach. "I couldn't." She picked up her glass and drank the last inch of wine. "I'll have to leave the car. I'll get Tom to collect me and get it tomorrow." She began tapping at her phone.

"Oh," she said, moments later, frowning. "He's had a couple of beers. He can't drive either."

"Get a cab," said Rupe, waving a hand. "I'll pay for it."

Ellie reached for her phone again. "Thanks, Dad."

"Or tell him to get one round here, and we'll have a bottle of red first!"

Noooo, willed Clare silently, as Ellie shook her head. "I've got to get up in the morning!" Clare smiled at her. They'd see Tom soon but right now, she wanted nothing to spoil this warm family feel.

"Do you want any money?" Rupe said to Josh.

"I'm all right, thanks." Josh spoke evenly but Clare knew it irritated him when Rupe became full of what he called wine-largesse.

She was glad Rupe did not pursue it. "Well, it's there if you need some."

Clare smiled at him. She was feeling more hopeful and relaxed than she had for a long time. Sometimes the only way Rupe knew how to show his love was by offering money, but at least he was trying.

"You'll be all right on that interview," Rupe went on. "The trick is to take control. Turn it round so that you're the one asking the questions. Say, 'Am I the sort of person you're looking for?'"

Clare could see Rupe undoing all his good work as Josh sighed.

"I'm sure Josh knows what he's doing," she said lightly, while Ellie laughed.

"Here we go," she said, rolling her eyes at her brother. "The 365th telling of how Dad got his first sales job…"

"You can snigger," said Rupe, "but it worked."

"It wouldn't now," said Ellie firmly.

"I don't know about that." Rupe was pouring more wine. Clare let him top her up and then let her breath out slowly, relieved Ellie had taken on the job of averting a spat.

"I do," Ellie was saying. "So shut up and let's talk about something else." Rupe shrugged. "Let's go back to your birthday," said Ellie.

"I'm going to bed." Josh closed the dishwasher door and stood up. "I'm at work at seven." He put a hand on Clare's shoulder. "Night, Mum."

"My cab's here in five." Ellie snapped her phone shut. She gave her brother a small shove. "Good luck with the interview."

"I think I'll go up too," said Rupe, when Ellie had disappeared down the path. He put an arm around Clare and she leant on him for a moment, feeling the old warmth run through her. "I'll just start the dishwasher and so will I," she said.

"That was a good evening," he said.

"Yeah."

"They're good kids."

"Yes, they are."

"That's because you are an excellent mother," Rupe said with a flourish. He drained the last mouthful of his wine and put the glass next to the sink. Clare picked it up. She heard his footsteps going upstairs, as above her a loo flushed.

If only it could always be like that, she thought as she went round switching off lights. The kids getting on, Rupe being mellow instead of winding Josh up. It seemed a while since they'd all laughed like that and nobody had fallen out. Was that why she found it hard that Ellie had met Tom? Because she missed all this?

Rupe drove her mad but he loved both his children and he loved her. She knew that. It would shake down – he'd get some more interests…

Tonight, she just felt grateful and loving towards him. She hoped he'd not fall asleep too quickly…

She got ready quickly in the en suite and slid into bed beside him, not bothering with her usual T-shirt and pyjama bottoms. He was naked as always, lying on his back with his eyes closed. She stroked a hand across his bare chest.

"Love you," she said.

"Love too," he mumbled, his voice thick with drowsiness and booze. He put out an arm and patted at her. Then he rolled over, away in the opposite direction so he lay facing the window and she was looking at the back of his head.

He was snoring already.

Chapter Fourteen

Tom was being the perfect host.

They'd had champagne and nibbles – small, salty biscuits Clare recognised as coming from M&S, together with cashew nuts, in matching bowls – in his flat before walking a few metres along the seafront to The Ambrette, where Tom had booked the tasting menu and started them off on an exceptionally nice Chablis.

The apartment had been a revelation. Clare had admired the high ceilings and stripped floors, the large windows overlooking Turner Contemporary, the minimalist furnishings and black and white art on the walls, with something akin to wonder. She had made sure she went to the loo before they left, not just to sample the beautifully-tiled grey and chrome bathroom, but so that she could sneak a look through the door of the large master bedroom, curious to see if her daughter had really undergone a complete personality transplant.

She was relieved to see that what was clearly Ellie's side of the room was lost under a jumble of dresses and shoes and bags, with a towel thrown across a chair, beads and make-up strewn across the dressing-table surface, and a pile of books and teaching materials teetering next to the bed. There was no need to worry that Tom had whisked her off somewhere sinister to post a Stepford Wife-type insert into her brain. Clare smiled and wondered how much mad tidying had gone on across the other rooms before they arrived.

She could see Rupe was impressed and she had to admit the place was very classy indeed. Ellie had looked proud, and slightly nervous, when they first arrived, but was smiling now. She was wearing the red dress Tom had collected a couple of weeks before, with her hair piled loosely on top of her head and a pair of green jade earrings that matched her eyes. She looked stunning. Once again, Clare thought what an arresting couple she and Tom made. He was wearing a soft, pale open-necked shirt, with the sleeves rolled back over his tanned forearms. Sitting side by side, wine glasses in hand, they looked like the cover shot for a glossy magazine.

"Josh would have been so welcome to come too," Tom was saying. "I was going to book for five but Ellie said he wouldn't want to…"

"He's got a preliminary interview tomorrow," said Clare, "on Skype or something. He wanted to do some prep."

"Give him my best," said Tom.

"I told Danny about the party," said Ellie, barely letting him finish. "And he and Mia will come for the weekend. I said to come before that too – we haven't seen him for ages." She turned to Tom. "You'll love Danny. It's weird that even though we've got different mothers, he feels so much more like my brother than Josh ... who is so bloody annoying."

"He seems like a good guy to me," said Tom.

Clare threw him a grateful smile.

Ellie snorted. "You wouldn't say that if you could see him stalking about at the moment with a face on. I popped by at lunchtime and he could barely say hello."

"He's worried about his interview," said Clare.

"You always stick up for him." Ellie flicked a glance towards Rupe.

"I stick up for both my children," said Clare, smiling at Ellie with what she hoped was a warning look in her eye. She did not want the evening to degenerate into a dissection of family relations before they'd even had the first course. Especially as Tom said there were a further seven to come.

Ellie smiled back defiantly and addressed Tom. "Mum let him get away with murder when he was growing up. I always had to be in early, do my homework, lay the table ... but Josh?" She made a scoffing noise. "He could do what he liked."

Clare shook her head. "That is so not true." She sipped at her wine and smiled again. "I seem to remember you getting away with rather a lot too. Especially where your father was concerned."

It did the trick. Ellie grinned. "Yes, Dad's always been a softie, haven't you?"

Rupe shrugged indulgently as Tom spoke. "I think this is a common family trait," he said. "My older sister always says I was spoiled rotten, but it's not how I remember it."

"Where does she live?" asked Clare, glad to be on safer ground.

"London. Both my sisters are there."

"And I still haven't met either of them," put in Ellie.

"I haven't seen them since Christmas myself," said Tom, sounding, Clare thought, a touch defensive.

There was a small silence. Clare filled it. "You will certainly like Ellie's other brother Danny when you meet him," she told Tom. "He's a lovely man."

"Claudia's a laugh too," said Ellie. "We'll invite her to the party too. Mum gets on fine with her, don't you? Even though Dad left her when Danny was young, she's always sent us cards for our birthdays. She has a few digs at Dad but lots of women would never have forgiven him. Running off with Mum like that. Danny was only about … eight, was he?" Ellie rattled on as Clare and Rupe exchanged glances. Clare saw Tom pick up on them.

"It's all a very long time ago now," said Rupe.

Tom changed the subject. "What sort of a week have you had?" he asked Clare. "Been at the shop?"

He was good company. They talked about films and books and Rupe's problems with the blackfly on his runner beans – on which he managed to hold forth at some length. Clare told a story about a woman donating sixteen designer ball gowns ranging from size eight to size twenty-two, who claimed to have worn them all.

"This is amazing," said Clare, indicating the soft-shell crab in front of them. "Just delicious. I didn't realise we were coming here."

"The new place is good but a bit basic," said Tom, as he ordered another bottle of wine. "I wanted to take you somewhere a bit more special. I thought we all deserved it."

"Tom's been a bit stressed with his flat that got trashed," said Ellie, stroking his arm. "Haven't you, babe?"

Rupe shook his head. "What's wrong with these people?" He looked at Clare as if she might supply the answer. She shrugged.

"It's just happened at an awkward time," Tom was saying, "when I'm busy with other things. I don't want to give out too many sets of keys and I've learned from experience that if you don't properly project manage the job, people turn up in the wrong order and then blame each other when things go wrong…" He pulled a face. "I was doing a flat once and the tiler went in and tiled the whole bathroom without waiting for the new bath to be put in. Oh, I thought that was it, he said. Like I'd want new tiles round a cracked tub."

"You need a foreman," said Rupe. "People are idiots."

"Yes, but that pushes the price right up, and it's already costing thousands. I'll work it out. I'll simply have to—"

"I'll do it." Clare felt a little jolt of shock at the way the thought had come out of her mouth while it was still forming. All three of them were staring at her.

"I'll help you out," she said calmly, as if it were the most natural thing in the world, even though her heart was thumping at her own audacity. "I can oversee the work, if you're busy. I'd enjoy it," she added. "I've always liked watching home improvements unfold…"

"When I was little, Mum wanted to go on *Changing Rooms* with Auntie Figs," said Ellie, giggling. "But Dad said no way."

Rupe took a swallow of wine. "Couldn't have coped with that fool with the long hair prancing about the place."

"He's hardly a fool," said Clare. "You should approve. He's worth a fortune. Anyway, while I've got the time, if you want me to supervise I will. Have you booked anyone to do the work yet?"

"I've got quotes coming for a new kitchen and bathroom," Tom said, still looking bemused. "And I can call David from Broadstairs Carpets to measure for flooring… I've got a couple of different blokes who do painting… But, are you sure? I mean, it's a lot of hanging around…"

"Just give me a list of what needs doing and any contact numbers. I can get some more quotes if that's helpful." Clare felt a little rush of excitement. "I'll enjoy it," she said again.

"Well, that would be brilliant." Tom was looking at her in wonder.

"My wife's a top negotiator," said Rupe proudly. "She'll get you the best prices on anything."

"I'll pay you, of course…" Tom said.

Clare spoke briskly. "I wouldn't dream of it."

She looked from him to Ellie, who hadn't yet spoken. "You can buy me a bottle of fizz when it's finished," she said lightly.

"Mum will kick arse for you," said Ellie. "It will be done in no time."

'I'll drop everything round. And the keys." Tom sat back and exhaled loudly. "Wow, I wasn't expecting that. I've been wondering how the hell I was going to be everywhere at once…"

"Busy in the skip world, are we?" Rupe leant back also, as a waiter cleared their plates.

"Crazy. And I've exchanged on this other place. The architect says planning will be approved, no problem, but there's been a lot of paperwork. I'm in the middle of costing it all out."

"You should have done that before you bought it!" said Rupe.

Tom smiled. "Well, of course I did, as a ballpark. But now I'm doing the detail…"

Clare's thoughts drifted off as a dish of lamb cooked with fenugreek was put in front of her and Tom described his conversion plans. She felt exhilarated. She wondered if Tom would allow her to advise on colour schemes. If she could choose tiles and kitchen units… It was a long time since they'd done anything at home. It was always shelved till they were "not so busy" and then "when we've retired". It had always been "we" but Clare wasn't ready for slippers and a pipe yet.

The lamb was incredibly tender and fragrant. Clare was

trying to identify the flavours in the accompanying velouté when Rupe's voice crashed through her reveries.

"On benefits, I expect," he said, with the tone of one who expects to be right. Clare's head came up.

Tom was shaking his. "No, she had a part-time job. More than one, I think."

"Drugs involved?"

Ellie was pouring wine. Tom was shaking his head again. "Just struggling, I think. The boyfriend left, and she wasn't coping with the kids..."

"She could still have cleaned!" said Ellie, indignantly.

They were back on the trashed flat again. Clare wondered whether to mention Ellie's near ineptitude with anything that involved a cloth, but let it pass. Tom, she would bet her life, had a cleaner. And a good job it was too, with her daughter there.

Tom was talking about local deprivation. Ellie was looking bored. When had she lost her appetite for politics? She'd been passionate as a teenager...

"You can turn things around if you really want to," said Rupe. "I had nothing when I started." Clare felt the familiar irritation rise in her. Rupe jerked his head towards her. "Though don't say that to my wife. Tell her everyone is born equal and we all get the same chance, and she'll eat you alive..."

Clare made a face at him as Tom shook his head. "I would never say that. My father was a rags-to-riches Italian. Grew up in real poverty and worked himself into the ground building up a business, but I'm very aware how hard it is. He was lucky he'd had some education. That's what can make the difference..."

Clare looked at him. She again felt a sudden doubt, hoping he meant all he said and wasn't just spouting what would go down well with her. She mentally shook herself. Why should he? Yes, he would probably prefer to get on with his "in-laws" but he had Rupe as an ally for any diehard views...

"What does your father do?" she asked Tom.

"Pizzas! Started off with one tiny bar, and built it up to six pizzerias. My brother runs one of them now. Dad sold the others when Mum wanted to come back to England when my sisters were small, before I was born. Then he started two more here. Sold them when they went back to Italy to retire. Dad still likes to get in the kitchen, when he can. He and Mum take charge whenever my brother and his wife want a holiday. It's still very much a family concern."

"When are we going to visit them?" Ellie leant against Tom's shoulder. "I've always wanted to go to Italy," she said dreamily. "I want to visit Venice and Florence and Rome... I've heard so much from the students. It all sounds so romantic..."

"Nothing very romantic about Potenza, I'm afraid," said Tom. "It will probably remind you of Ramsgate. And it's about 500 miles from Venice so we can't just pop over there."

Ellie looked disappointed, and for a moment Clare caught a fleeting glimpse of her as a small child. Tom immediately put out an arm. "But I will take you to Venice too..."

Ellie smiled at him, her face alight again. "We could get married there," she said.

"Why not?" Tom's tone was light, but his smile didn't quite radiate all the way.

"You'd prefer that to Ramsgate Registry office?" As Rupe guffawed at his own quip, Clare caught Tom's eye.

The smile he gave her was brighter. "More wine?"

Chapter Fifteen

"**A**nd there'll be wine," Simon told Anna, as if this clinched it.

"And I'd love you to," added Nick, which sort of did.

"Oh, I don't know," she protested again. "I'm not really a murder-mystery sort of person. I can't strut my stuff, like you do." She smiled at Simon, who delighted in any opportunity to perform.

He shook his head. "Oh darling, you don't need to. You just have to look exotic and mysterious and then answer a few questions."

Anna pulled a face. "Exotic?"

"You're a countess with a mysterious past. You were once a great dancer but since your husband died you have become a recluse, living alone with your faithful butler..."

"Me," put in Nick, grinning.

"You'll be perfect, darling."

"You will," said Nick.

"And we haven't got anyone else," added Simon.

Anna laughed. "That's more like it!"

"They've been falling like flies," said Simon dramatically. "It's left to us and Ellie to save the day."

"And Janine," said Nick.

"I don't really count her, darling," said Simon, "when it comes to creative talent. We'll make her a serving wench."

Anna and Nick smiled. "Don't be mean," said Nick. "She's very kind."

"And boring as batshit," said Simon.

"Who is?" said Ellie, joining them. They were sitting around a wooden table in what was known as the school garden, but was really more of a yard with a few tubs. A handful of students lounged in the corners with cans of Coke, but most of them were sprawled on the grass in the park across the road. It was only morning coffee-break but already it was very hot. Anna wondered how many of the latest excitable Spanish group would be back for lessons this afternoon and how many would slide off to the beach if they could dodge their fierce group leader.

"What do I wear?" asked Anna.

"Just dig out an evening dress that's vaguely 1920s," said Ellie, as if she were talking about selecting a pair of socks or a T-shirt, "and I'll sort the accessories. We've got a box of headbands and feathers and cigarette holders from last summer." She shone a smile on Anna. "I'll do your make-up, if you like?"

"I'll give out the character studies tomorrow lunchtime," said Simon.

"What?" Anna heard the squeak in her voice. "But I'll be working till six. I won't have time to..."

Simon threw up one hand in a gesture of dismissal. "Darling, relax, really. We make it up as we go along. It's the students, darling. It's not the Old Vic."

The dress had to be twenty years old but gratifyingly it still fitted. It was silver-grey and encrusted with small beads and sequins – a heavy, lined sheath, held up by two thin silver straps. Anna remembered it had been expensive. She'd worn it to the leaving do of one of Jeremy's colleagues – after Jeremy himself had retired and was doing consultancy work and flying round the world, lecturing. He had been happy and vibrant doing that. Excited by the places he'd been and the people he'd met. She'd been with him on some of the trips, when they'd been able to farm out the teenage boys. She remembered the wonderful five days they'd spent in Chicago, making love in the luxury hotel in Geneva, looking over the river in the beautiful restaurant in Rome where he'd given her the eternity ring…

"Why are you wearing that?" Jeremy was in the doorway of her bedroom. She thought he sounded alarmed.

"It's fancy dress," she said. "A murder-mystery evening I'm part of for the students." She looked at herself in the full-length mirror. She'd have to wear a wrap. She was too old for bare shoulders and upper arms.

Jeremy frowned. "You don't usually do things like that."

"I know. But they're short of people and…" She shrugged. "It will be a bit of fun. Simon twisted my arm."

Jeremy nodded. He'd met Simon a couple of years

before, the last – and final – time he had made it to the staff end-of-summer barbecue. "Well, have fun," he said.

Something twisted inside her. "We'll do something nice this weekend," she said. "Watch a film or … maybe we could go out somewhere in the car? We haven't been out anywhere together for ages. A pub garden for lunch?" Her voice trailed away.

Jeremy nodded, his voice heavy. "Maybe."

———

Driving back towards the school, the dress in a carrier beside her, Anna tried not to feel guilty. She was not yet sixty. It was nothing these days. The new forty, they called it. When Jeremy was forty, he had been, by all accounts, an insatiable party animal. Come to think of it, he had been at fifty-nine. She suddenly remembered a murder-mystery evening they'd done together – a fund-raiser for the PTA, when the boys were at primary school. Jeremy dressed as a vicar, hamming it up, making everyone on their table laugh, the other mothers looking at her enviously. Everyone used to fall a little bit in love with Jeremy. She had adored him.

And you still do, she told herself fiercely, as she swung the car left at the roundabout to Margate. The old Jeremy was still there underneath it all. They just needed to spend some time together.

She'd get him out this weekend. Refuse to take no for an answer.

As she got closer to the school, the twinges in her middle deepened. They were probably from hunger – she'd only

172

had time to grab an apple and a piece of cheese and bung a frozen boeuf bourguignon in the oven for Jeremy – but it felt like anxiety. Anna breathed deeply. She felt nervous. And not just because she'd barely looked at the print-out from Simon and still didn't have a clue what the Countess of Exotica was supposed to reveal about her shady past…

"Ooh, ding-dong," said Simon as Anna emerged from her office and prepared to descend the stairs to the large common room. "You look fabulous, darling."

Nick whistled and then pulled a face. "Sorry, is that terribly sexist?"

"It sounds good to me!" Anna smiled at him. "It's been that long…"

"Seriously, you look wonderful," he said, as Anna sat in a chair and allowed Ellie to apply eyeshadow.

"And you certainly do," Anna told the younger woman. Ellie looked amazing. She'd donned a short black bobbed wig which was dramatic with her smoky eyes and dark-red lips. She was wearing a headband with a feather and long strings of fake pearls that set off the Twenties-style dress with a fringed hem.

"It's a great dress, isn't it?" said Ellie. "Mum bought it from the charity shop she helps in. She got me a great suit too, with a nipped-in waist – I'm going to get Simon to set the next one in the Forties…"

As she chatted on, dabbing and brushing at Anna's face, Nick pressed a plastic cup of wine into Anna's hands. "A stiffener," he said. "Ready for one, Simon?"

Simon struck a pose, making Ellie laugh. "Is the Pope a Catholic? Darling, I thought you'd never ask."

Anna sipped at the wine slowly. She couldn't drink much, but already she could feel it relaxing her. As they bantered around her, she glanced at the character notes in her hand. Simon was right – it was only a bit of fun for the students... She was glad she'd come. Nick touched her softly on the shoulder. "OK?"

She nodded.

"Hey!" he went on, as Ellie finished Anna's lips with a flourish and handed her a mirror. "We must take a photo."

Anna looked in wonder at the face in the glass. She hadn't worn this much make-up in years and wouldn't dream of going out in public like it but ... she had to admit, she did look good. Ellie had defined her eyes and lips, and swept on some bronzer that had really brought out her cheekbones.

"And now..." Ellie placed a headband similar to her own around Anna's forehead and handed her a long black tapered holder with a mock cigarette in the end. "You look brilliant!"

Nick was snapping her with his phone. "Come on, all together!" They'd just got close for a group selfie – Nick's cheek was almost brushing hers – when Janine appeared. She too, had undergone a transformation. She was wearing a low-cut milkmaid-type dress with what was clearly a pretty dynamic push-up bra, had piled her hair on top of her face, and was also made-up to the nines.

"You look fab!" cried Ellie.

"Come in," Nick pulled Janine into the huddle.

"Very Barbara Windsor," breathed Simon.

"You look beautiful," said Anna, as they all beamed into

the phone once more. Janine blushed, whether from the compliment or Nick's arm around her shoulder, Anna couldn't be sure.

Nick flashed the screen around. "Everyone OK if I put this on the school Facebook page?"

"Sure thing – oh bloody hell, they're arriving!" As the first students began to sit down, Ellie sprang up, sweeping mascaras and lipsticks into her bag and gathering up the props. "Let's go! Break a leg everyone…"

It was fun. The room was full, with almost every one of the rows of plastic seats taken, and the students clapping and laughing as the five of them acted out the various scenes Simon had concocted. Anna found herself adopting a broken accent of indeterminate origin, which seemed to amuse the onlookers, and she found it surprisingly easy to improvise in her new persona, enjoying herself as she instructed Nick, who was channelling his inner Jeeves, to fetch her a drink, bring her slippers, and answer the door to Simon as the dastardly stranger who turned up announced.

Janine was actually very funny, and stole a few laughs from Simon with her great comic timing. As she walked up and down the rows of students, answering questions, Anna began to wish she'd been asked to this before.

"Why you kill the doctor?" said Carlos.

"Me?" Anna affected shock-horror and sucked on her cigarette holder. "I am a respectable lady. I wouldn't dream of murdering anyone…"

"But the servant say you go quickly and change dress," put in Juan. "It was because blood?"

"No, no," Anna shook her head vigorously. "You cannot believe anything my butler tells you."

"I am aghast, Madam," said Nick, coming up behind her and speaking in an exaggeratedly cultured tone. "Are you suggesting your faithful old retainer would tell untruths?"

"What is a *gast*?" asked Gabriella. "I do not learn this word."

"Fetch me more champagne, Jeeveson," drawled Anna. "And be quick about it."

Nick nodded gravely and glided off. Across the room she saw Simon wink at them both. She moved across the room to the next group waiting to question her. Nick caught up with her. "You suit that look," he said. "You're so elegant."

"Oh, I don't know about that…"

"It was the first thing I noticed about you." Nick was looking at her intently. "How beautifully you hold yourself. You could be a dancer. Were you? You remind me of the way Darcey Bussell walks."

"Oh my gosh, that is praise indeed." Anna laughed self-consciously and looked across the room. "Ellie looks like Lady Mary from Downton," she said, keen to divert his attention elsewhere.

Nick nodded. "Yes, she looks stunning. I'm modelling myself on Carson."

"Oh, I love him. Are you a Downton fan? Jeremy thinks it's dreadful rubbish, but I've been through the whole series twice."

"I loved it," said Nick firmly. "Seen the film?"

"Of course! Longing for the sequel."

"Come on!" Simon was behind them. "Last few questions then we hand out the sheets for them to guess."

The students were soon milling about, bending over their forms and talking at top volume in a babble of Italian, Spanish, and every language apart from the one they were here to practise. Anna saw the door at the back of the room open, and a tall, good-looking man come in and lean on the back of a stray chair. Seeing Ellie wave and smile, she assumed it was Tom and hoped Ellie would introduce them. Her words of caution had never been mentioned again and Anna still cringed at the thought of her outspokenness. She was keen to show Ellie how warm she could be towards him.

But Simon was instructing the room loudly to sit back down and she was employed to help collect the forms and then read them.

"Put all of them who've guessed Janine in a pile here," Simon said, when they'd amassed a heap of papers. "And Nick, you start going through them and see who's come up with the best reason why. If there's a tie, choose the one who's made the most effort with their English..."

He sat down opposite and began to help him.

"Shall we collect the empty cups?" Anna said to Ellie. "And are you going to introduce me?" She nodded to where Tom was talking to the Italian group leader.

"Yes, of course." Ellie led her across the room. Tom had a nice direct smile and a firm handshake. He had heard all about Anna, of course. He made easy chit-chat about whether she'd enjoyed herself, and complimented her on her costume. He was very attractive indeed. What young woman wouldn't fall for him?

"We're going for some food," Ellie said, when they'd finished clearing up and the students had gone noisily into the night. "GB Pizza maybe or the new bistro? Simon and Nick too. Do you want to come?"

"Oh do!" Nick was suddenly behind her. "That would be great. And you, Janine?" As Janine's face lit up, Anna saw Simon give a small eye roll. He nudged Nick. "Come on, let's move those chairs."

"I can't," Anna said to Ellie. "I've got to get home." She looked at her watch. "It's already half past nine. I told Jeremy I wouldn't be late, and you know it's a half-hour drive..." Her voice petered out. She realised she sounded – and felt – disappointed. "Another time?" she added brightly.

"Sure," said Ellie. She looked over her shoulder to where Nick and Simon were stacking up the last of the seating, laughing about something, with Janine hovering nearby.

"You coming, boys?"

Are you coming?

Figs looked at the text message. Why shouldn't she go? It was only like a school reunion; people went to them all the time. She'd enjoy it – from the pictures on the Facebook group, she'd worn a lot better than most of them.

She hadn't hesitated when he'd sent her the friend request. Quite a few of them had – after Nerdy Pete from school had set up that group. It was fun looking at all the old photos they'd posted. Her hair! Some of them looked the same – just older. Others she couldn't recall at all. Not even the names.

But Dave was still looking pretty good for almost fifty. You could still clearly see that gangly, floppy-haired sixteen-year-old she'd fallen so hopelessly in love with – until he'd dumped her for a short-lived romance with Amy-Marie – sex siren of the fifth year.

Now he was married with kids too. They were only chatting about their lives.

So why did she hastily close the laptop lid when Tilda appeared? Why had she turned the sounds off her phone so the kids wouldn't wonder why she got so many messages?

It had been strange to hear his voice. At first it could have been anyone's – the forty-nine-year-old tones of a stranger. But when he laughed, she'd felt that old tug. She remembered his arms wrapped around her at a bus stop, the time they were caught kissing at the back of the Geography room, the first night he walked her home...

In the second call, he said he was coming to London in a few weeks' time, and why didn't they set up drinks or a lunch? Put out a Facebook message and see who else could come?

She already knew they'd only have eyes for each other.

Because her heart thumped when it was *him* on WhatsApp in a way it never did for Don.

Her fingers hesitated over the keys. It was a lunch in

London. There'd be a group of them. Three others had already said yes. It wasn't like she'd be closeted with him on her own. She'd only go to the restaurant. He'd already mentioned casually the hotel he'd be staying in...

Figs looked at the screen. He was online right now.

She pressed keys.

Maybe.

Chapter Sixteen

"Clare!" Tom's voice was warm as he answered his phone. "What a nice surprise."

"Hardly a surprise, I'd have thought," said Clare drily. "Considering you knew today I'd be standing on your health hazard of a carpet. You're right – it's not very pretty in here."

She heard him sigh. "I know. I'm sorry. I really should have—"

"But I've been through all the quotes," Clare went on briskly, "and I really don't think we need to spend as much as this. Are you happy for me to look at some alternatives?"

"That would be brilliant."

"OK, good! I've had a few ideas. I'm going to need a float, because some of it might involve cash. I can sort it all if you transfer it…"

"OK," he said, immediately businesslike. "How much?"

She'd recoiled when she'd first come through the door. The vinyl flooring in the kitchen was filthy and one kitchen cupboard was hanging drunkenly from its hinges, the knob missing from the top drawer. The once-white sink was brown and the hob was encrusted. She could see now why Tom had instructed the kitchen should be gutted and new units fitted.

The bathroom was equally unsavoury and the carpet in the living room had a large patch on it that did not bear close inspection. A dirty sofa had been left behind. How did people live like this? The main bedroom was dusty but undamaged, apart from a crack in the mirrored door of the built-in wardrobe – that would probably be a pain to get fixed – and a socket that looked wobbly.

The smaller one – which had clearly been a child's room – with pink carpet and pink princess walls – was the only civilised corner of the apartment. It should have been lovely. It was spread over the top two floors of one of Ramsgate's many Regency buildings, light and airy from the long windows with a distant view – if you stood on tiptoe in the larger bedroom – of the sea.

She'd thrown as many windows open as she could, and held her nose as she'd taken out the bag of rubbish left in the corner of the kitchen in the heat.

Then she'd taken a long, hard look around and started making phone calls.

"It's going to take a couple of weeks, I should think," she told Tom now.

"I expect longer…"

"Leave it with me," she said, warming to the challenge. "Don't come here till I tell you…"

Clare was there the next morning at seven to let the plumber in. She was armed with disposable gloves and a box of cleaning stuff that was heavy on the bleach and anti-bac. She'd picked up a cheap kettle, tea, coffee, and bottles of water, remembering a pack of loo rolls at the last minute. Rupe had laughed the night before when he'd seen her clipboard and long typed list, but Clare was filled with an energy and sense of purpose she hadn't felt since before they'd sold the business.

"So it's all coming out?" Wayne the plumber looked around the murky bathroom, taking in the mouldy tiles around the bath and the furred shower curtain.

"Not quite."

Wayne frowned while the lad with him stopped looking at his phone and regarded Clare with interest. "Tom told me—"

Clare gave him her brightest smile and spoke firmly, as behind her the doorbell rang again. "Yes. But there's been a change of plan."

By midday there were six of them in the flat, and the faint air of something that had died had been replaced by the smell of disinfectant. Clare wiped her brow and smiled at the two women who'd been working in the kitchen with her. "I'll go to Waitrose. What do you want?"

As she walked down Grundy's Hill towards the supermarket, Clare realised she had quite a jaunt in her step. She had that buzzy feeling she used to get when the business was growing and she was sending staff out across the country to clients, managing it all on a big spreadsheet and juggling half a dozen diaries as well as being the unofficial Head of Human Resources, Office Manager and Bought Ledger, listening to marital woes while she ordered more toner for the printer and sent stern emails about unpaid accounts.

This was just revamping a grotty rental property but it felt good to be in charge of something again – something that wasn't a blocked hoover or what vegetables to cook.

As she grabbed a mini trolley and headed up the first aisle, she saw Harriet from the Oasis shop coming towards her. She was dressed smartly in a crisp white shirt tucked into tailored trousers and heels. She gave Clare an enormous smile and swung her shiny ponytail, Clare was conscious of her own paint-splattered cut-off jeans and sweaty vest top, her hair pushed pack from her no-doubt-grimy forehead.

"Hello!" Harriet looked genuinely pleased to see her. "How's it all going?"

Clare explained briefly what she was doing. "And you look very well?" she said, looking at the other woman's glowing face.

"Working again!" said Harriet, happily. "Just been for a meeting about redesigning the logos for the Wainwright chain. I'm freelancing but it's *so* good to be doing something useful once more…"

Clare remembered her fervent words about staying at home with her daughter. "That's great. And how is Millie?"

"She's totally good, thanks."

"You got that school problem sorted?"

"Oh yes – you know what kids are like. We had them all round for tea. All soon forgotten."

Clare was silenced for a moment by her airy tone. The woman was transformed.

"To be quite honest," Harriet confided, as if sensing Clare's confusion, "it was always Luke who was so keen that I shouldn't work. He wanted me to be at home with Millie. But as I said to him, I can work around the school hours if I'm self-employed and I think it's rather more important that she has a mother who's fulfilled, don't you?" She sounded almost as if she needed Clare to agree.

"Oh, absolutely," said Clare. "I'm rather enjoying this little job myself."

She saw Harriet's eyes flick to her scruffy trainers. "It sounds very interesting," she said politely.

"I'll see you in the shop sometime," said Clare, pushing her trolley forward.

"Well, if I have time…" Harriet hesitated. "Luke…" For the first time the other woman looked uncertain. "It's like having two children sometimes…" she trailed off.

"Good luck with it all." Clare pushed the trolley forward, suddenly feeling an irrational dislike of the totally unknown Luke. She hadn't liked the look in Harriet's eyes when she mentioned his name…

Give Rupe his due, he had been obsessive about the business and had wanted and needed Clare involved, but he had never made her feel she couldn't make her own decisions. She looked around but Harriet had disappeared. She gave herself a mental shake. It was none of her business. But she still wished they'd swapped numbers…

She was coming out of the shop again, loaded up with sandwiches, fruit, and chocolate, when she spotted a scrawny-looking dog in the doorway opposite, sitting next to a familiar figure. She crossed the road.

"Tony!" He looked touchingly pleased to see her. "Still nowhere to live?"

He pulled a face. "Not that will take animals." He indicated the dog next to him. An old ice-cream carton filled with water was further back in the entrance to the empty shop, next to a rolled-up sleeping bag.

"Where did you get him?"

"He was just wandering about down by the harbour. One of the cafés was feeding him scraps but they said he'd been around for a couple of weeks…"

Clare frowned. "How are you feeding him? Have you got money?" *And poo bags?* she wanted to add.

He was nodding. "A little bit." Clare felt in her pocket for her wallet. "What are you doing about finding somewhere?"

"A guy from Porchlight – Steve, he's trying to do something."

"How long will that take?"

Tony shrugged. "It's OK. We sleep on the beach. There's a couple of others down there. We look after each other's things – I'm just here now cos…" He nodded to where a polystyrene cup had a few coins in it. "They buy me sandwiches sometimes." He nodded at a shopper coming through the glass doors opposite.

"Do you want one now?" Clare pointed to her carrier bag. "I got extra."

She put the bag down and pulled out an apple and a ham and mustard on brown. "You still got a phone?"

He nodded. "But no credit."

"Here, put this number in it." She reeled it off and handed him a note. "Get some credit, eh? In case you need it. And let me know what Steve sorts out for you? I could try to help too?"

"OK!" He smiled. "Thanks."

She gave the dog a brief pat. She wasn't good on breeds but he looked like a lurcher crossed with something shaggier – leggy, with soulful brown eyes. She thought Tony probably had enough to contend with already but could understand him being drawn to a companion. "What's his name?"

"Belter."

She nodded. It was as good a name as any.

_____

Chapter Seventeen

She got it all done in thirteen days. On the afternoon of the fourteenth, she made a final coffee for the chap from Willow Fabrics, packed up the last of the cleaning materials, and put them in a plastic box in her boot.

Then she walked back to the flat, let herself in, and sat cross-legged in the middle of the living-room floor that two weeks earlier she hadn't even wanted to walk on. The sun poured through the window and heated the top of her head. She noticed a small smear on the glass and jumped up to wipe at it with the bottom of her T-shirt, looking critically around the room for any other missed imperfections. She nodded to herself, satisfied. She was good at this.

She thought wryly of her messy kitchen at home, that had become increasingly so, with Rupe left holding the domestic reins while she was here ten hours a day. He'd been bemused by her fervour for the job but uncomplaining. In fact, he'd been in rather good humour – listening to work tales each evening with apparent genuine interest, and recounting his own entertaining battles with Mrs P next door.

Perhaps having more to do suited him too. He'd looked up a recipe for chicken pie, he'd told her this morning, and was going to make it for tonight, with what was left of his home-grown runner beans (the blackfly had finally got the better of Rupe, a defeat he'd not yet got over). She'd deep-clean the surfaces tomorrow...

She jumped as the doorbell rang, although she was expecting it. She'd been very specific about him not using his keys...

Clare opened the flat door and ushered Tom into the tiny hallway. "Hold on a second," she said, putting a hand up to stop him going further. "I want you to hold in your mind the image of the flat the last time you saw it."

He made a face. "How could I forget?"

"Are you visualising?" she persisted. "Are you seeing that manky bathroom and squalid kitchen, the stains, the rotting rubbish smell..."

"Yes! *Yes!*" He grinned at her. "And I can now smell new paint. Show me..."

She stepped back with a flourish and waved him through the newly glossed inner door.

"Oh wow!"

She laughed in delight as he looked in wonder around the kitchen. "And all at under a third of the budget."

He shook his head slowly. "You haven't replaced it?"

"Nope. It's been scrubbed to within an inch of its life, and painted. Those are all new handles, of course. The tiles have been cleaned."

"Is that a new hob? Or...?"

"No! My wonderful help – Terri and Charlie – who usually clean for me – did it. We ordered some special pack from amazon – it did the oven too. The fridge is new – the old one was beyond disgusting – but I got it in a sale." She could hear herself almost babbling.

"You are brilliant."

She led him into the living room and showed him the new carpets and freshly painted walls. "Oh, you've done curtains too! Thank you."

"They were cheaper than blinds – which were so dirty and broken we chucked them – and I thought, if you're renting it out..."

"Sure, yes. I don't know what to say."

"Wait till you see the bathroom!" They mounted the newly carpeted stairs. "I thought we'd just have a tiny go at cleaning it first."

She pushed open the door, pleased to see Tom's eyes widen. "The tiles have all been re-grouted and I bought a new loo seat and shower screen – there was enough bacteria growing on those curtains to wipe out Milton Keynes. And new flooring of course. Oh, and new plugs for the bath and basin. They had a life of their own too. New towel rails and the radiator painted. But apart from that – elbow grease!"

Tom laughed. "Amazing!" He looked in the bedrooms.

"That cost money!" Clare indicated the repaired mirrored wardrobe.

"Fairly ghastly, isn't it?" said Tom

"But it makes the room look a lot bigger," said Clare practically.

It did look good, with the cream walls, white gloss, and long, pale voile curtains floating in the breeze from the open window. "The carpets are 'desert sand'," said Clare. "I thought they'd last a bit longer if they weren't too light in colour. But make sure you get decent references this time, eh? Get someone with some pride in the place?"

Tom was still shaking his head. "I'd have simply ripped it all out. Astonishing."

"You've clearly had it too easy," smiled Clare. "Never had to make do and mend!"

"I've had to make do with a big overdraft!" He laughed again. "I can't believe how quickly you've done all this."

"Terri and Charlie are brilliant. We're a good team. Charlie did a lot of the painting too with a guy I know who does odd jobs for us. He knew someone who could fix the wardrobes. Not sure Wayne was too pleased with me, mind. Thought he was getting a whole new bathroom to install!"

Tom shrugged. "He's earned thousands from me and will do again. There are at least three shower rooms to install in the new place. Plus kitchens."

He suddenly wrapped her in a hug, taking Clare by surprise. "Rupe was right," he said, letting her go again. "You are clearly a top negotiator. I've got to give you some of the money you've saved me. It's only fair."

"No, really. I've enjoyed it. Anyway," she said awkwardly. "You're family now, aren't you? Take Ellie out somewhere nice."

"I'll take you as well! Hey, come for a drink now."

"Oh, I don't know."

"Why not? Come on, I want to celebrate. This is bloody

marvellous – such a stress lifted. Let's go down to the harbour and drink champagne. Come on!"

His enthusiasm was catching. Drinking champagne in the afternoon sunshine suddenly sounded deliciously decadent. But also a bit odd.

"What about Ellie?" she said. "Won't she be finishing soon?"

"I'll text her and tell her where we are."

"Oh of course. Yes, it will be nice to see her…"

"What are we waiting for then?"

They walked down Jacob's Ladder, the three flights of dog-leg concrete staircase leading to the harbour. It was hot, and the sun was bright and bouncing off the yachts on the water beyond. They stopped and peered into the small Sailors' Church before wandering on past the cafés, galleries, and chandler's shops that filled the historic arches set into the cliff. "I thought we'd go here," said Tom, turning into The Arch, a café-bar fronted with tables and jaunty umbrellas. "Hey, Miles!" he called to the man seated on a vast leather sofa in the corner. "We need a bottle of your finest bubbles." He turned to Clare. "Have you met Miles? Owner of this fine joint."

Miles stood up and held out his hand. "Delighted to meet you."

"And you," Clare smiled, saying to Tom, "A bottle? I've got to drive later…"

"Where's your car?"

"Spencer Square."

"Be fine there," Tom said decisively. "I'll get you a cab

home. And one for us too. We might want a second bottle, who knows…?"

"Gosh, well, I don't often say no to fizz."

"Gabbi!" Miles called to a pretty, dark-haired girl behind the bar. "Bring the Laurent-Perrier Rosé please. And some pretzels."

"Blimey," said Clare to Tom. "You sure?"

Moments later, Miles came to their outside table with an ice bucket draped in a white cloth.

He grinned at Tom. "I had heard. And I've been waiting to meet the lovely new lady friend. I don't miss much in here." He smiled at Clare. "You make a very handsome couple." He looked at her questioningly, as if waiting for her to provide further details.

Tom jumped in. "Clare's my girlfriend's mother actually."

"Sister, surely?"

Embarrassed, Clare rolled her eyes. "That old chestnut!"

"Where've you been?" Miles was saying to Tom. "Not seen you for ages. Thought you were so loved-up you weren't coming out any more."

"Just been busy," said Tom. "Ellie should be here a little later; you can meet her then."

He raised his glass when Miles had poured and gone back inside.

"To you!" he said, to Clare. "Thank you."

She sipped. "Gosh, this is lovely," she said, feeling slightly awkward.

"And it's such a wonderful setting," said Tom, waving

an arm towards the boats bobbing on the water opposite. "We're so lucky to live here."

"Yes." Clare took another mouthful of the crisp, cold bubbles. "I'll certainly drink to that."

"Ellie said you moved back here when she was small."

"Yes, when they were both quite young. We ummed and ahhed. Rupe didn't want to be too far away from his son Danny, but the schools are good here and I wanted to bring the kids up by the sea." She looked out across the water in front of them. "And it was nice for Danny on the weekends when he stayed with us."

"I'm looking forward to meeting him. Ellie's always saying what a great guy he is."

"And how critical she is of me for breaking up his parents' marriage?" Clare asked drily.

"No, she's never said that."

"In her teens she always used it as the ultimate coup de grâce," said Clare wryly. "Any time she thought I was being overly moralistic or was warning of the pitfalls of, say, going to a rave when you're only fifteen, anything like that, she'd trot out, *but you had an affair with a married man…*" Clare gave a short laugh. "Rather missing the point that if I hadn't, she wouldn't be here at all!"

"Well," said Tom, turning the champagne flute in his hands. "These things happen. I've not been perfect. Perhaps…"

Clare felt suddenly compelled to defend Rupe. And herself. "Their marriage was over before I got there. Claudia was already having an affair and Rupe had given up on it all. But Rupe never tells anyone that. He was pretty honourable about it. He didn't want Danny to think badly of his mother, so since the boyfriend had petered out by the time I was officially on the scene, we took the rap. Claudia drives Rupe mad at times, but he still never says anything against her."

"And you get on all right?"

"Oh yes – I see her as family. I don't find her any more difficult than some of my lot. Easier actually!" she added, thinking of the string of WhatsApps she'd had that morning about Angie's latest feud, which Clare knew she would be compelled to hear about in considerable detail any day soon.

"And to be honest, Rupe knows he deserved it. He says himself he was a useless partner back then. He was literally never there – he was always chasing the latest deal. Made a shedload of commission but Claudia was very much left to hold the baby. If I'd been Claudia, I would've had an affair too."

Tom looked at her shrewdly. "Ah, but would you? You strike me as very principled."

She looked back at him. "Yes, I guess I am."

"I expect Ellie has told you about my previous girlfriend?"

"She's told me very little about your personal life. Nothing really, in fact."

"Oh, well, we lived together just outside Canterbury and it was me who was never there – I was building up the business and she was always complaining she never saw me. It was getting pretty bad between us so one day I knocked off at lunchtime and bought flowers and champagne and arrived in the middle of the afternoon to find"—he paused for dramatic effect—"her tucked up in bed with a bloke from her life-drawing class."

"Oh dear!"

Tom smiled. "Yes, it wasn't quite the same after that. Although actually," he continued, "it made quite a pleasant change to see the view from the moral high ground, for once. Before that it had always been me caught in flagrante with the wrong woman."

Clare felt her eyebrows shoot up. She deliberately gave him what she intended to be a very old-fashioned look. "I do trust you are now a reformed character."

"Of course. I'm talking about when I was young and stupid."

"Because despite what my daughter says, I am protective of both my children, and if you did that to Ellie I would—"

"Kill me?"

"Be none too pleased."

"Why would I look at anyone else when I'm with a beautiful girl like Ellie?"

Clare nodded. "Right answer."

Tom leant over to the ice bucket and topped up both their glasses.

"But there's something I want to ask you before she arrives."

"Oh?"

"I want to offer you a job."

A flare of excitement went through Clare. But as her mouth opened, he swept on.

"Would you consider working for me again? I mean properly, with a proper wage. For the next six months at least. To oversee the conversion of the new house. And then, who knows, there might be other projects after that…"

He leant across the table and topped up her glass. "This time we really do need new kitchens and bathrooms. There's a set of plans, and we've got to adhere to building regs and will be inspected. I've already hired the builders to do the structural stuff and promised some work to Wayne, and Barry, the electrician I usually use."

"I got ours to do the dodgy socket and put new light switches in the kitchen. Just seemed easier."

"Yeah, and that was great. But this is a total rewire and I've already agreed a price. But you can hire the decorators and choose the tiles and carpets and blinds. Or I can suggest—"

"No," she said quickly. "I'd love to do it."

She pushed away the thought of how Rupe might feel if she was out working all the time, instead of just for a couple of weeks. It was up to her, wasn't it?

"There might be the odd day I need to—"

"Of course. You can manage your own time. I don't care how you do it, as long as it gets done." He raised his glass to her. "I hoped you'd say yes. When I saw you today… You look different somehow, like you've been enjoying yourself."

She nodded slowly. "Yes, it's been good to have a project."

"I thought so." He paused. I thought when I met you the first time that you seemed … sort of … unfulfilled."

She shook her head dismissively, feeling herself bristle. "Not at all. Just deciding what to do next with my life."

"Sorry."

She softened. "Slightly at a loose end, maybe." She grinned. "And now I won't be."

"Are you happy to pick out the kitchen and bathrooms if I give you a budget?"

"Absolutely."

He chinked glasses with her. "Brilliant. When can you start?"

Chapter Eighteen

"Even my mum can get a job more easily than I can!" Clare could hear the frustration beneath Josh's bantering tone.

"It's only for a few months," she said. "And hardly the sort of thing you'd want to do. Any more news?"

"Nope. And even if there was, it wouldn't come to anything."

"Something will. You got down to the last four, they said, last time. It's only a matter of time…"

"They said I could apply again next time they have vacancies."

"There you go then."

"But when will that be?"

"I don't know. How is Nikhita?"

Josh nodded wearily. "Yeah, she's OK."

Clare smiled at him. "Did you ask her if she'd like to come down for the weekend sometime before Dad's party?"

"Not really."

"Well, she's very welcome, as I've said." *About six times*, she added silently. "And I'm happy to call her mother. Or should I post her a card perhaps?"

"I dunno."

"But she's coming to the party?"

"I don't know, Mum. Can you stop going on about it?"

"OK. Sorry."

Clare would have been quite happy never to mention the damn party again. But Ellie was in overdrive about it and only that morning had sent her mother pictures of various styles of birthday cake, all of which Clare knew Rupe would think ridiculous.

"Your sister is very keen we give Dad a good time," she tried. "She wants me to get hold of some of the staff from the company and some of his old tennis friends.

"He hasn't played tennis for about ten years, has he?"

"Longer probably, but he goes to the pub with some of them still." She laughed. "They all compare notes on their creaky knees. Anyway, if you can think of anyone we can invite – or you want any of your friends to come?"

"Yeah, that'll be a can't-miss, won't it? My Dad's seventieth."

"Well, you know your father – at least there'll be plenty of booze."

Josh suddenly grinned at her. "That's true. Are we going to have a barbecue?"

"Hopefully. If the weather's OK. You can never tell in September. Some years we've been sitting in the garden, and sometimes there's been rain and a howling gale."

Clare looked at the list Ellie had made her of "Things to

Think About". She slid it to the back of her folder, making a mental note to mark half of them for delegation back to Ellie to "Think About and Preferably Action While You're About It", before turning gratefully to the bathroom brochures she had spread across the kitchen counter.

Ellie had said very little about her mother's new role. A simple "Oh good," when Tom had announced it in The Arch, followed by a lot of chat about her own day and the dynamics between various colleagues that Clare had never met, and in which Tom appeared to be only feigning interest.

Rupe hadn't said much either. Clare had made a piece of cheese on toast to mop up the champagne and gone to have a shower and when she'd come down, Rupe had put his chicken pie in the oven, leaving an astonishing amount of washing-up, and then disappeared into the garden. They hadn't spoken about it on any of the days since.

At that moment he poked his head in at the back door. "Your sister's lurking about looking for you."

"Where?"

"I don't know – sticking her great nose in my geraniums last time I looked."

"I was talking to Mrs P," said Angie from behind him. "She said Rupe was out there in only his boxers this morning and it put her off her breakfast."

"She shouldn't be looking, should she?" said Rupe. "I was turning the hose on."

"I think she'd rather you kept your hose to yourself." Angie laughed loudly at herself.

Clare sighed. "You didn't say you were coming."

"I did. I sent you a WhatsApp saying I might pop in on my way home. I can't stay for a drink – I had to bring the car."

"That's a disappointment," said Rupe.

"I'm going for a shower," said Josh.

"Ah," Angie sounded sympathetic. "You been working today?"

"No, he always dresses like that," Rupe said, nodding towards Josh's delivery suit.

"Yes, I have," said Josh nicely to Angie. "And it was very hot and very difficult. Almost everyone I went to was complaining about something. One woman sent her bananas back because they were too big and she only liked small ones."

"I can't stand people like that," said Angie.

Rupe made a deliberate choking noise. "And what complaint have you come to entertain my wife with today?"

Angie turned her back on him. "I'm not stopping," she told Clare. "I just wanted to bring you up to date on what the bitch has done this afternoon. You are not going to believe this. If it wasn't so ludicrous, I'd be really upset."

As Clare closed the brochure again, Rupe came past her to the wine rack, giving her a wink. "Don't they always say," he began conversationally, "that if you have a problem with one colleague it's probably them, but if you have a problem with three then it's probably you?" He paused. "By my reckoning, you've had about seventy-six work disputes since I married your sister so I think we can say that's fairly conclusive." He pulled out a bottle of rioja and roared with laughter.

"Go away, Rupe," said Clare calmly. She looked at Angie. "This is going to have to be quick – I've got work to do this evening."

Angie looked from her to the photographs of shower cubicles. "What sort of work?" she said sharply. "Are you redoing your en suite?"

"No, I'm working for Tom."

Her sister's jaw went slack. "That's sounds rather strange."

"Why? I've just refurbished a flat for him after the tenant left it in a bad way. Now I'm going to project manage the conversion of the house he's bought. Into three flats," she added, as her sister continued to stare at her with what looked like indignation.

"You didn't tell me about the flat!"

"I haven't seen you. I don't tell you everything—"

"Isn't it a bit incestuous?"

Clare looked at her hard. "No, it is not. He needs help, and I want something to do."

"What about the shop?"

"Something challenging."

"I meant," said Angie heavily, "what about letting them down?"

"I've told Karen I'll still do some shifts, just not twice a week. She's got a couple of new people. She's fine."

Angie was still looking put out. She liked to be informed of family developments in real time.

"Anyway," finished Clare wearily, "what's happened now?"

Angie sat down on a stool. "She has issued a disciplinary," she said dramatically.

"I'll call Sky News," said Rupe. He held up his glass to Clare. "Don't worry! I'm going!"

Clare waited till he'd left the room. "What does that mean, exactly?"

"It's like a first warning. It's on my record and she's put it up the line so now I've got to see *her* boss."

Clare sighed. "So what is it this time?"

"She's still banging on about this lunch-break thing. It's a trumped-up charge and she knows it."

"But you said you were going to be deliberately late, so…"

"Once," said Angie firmly. "How did she know I hadn't had some sort of problem? I said to her I could have been stuck in traffic; I could have felt unwell. I was fifteen minutes over time."

Clare felt her irritation rise. "Yes, you could have been, but you weren't. The day you had lunch with me and Figs, you said—"

"It's not that time she's talking about. It was this Monday and Tuesday."

Clare raised her eyebrows but said nothing.

"I took fifteen minutes on Monday just to pop out and get a sandwich because I was right in the middle of things that really needed to be done; she doesn't appreciate commitment. Instead, she went off on a great rant about the full half-hour again, so I intended to take an hour and fifteen on Tuesday but I misjudged and it was an hour and twenty. Next thing I know she's written me a formal notice."

"Yes," said Clare deliberately, "because she knows you're being intentionally awkward!"

Angie shook her head. "It's because *she* is a control freak..."

"Well, if you know that, why are you going all out to wind her up?"

As Angie launched into another tirade against her boss, for whom Clare now had infinite sympathy, Clare's phone beeped. She fell on it gratefully. "WhatsApp message from Ellie," she said to her sister. "Sorry, Ange – she wants a pow-wow about Rupe's birthday party."

"Oh," said Angie with interest. "Is she coming over?"

"No, no," said Clare hastily. "By phone. She wants me to call her shortly. Something online she wants me to look at with her. It's going to take a while."

Angie frowned. "What sort of thing?"

"Catering options."

"I thought you were having a barbecue."

"Yes, we were, but you know how the weather can be. So, we're just wondering... Maybe a hog roast," Clare improvised. "Lots to discuss."

"You told Figs you couldn't be arsed with it."

Clare scowled at her. "Shh," she said, lowering her voice. "I was just in a bad mood. Of course we're going to make it all as lovely as possible for him. Seventy is a big milestone and he did a lot for me when I was fifty."

"You didn't have a party," said Angie, as if it was a grievance she was still nursing.

"We had a weekend in Paris. And a nice family dinner. It was what I wanted."

"They all thought it was weird at work the way I hadn't celebrated my sister's half-century with her," said Angie peevishly.

Clare shook her head. "You did. You and Figs and Mum came round for drinks when we got back. You know you did."

"And you know what I mean," said Angie, in the tone she used when she felt confident she'd dealt the winning blow.

"I did what I wanted," said Clare. "And I don't remember you dancing on the table around your fiftieth yourself."

"I wasn't well," said Angie.

Clare let it go. There was no point reminding Ange that her decline had actually been due to Zach clearing off as usual, having completed another stint of being fed, housed, and bankrolled for a few weeks in between, Figs and Clare always suspected, his managing to find someone younger to shack up with who hadn't yet discovered his innate aversion to earning a living.

Angie liked to think she and Zach had a "connection" and that, unlike her family, he "got her", so would always excuse his comings and goings as him being "a free spirit".

As Figs had observed drily, the only free spirits around were in Angie's drinks cupboard, to which he liberally helped himself .

"Let me know if you want me to do anything," Angie

said now, surprising Clare. "I can come early and help set up, if you like."

"Thank you," said Clare, making a further mental note to tell Ellie, if approached, to refuse this at all costs. "I'm sure we'll be fine but I'll let you know."

"Sometimes nice to have a drink first, isn't it?" said Angie, "to get us all in the party mood."

"There might not be time for that," Clare said briskly. "Right, I'd better call…"

"OK." Angie stood up and made a performance of heaving her handbag over her shoulder. "I'll let you know what happens."

"Yes, do," said Clare without conviction.

"Oh no, are you leaving?" Rupe appeared in the doorway with an empty glass. "So soon?" He affected a stricken look.

"You think you're so very funny," said Angie. "But actually, you're just plain rude."

"Talking of rude," said Rupe, when Angie had swept off into the evening, "what's he being such a misery about?" He jerked his head to indicate upstairs.

"He's fed up and you can't blame him. He'd set his heart on that job; he was really disappointed. Especially to get so close and then—"

"That's what life is like. You win some, you lose some. You have to learn from the rejection. Has he asked himself why he didn't get it when he was down to the last few? Hmm? Shall I—?"

"No! Leave him alone."

"He should have persevered with his training."

"He should never have started it in the first place. And it's your fault he did," Clare went on hotly. "Anyone can see he's not the personality type to be an auditor. You went on and on about it."

"I was trying to help him get a solid career and earn enough money."

"It's not all about money!"

"No, but it helps. It's pretty difficult to have a good life without any."

"He doesn't have to judge everything by the salary though, like you do."

"What does he want to do?"

"I don't think he's sure. Something creative where he can come up with ideas – write things, think through stuff. I don't know."

"That should narrow it down."

"You are so irritating!"

"And you are very bad-tempered. Is this new job of yours going to cheer you up?"

Clare looked at him. "I hope so."

"Do you want a glass of this?" Rupe indicated the bottle of red he was drinking.

Clare shook her head. "Don't think I do."

"What's wrong?"

"Nothing, I'd just rather have a cup of tea."

"I didn't mean that."

"I just feel…" she began. "It seems to me…"

He was looking at her questioningly, not helping at all. Clare felt annoyed. He must realise too. It must have at least occurred to him – not that Rupe wasn't very good at putting his head in the sand, when it suited him. "Since you've been at home all the time," she said, "I've noticed that…"

"What?" said Rupe, as they both heard the sound of a key turning in the front door. 'Hello, poppet," he said warmly, seeming relieved, Clare thought, to be interrupted, as Ellie appeared in the kitchen doorway dressed in a short turquoise sundress, her hair piled up on top of her head. Her tan had deepened even in the few days since Clare had last seen her, accentuating her green eyes, long, glossy legs, and slender feet in their matching jewelled flip-flops.

"Didn't you get my message?" she said to Clare. "I've just come in for the tennis shoes. I've got this tournament with the students. Tom's outside in the car."

"Isn't she beautiful?" said Rupe, as Ellie ran upstairs.

Clare nodded. Her daughter was exquisite. Beside her, Clare was conscious of her own softening fifty-year-old flesh, the slight wobble to her upper arms and the beginnings of a jowliness around her jawline. She only wore shorts if she was staying at home now, and no longer selected dresses with spaghetti straps…

"See you soon!" Ellie was out of the door again. It banged behind her.

"She reminds me of how you used to look," said Rupe.

"Thank you," said Clare tightly.

"I mean it," said Rupe, oblivious. "You were really, really beautiful in your day…"

Chapter Nineteen

"I know he doesn't mean to upset me but..." Clare shook her head as Figs handed her a coffee.

"Of course he doesn't," said Figs. "You know Rupe – he doesn't think. Opens his mouth and his whole brain falls out."

"Yes, but it's about the third time he's made some comment about how I looked when I was young. He obviously doesn't find me attractive anymore." Clare felt a lump in her throat and took a swallow of the coffee. It was too hot.

Figs put her own mug on the table and sat down opposite. "Don't talk bollocks. Rupe adores you, and he's dead proud of how you look – which is fabulous. You do look like Ellie – nobody would think you were fifty. You could be her older sister. Ange, on the other hand, looks like your bloody aunt!" Figs swept on. "How she can think that Zach is interested in her I do not know. It's so obvious he sees her as his own personal food and booze bank.

Remember when she brought him round to yours that time and Rupe was pissed off because he drank all his scotch?"

Clare smiled. "She said she was seeing Chrissy last night."

"Oh well," Figs shrugged. "Maybe that will come to something – until Chrissy gets fed up with her too…"

"She seemed really nice, didn't she?"

"She'll need to be to put up with Ange. If I were you, I'd tell her that Chrissy is invited to Rupe's knees-up and the wanker Zach very definitely isn't."

"I'm dreading that party," Clare said.

"Why? You usually like entertaining."

"I don't know – I've got a bad feeling about it. A sort of premonition of doom."

"Pah!" Figs looked unimpressed. "You're just a bit fed up at the moment – though I thought you'd be full of the joys now you've got this job and all those men to order around…"

Clare gave a short laugh. "Yes, I am quite enjoying that – we have a laugh. They call me Guv. I feel like I'm in a police drama!"

"I wouldn't mind having something like that to do." For a moment Figs looked almost upset.

"What's the matter?" Clare frowned. "You're always doing things."

"Not at the moment."

"Why not?"

"I dunno. I'm a bit…" Figs shrugged again. "I feel like I'm just hanging around. The kids have got their own stuff.

Don is out there. I need some work to distract me, but there's nothing at the moment…"

"You've got your classes and your pottery. How's that going?"

Figs ignored her question. "I need to network a bit more so I was thinking of going to this thing…"

There was something about the way she said it that made Clare look at her sharply. "What thing?"

"Do you remember Dave Roberts? When I was at school?"

"How could I forget? You mooned over him for months. Didn't he go into the army?"

"RAF. But he didn't last long – he only did it because his dad wanted him to. He's some hotshot in insurance now."

"Oh?"

"We've been chatting on Facebook. There's some group set up by one of the nerdy boys – Caroline sent me the link and said I should join."

"And?"

"Nothing. It's just been nice to be in touch with some of them again."

Clare frowned. "Him in particular?"

"Yes, I suppose. We still get on really well."

"You haven't seen him for more than thirty years!"

"I know but there was still that … connection, you know."

"That sounds like something Ange would say."

Figs got up and went over to the coffee machine and put a new pod in it. "Well, I'm just curious," she said, with her back to Clare. "Can't do any harm, can it, just to go to a lunch with a group of them?"

"You clearly think it can," said Clare, knowing she sounded disapproving. "Or you wouldn't be asking me…"

"I'm not asking you really – I'm just telling you I'm thinking of going."

"Oh Figs, don't get carried away. Suppose you fancy him all over again?"

"He's married."

"Huh. Since when has that ever stopped anyone?" *When has it ever stopped you*? She added silently. Clare didn't know for sure if Figs had ever been unfaithful to Don, but she knew she'd thought about it. Knew there'd been drinks and lunches and flirtations with males various. Figs always laughed it off if Clare showed any concern.

"He lives in Newcastle," she said now. "So nothing would come of it anyway."

"And you're married too."

"Yes. Well, who knows what Don gets up to – he's got all the opportunity, hasn't he?"

"I thought you once said you wouldn't want to know?"

"I wouldn't." Figs said firmly. "Because then I'd have to divorce him and it would all be a hassle and I'd have to live in a smaller house." She laughed.

"Well, be careful he doesn't feel *he* has to divorce *you*, then," said Clare darkly. "Or the end result might be the same."

"God, Clare, you're such a stiff sometimes!" Figs pushed the button on her coffee machine. "Do you want another one or are you off to dispense joy and happiness elsewhere?"

Clare made a face at her sister. "I'll have another one. Go on, show me a photo of Mr Roberts in middle age."

Figs reached for her phone and opened up Facebook. "There!"

Clare nodded. "Wearing well," she conceded. "Be careful…"

Figs took the mug from her and busied herself making another drink.

"Who's coming to Rupe's party?"

"Usual suspects. I thought I'd get his favourites from the company. Even Polly."

"Was she one of his favourites?"

"Well, we never found out, did we?" Clare felt a little stab of something in her solar plexus.

"I think you were imagining it," said Figs. "Remember you were in a strop with Rupe generally because he was never there and you were stuck with the kids? You were going to hide out in the London flat for a bit, weren't you? Give him a fright."

"Oh yes," Clare smiled. "I'd forgotten that. I started packing and filled about half a suitcase and then couldn't raise the energy. I shouted a lot instead!"

Figs laughed. "I wish Don still had that place. It was so great. Must be worth an absolute fortune by now."

Clare nodded. "I should say so. That near the tube."

Figs scrutinised Clare. "Anyway. Why are you thinking about Polly after all these years? I certainly wouldn't invite her to his party if it's going to set you off again. I bet Rupe barely remembers."

"He's still got a birthday card from her!"

"What?"

"I picked up a book on his shelf and what had he been using as a bookmark?"

"A recent one?"

"No, it was from years ago. It was some stupid cartoon he'd thought was funny. Said he'd never finished the book and didn't know it was there."

"Well then! He'd hardly leave it lying around if it meant anything."

"Hmm."

"What's really going on?" Figs frowned at her some more. "You're all…" She stopped, searching for a word. "Sort of crabby. Finding fault. All that fuss about Tom, and—"

"It wasn't fuss. It was being protective of my daughter. If Tilda—"

"Tilda is. I'm sure she's done badly in her AS levels because she spent all her revision time with, or Facetiming, Ryan. And then she thinks they're going to go to the same university and live together! But he'll be there for a year first, and he's going to get himself a new girlfriend within the first month, isn't he? And even if he doesn't, it won't last a whole year and she'll have made all her choices based on being with him…"

"But you like him?"

"He's OK – as eighteen-year-old boys go. But I just know he's not the marrying-his-childhood-sweetheart sort."

"You don't *know*…"

"I do. I can smell it."

"I'd be concerned too," agreed Clare. "Perhaps she'll find someone else when he's gone?" she added hopefully.

"She won't," said Figs grimly. "All I can do is try to keep her studying so at least she doesn't throw away her A levels on the twat."

"That's a bit strong."

"I know. There's nothing wrong with the kid but that's what they are – kids. And you still haven't told me what's wrong with you?"

Clare hesitated. Figs might have good advice. Or she might make inappropriate jokes. Whichever it was, Clare would be embarrassed and once she'd told her sister, she couldn't un-tell her. And it didn't seem fair to mention it – not when she hadn't even managed to discuss it with Rupe.

"I'm just…" she paused. "Up and down," she offered. "I think it's my hormones."

"Ah," said Figs. "Those bloody bastards have a lot to answer for." She sighed. "I sometimes wish I'd stayed in Dubai. Hope those damn kids realise the sacrifice I made for them – just so they could go to good schools here. I could be round the pool now, lounging back on a sunbed with a mojito."

"You said it would drive you mad living there all the time."

"Yes," Figs conceded. "It would. But Don might go to Singapore next. When Tilda's at uni. And maybe Alex can do his A levels out there – we'll find him an international school. I wouldn't mind giving that a whirl for a couple of years. I'm ready for a change."

"Well, don't jeopardise anything then," said Clare sternly.

"For God's sake, Clare – the worst that would happen is we'd get drunk and have a shag in his hotel room. Not run off into the sunset."

"Oh, so he's got one set up then?"

"He's got business meetings – he's there for three days. Where is he supposed to sleep? Underneath the arches?" Figs shook her head, sighing. "I haven't seen Don for nearly two months. And sometimes I miss sex. Do you find that so very surprising?"

Clare didn't.

Chapter Twenty

Who knew sex could be like this? When he touches me, it's different from anything I have ever felt before. My body dances and hums – an explosion of small electric shocks, as his fingers trail across my skin. Even the anticipation is a delicious agony. I tremble inside when I think of us entwined; I imagine, as I dress, the moment when he will be slowly undoing it all again and I, too, will be undone...

Ellie arranged herself along the length of the leather sofa and draped a bare leg across Tom's thigh.

"Are you nearly finished?" she asked, as Tom continued to tap at his laptop.

He didn't look up. "Not really."

Ellie looked at his tanned, muscular legs in the cotton shorts he was wearing. She sighed and twisted herself back up to a sitting position, moving in close to him, leaning over him so she could put a hand on each of his shoulders. She began to knead the hard muscles that ran down from his neck.

"Mmm, that's nice," he murmured, still typing.

Ellie massaged on. "If you put that away and lie down, I could do it all over…"

"I've got to get this done."

She began to stroke the base of his hairline. "It's Sunday. And you've been doing it for ages."

"It's a big contract. I need to get it right. You know I want to build up my commercial clients. If I can get that bit of land for the recycling plant…"

He stopped as Ellie began to nibble at his ear. "Look, just let me get this done," he went on. "And then we'll do something."

Ellie pressed herself closer. "You said that an hour ago."

"And every time you interrupt me, it takes a bit longer."

She drew back. Tom turned and smiled at her, though she could see his impatience. "Haven't you got any work to do for tomorrow?" he asked.

She shook her head. "I've taught these summer courses so many times…"

"Well, have a tidy-up or something then." He waved a hand around the room where Ellie's possessions – a cardigan here, a make-up bag there – adorned most of the surfaces.

"Fine!" She got up abruptly and began to gather things, filling her arms with sunglasses and clothing and books before stalking into the bedroom and dumping them on the floor next to her side of the bed. She heard him call "Ellie," in a weary tone, and she undid another button on her vest top, picked up a magazine and lay back on the pillows, flicking through it, waiting for him to come in…

Rupe and Clare were both on the patio – Rupe in a canvas chair with a glass of wine propped in the arm holder, and *The Sunday Times*, Clare lying on a sunlounger with the latest Joanna Trollope.

She felt warm and relaxed, glad to have nothing more taxing to listen to than the sounds of small bees buzzing round the lavender. She loved her kids, but feeling she had to constantly jolly Josh along while keeping a lid on Ellie's party mania could be draining.

"Your shoulders are getting a bit red," Rupe observed as he rose to refill his glass. "Do you want me to rub something on you?"

Clare considered. There was a time when anything involving a "rub" had been guaranteed to be a precursor to sex, when they'd had an array of massage oils and perfumed lotions in the bedside cupboard, when "Do you want your shoulders done?" or "My back's a bit stiff" was code for *Let's get to it*. She thought Rupe probably didn't mean that now and was not entirely sure if she would have the energy if he did.

They'd have to go upstairs – they couldn't risk Mrs P poking her head over the hedge or Josh returning early from work – and she was keen to see if the heroine of her novel stuck to her guns and married the man of her dreams, or gave in to the petulant demands of her adult children. But she could feel her back glowing and knew she needed either some sunscreen or to go in for a T-shirt to put over her bikini. "There's some on the windowsill," she called.

"Do you want a drink?" Rupe called back.

"Just some water."

Rupe put a tumbler down beside her and crouched alongside her sunbed. She heard a squelching sound as he squeezed at the tube and jumped as a cold splodge of cream landed on her hot skin.

His hand smoothed it into her shoulder blades, and down the tops of her arms, moving rhythmically in large circular movements. As he moved down her spine, Clare shifted on the cushioning. Maybe she could finish the book later…

"Feels good…" she murmured.

But Rupe appeared to have finished. He wiped the last of the lotion from his hand with a flourish across her lumbar region and rested a hand on the back of her thigh. "You've still got such a great body," he said. "I was looking at your lump of a sister and thinking I am so fortunate to be married to you."

"Thanks, Rupe." Clare closed the novel.

His hand was warm on her leg. He gave it a stroke. "You know what we could do later," he said, thoughtfully. "I mean, I will do it – for you."

She dropped her head onto her folded arms and stretched languidly beneath his fingers. "What's that?" she asked slowly.

"I haven't done it for ages," he said teasingly, as if inviting her to guess, "but you always like it when I do."

She twisted round and met his eyes, feeling the first ripples go through her. "Tell me…" she said.

He smiled. "I will open that last bottle of Gevrey," he

said, eyes bright. "And make you my special recipe corned-beef hash."

Tom still hadn't appeared. Ellie threw the magazine onto the floor and picked up her phone. She began to compose him a WhatsApp. Then she heard the loo flush.

She got off the bed and walked back into the living room, glancing out of the big window towards the sea where knots of people stood around outside Turner Contemporary in colourful T-shirts and bikini tops, or wandered along the open steps with beers and ice creams. She watched a couple snogging and sighed.

Tom's laptop was still open on the sofa. She looked at the screen. His emails were open and he'd just started a new one. It was addressed to Clare.

Hi there. Hope you're having a good weekend…

"This isn't about the contract," she said, as Tom strolled back into the room. "You're writing to Mum."

He sat back down and moved the laptop onto his knees. "Yes," he said with measured patience. "I need to tell her about the gas lot coming to look at splitting the meters." He looked up and held Ellie's gaze. "I'm so glad I've got her to help me at the moment. I'd be tearing my hair out."

"I could work for you."

Tom smiled at her. "You're teaching full-time."

"I could give it up. I'm getting a bit bored there anyway. I could be your personal assistant. With benefits."

She leant down and moved the laptop onto the floor and sat down beside him. "You can just give me a cuddle for two minutes."

As he turned towards her, she moved quickly and sat astride him, bending her knees and letting her dress ride up to her hips before leaning in to kiss him. Holding his head in both hands, she pressed against him, feeling him respond.

"You are incorrigible," he said, kissing her back deeply and holding her tightly. Ellie felt something inside her shift in relief as the fervour began to build between them and she felt stabs of desire shoot through her.

He moved forward and she wrapped her legs right around him, gyrating her pelvis as he gave a small groan. He stood, lifting her with him, and as she wound her arms around his neck, her mouth still on his, he carried her into the bedroom.

Figs was in bed too. She'd poured herself a glass of wine to give her Dutch courage.

Tilda was out with Ryan; Alex had gone skateboarding with Connor and Jamie from school. Figs had her dressing gown nearby, ready to throw on in case anyone came home unexpectedly. She would tell them truthfully that she'd been in the shower. She often had one after using her potter's wheel. It had a tendency to splatter.

She wouldn't say that Dave had phoned just as she'd stepped out onto the tiles and that somehow she'd ended up telling him she was naked. It was he who'd suggested laughingly that they had a video call, that he could lie on his hotel bed – he was in Birmingham for some reason – and that she could get into hers, so they could "pretend".

She'd laughed too, protested that she couldn't possibly. Had, at first, flatly refused to turn the camera on. He'd told her he could imagine how beautiful her body still was, and had begun to describe how special he would like to make her feel...

She felt as though she were above herself looking down. She couldn't remember the last time she'd been under a duvet in the middle of the afternoon, much less with no clothes on, breathing down the phone to someone she hadn't seen for more than three decades.

Part of her wanted to giggle hysterically with the ludicrousness of the scene. But as he went into more and more detail, and she heard his breaths get quicker, she stopped making jokes, lay back on her silk pillows, and let the heat flood through her...

———

Anna put a cup of tea down next to Jeremy. "Why don't you come and sit in the garden?" she asked.

He didn't look up from his book. "Because I'm all right here."

"It's really lovely out there," she tried. "The vitamin D would do you good."

"I'm fine."

"Suppose I'm not?" she said in sudden irritation. "Suppose I would like to sit outside in the sunshine with you and have a conversation?"

Jeremy laid down his book and regarded her. "What would you like to talk about?" he asked calmly.

"What is there?" she said hotly. "We don't go anywhere, or do anything. Nothing much has happened in the news. There's nothing fresh to say about the boys. I could tell you that Nigel has just had a stand-off with a seagull. Would that interest you? But it's not as if we can discuss our plans because we don't have any!"

Jeremy sighed. "Aren't we going out next weekend when Steven comes?"

"Yes, in theory. If you don't find an excuse not to." Anna tried to make her voice reasonable. "I know it's an effort, Jeremy. I know you're probably a bit depressed, but you can't just sit here for the rest of your life, reading a book or staring at the bloody television. I want to do things."

"I'm not stopping you, am I?" He looked at her steadily.

"I'd like to do something with you," she said, wondering, as she said it, if that were even true. Was it all too late now to even bother?

She could have gone out last night. Nick had told her there was a group of them from school going to something at the Tom Thumb Theatre. They were having drinks in the Fez and an early supper somewhere in the old town first.

During the evening, he had sent her a picture of a gin and tonic and a smiley.

Wish you were here!

This morning, she'd sent him a picture of her cat Nigel asleep on his back with his legs in the air.

How's the head?

They exchanged WhatsApps a lot. Silly jokes and pictures. Nick hugged her daily, kissed her on the cheek, always...

He'd never taken it any further. Because he knew she was married. Because she'd said often, or implied anyway, that she could never leave Jeremy.

But if she made a move – if she were to lean forward one day, move her face to the right, make sure it was her mouth he kissed, he would respond, she was sure he would. Why else would he tell her so often how special she was, how coming to Margate had changed his life? "I know what I want now..." he had said, on Friday, looking so seriously at her. She had been the one to change the subject, quickly, almost fearfully.

She couldn't remember the last time Jeremy had spontaneously put his arms around her. As he remained silent, she looked at him in exasperation. "Do you ever think about what I want?"

Chapter Twenty-One

The thing about Jeremy being so much older, thought Anna, as she drove down the Thanet Way towards Margate, was that it had always made her seem young. And also feel it.

When they'd first got together, his friends would joke that she was a mere child, and had laughed with delight when she hadn't heard of the actress they all fancied when they were in their teens or the music they played at parties. Anna had liked it. She felt fresh and pretty next to the other wives and girlfriends with their more dated clothes and hair. Women who, she now realised wryly, were only in their forties – no doubt she'd think they were all stunning, if she saw them these days.

Friends her own age pulled faces about being thirty, had crises about forty, lay in darkened rooms weeping when fifty loomed, but Anna had always felt fine about her age. Bemused, for sure – where did those years go to? But never upset. Because Jeremy was still always so much older and had never stopped making her feel precious and protected, special and beautiful. Today, he hadn't even got her a card.

And Anna felt old. Sixty!

There was no getting away from this one. Sixty meant you were officially aged. You got pensions at sixty, a pass for the bus, and you could no longer kid yourself you were middle-aged. You were an "older" woman. Bordering on elderly. And no amount of encouraging talk about sixty being the new forty or how great she looked for her now-great age – her daughter-in-law Fenella had done her very best to say all the right things this morning – could compensate for that.

Anna gave herself a little shake. She was healthy – she could still touch her toes and do the plank when she did her Pilates video. Her back was straight and her hair not entirely grey by any means, though it was so many years since she hadn't had it regularly coloured it could be worse than she thought. She would see Stevie and Fen and baby Tay at the weekend, and Marcus would call later when he got up on his side of the world. She was blessed. She took a deep breath as she reached the Birchington roundabout. It was not like her to want to cry.

Jeremy couldn't get out to buy her anything – it wasn't that he didn't want to. He had said this morning that he was sorry for the lack of card and that she knew she could have anything she wanted as a present. She was to think about what would be nice and they would order it. He'd offered a new car. She'd shaken her head at that. Her BMW was twelve years old now but it started every morning. It was comfortable. It was a friend.

She had wondered if maybe, after their exchange at the weekend, he would make an effort to get them out to dinner tonight but it seemed not. Stevie had booked The Oyster Company for dinner for tomorrow, she knew, and would insist that Jeremy came too. They were going when Tay was asleep and Anna's neighbour, Helen, was coming in to sit with him – she would phone if he woke and wouldn't settle.

Anna was glad that Fen would have an evening to relax. She would offer to do any night feed needed, so they could have a proper rest. Fen had finished breast-feeding after Tay was four months old. Anna would have continued until at least six, but she hadn't said a word. She was never going to be one of *those* mothers-in-law.

When she thought about Tay it made her want to cry even more. She couldn't wait to cuddle his warm little body, see his wide, toothy smile, hear the way he cried out in glee when he saw their cat, Nigel.

She hoped Stevie and his little family were looking forward to the visit too. That it wasn't just duty…

———

Nick looked genuinely thrilled to see her, his face alight with happiness as he put a card and a lush, heavily flowered potted orchid on her desk. "Happy Birthday to the most glamorous sixty-year-old I know!" he said, kissing her on both cheeks and standing back as if to appraise her. "You are astonishing."

Simon appeared behind him. "I'm looking forward to celebrating later, darling!"

"Simon, you are bloody hopeless!" Ellie and Janine were crowding in now too. "It's meant to be a surprise!"

"We're having a little drink for you after work," Ellie told Anna. "In the common room – at five."

Anna smiled at her. She could have a small one. Just a couple of mouthfuls – it would be churlish not to, even if she did have the car. She'd take some water down there with her. She knew the teachers here well. There wouldn't be anything soft in sight. "That's really kind of you," she said.

Ellie pushed a card into her hands as Janine hugged Anna. "Happy Birthday," Janine said, also looking a lot happier than she usually did. "I've got something to give you later."

"You really didn't need to—"

"It's only small."

Anna made herself keep smiling as the four of them gazed at her expectantly. "I hope," said Ellie, "that I look like you do when I'm your age."

So very old, thought Anna.

"Shit," said Nick, looking at the clock. "I've got to do some photocopying yet." He blew Anna a kiss. "Later!"

When they'd all disappeared to their classrooms, Anna sat staring at her screen. There were at least fifty emails to answer, she had a meeting with her boss Aaron at ten, and a woman from one of the host families to phone back about a student who was still allegedly smoking out of his bedroom window despite several warnings. Something the student, Miguel, flatly denied, while the host-mother, from a fairly new family to the school, insisted her husband could smell it from the landing.

Anna wrote a note for Lisa – Miguel's teacher – asking her to send the student to see her, and walked down the stairs to the staffroom to put it in her pigeonhole.

She wondered, as she went, if it wouldn't be easier to just move Miguel to another family and have done with it. The Harrisons near Dane Park had a space at the moment. Mr Harrison was a huge man, ex-services and very popular with the students who stayed in the large, rambling house with his wife and two daughters. But he didn't stand any nonsense. If Miguel smoked in a Harrison bedroom, he'd only do it the once.

The school was quiet. The incredible din of a dozen different languages at top volume that had greeted her as she walked in this morning had been siphoned off into lessons. Anna heard a faint burst of laughter from behind one of the closed classroom doors, and the rattle of cups coming from the small coffee-bar area at the back of the common room.

"Happy Birthday," called Mo, who had been serving the morning refreshments for as long as anyone could remember and was the only person to whom Aaron ever deferred.

"Thanks!" Anna answered as brightly as she could.

"Do you want a cappuccino?"

Anna smiled. "Just a black one would be great."

"It's an Americano these days, don't you know," said Mo, jerking her head at the blackboard behind her. "We remember, don't we, love, when it was plain do-you-want-milk-or-not? I went to a coffee place with my daughter the other day and I didn't understand half of what they were selling. She had a macchiato or some such. I said it sounds like a character out of *The Godfather*."

Mo gave a great hoot of laughter and Anna made herself grin too. She knew Mo was at least fifteen years older than her, but she always spoke as though they were the same age. Normally, it amused Anna. Today she felt that small twist of anxiety inside her as if something traumatic had happened.

"Have a shortbread finger." Mo put two biscuits on a saucer.

"I'll grab it on the way back." Anna ran down two more steps and along the corridor to the deserted staffroom and deposited the note.

Blake appeared in the doorway. "Many Happy Returns. How are you feeling?" he asked, smiling at her.

"Old."

"You don't look it." He grinned. "And you've still got all your hair."

Blake had turned forty a few months earlier and had come into school having shaved his increasingly thinning head. They'd all agreed it really suited him and knocked years off. "Even my dad doesn't have a comb-over," Ellie had said boldly. "And he's nearly seventy."

Blake had started wearing better clothes since too – he had a very nice floral silk shirt on now. Anna knew a lot of the female students were deeply disappointed when they learned he had a wife and a toddler.

"I'm sitting in on your ten o'clock," he said now. "We're

at capacity really, but Aaron wants to take one more group – a late addition. One of the agents needs to divert them from Brighton for some reason..." He and Anna rolled their eyes. Terrific. More host families to find in a short space of time...

Nick came back at lunchtime when she was doing her best to secure these. She was praying the new group would be largely female after the third potential family had said they'd be happy to take a couple of teenage girls but not boys. "Not after last time," as her most recent host-mother had put it. Anna didn't blame her. The last group of Spanish youngsters had been great fun but, as Ellie put it, "pretty lairy". Mrs Wilton, to whom she'd just been talking, had reminded Anna about her bedsheets being knotted together into a makeshift rope-ladder. Anna, who recalled the photographs of the mock escape the boys had staged, had suppressed a smile and assured her gravely that this would not be permitted to happen again.

Nick was hovering as she tried to bring the conversation with Julia Wilton to a close. "I can't promise they won't be vegetarian," Anna said again. "But you know we will pay a supplement if you need to buy anything extra that's lactose-free..."

She shook her head when she was eventually able to replace the receiver. "She's still going on about the gluten-intolerant girl with the custard creams under her bed," she told Nick. "I will be so glad when we get to September and it all slows down again."

He nodded. "Have you got anything planned with Jeremy tonight?"

"No, nothing special. We'll celebrate with Stevie at the weekend."

She thought he looked relieved. She wondered if he was going to suggest dinner. She couldn't do that. Jeremy would expect her back at the usual time, even if it was only to watch TV. She felt a stab of disappointment.

Nick seemed twitchy. "That will be nice," he said distractedly.

"Are you OK?" she asked him.

"Yeah, I'm really good. I was, um, hoping to talk to you..." He shone a huge beam on her. "I want to tell you, well, explain..." He stopped. "You've become my best friend these last few weeks," he began again. "And if it wasn't for you..."

Anna had that feeling of panic again, as if he was going to say something that could never be unsaid. That she would need to respond to.

"What's happened with the flat?" she asked quickly.

"Oh, yes – good," he said vaguely. "The solicitor thinks we should be able to exchange soon. Just a couple of searches to come back or something. But as there's no chain..." he trailed off. "But Anna, right now—"

At that moment the phone on her desk rang again. She looked from it to him. "I'm sorry, I need to..."

"Sure, I'll catch you later." He leant across the table and squeezed her hand, hesitating for a moment as she picked up the phone. Then he blew her a kiss and went out.

Anna looked at the card from him. She'd propped it up on top of the filing cabinet, with the ones from Ellie and Aaron. It was a watercolour of freesias.

With very much love and thanks for everything. Yours always,
Nick xx

She could still feel the pressure of his hand on hers. She suddenly wanted him to come back and hug her.

She gripped the phone tightly and adopted her most professional tones. "Anna Ward speaking…"

Chapter Twenty-Two

Anna had a lump in her throat as she looked around the common room. Ellie had banned her from going downstairs for any reason after lunch was over and now she knew why. Balloons filled every corner and a big foil helium affair bobbed from a white-clothed table that stretched along one wall. *Happy Birthday Anna*. And, as it turned in the breeze from the open door, *6-0*. It was lucky she hadn't intended lying about it!

Bottles of fizz poked from buckets of iced water, and white and red wine bottles were grouped at one end together with – now here was a departure – a selection of fruit juices and bottles of sparkling water. There were bowls of savoury biscuits and cheese straws, nuts and olives, plates of tiny sausage rolls and various stylish-looking canapes, together with mounds of strawberries and miniature cupcakes. All the staff were gathered, including Mo and Paul – the school handyman and gardener – as well as a selection of their older, longer-term students, and couples from her favourite, most-established host families.

"Oh!" she said, overwhelmed. "I wasn't expecting…"

Ellie had put a glass of champagne in her hand. "We couldn't just let it go by…" Ellie chinked glasses with her. "Happy birthday!"

Anna took a tiny sip as the rest of the staff began to gather around her. "It's so lovely of you," she said. "I can't drink too much because—"

"You can!" Ellie grinned at her. "Aaron has ordered you a cab home. We just phone up when you're ready and—"

"A cab? All the way to Whitstable?"

"Yes! And he is personally going to pick you up again in the morning." Ellie raised her eyebrows at Anna to emphasise the momentousness of this gesture.

"Where is he?"

"He's coming down later to make a speech."

Anna took a swallow of the crisp, dry bubbles. "Gosh!" she said. "Guess we'll all need a drink…"

The noise levels rose quickly, everyone rapidly getting into the party mood. Anna opened a huge card with dozens of signatures, Janine gave her perfumed shower oil, Mo a box of chocolate-covered ginger. Anna felt light and excited and happy. She accepted more champagne. She didn't have to rush back – there was nothing to rush for. Nick appeared at her side and put an arm around her, squeezing her in tight to him – in front of everyone. "It's so lovely about him and—" said Ellie, but then Aaron clapped from the stairs, standing above them all several steps up.

Anna wondered what she had been about to say. About

him and you? Did Ellie realise there was something unspoken between them? Had Nick perhaps confided in Ellie about his feelings? Was it those feelings he'd so wanted to talk about earlier?

Aaron was talking about a special person in their midst, for whom it was a very special day. He looked awkward, his eyes not quite meeting Anna's although he was apparently nodding at her as he spoke. He quoted the exact date Anna had come to work at the school as an administrative assistant and how many years and months had passed since. Talked about the great contribution she had made to the growth of the business so that this summer the Margate Academy had welcomed more than nine hundred students who had been placed with over two hundred and fifty host families.

It began to sound like a company report, and across the room Anna saw Simon whisper something into Nick's ear. Nick grinned. Then he caught Anna's eye and winked. Anna felt the warm glow go through her that she always felt these days when he looked or smiled at her. She turned back and kept her eyes fixed on Aaron, who, she trusted, was heading towards some sort of finale. She hoped it was not going to be a rousing rendition of "For She's a Jolly Good Fellow", which he had led them in when Mo had completed twenty-five years of service.

But Aaron had a couple more statistics to impart before thrusting out an arm. "I give you Anna Ward!"

He nodded regally towards Janine who scuttled forward with a massive bouquet. "From all of us in appreciation of all you do for the school," intoned Aaron.

"And because it's your birthday, darling," shouted Simon. Aaron shot him a brief look. "And to wish you many happy returns," he concluded stiffly. They all clapped and Aaron withdrew upstairs again. Anna made a mental note to find him before she went home and thank him for his generosity. She knew he wasn't comfortable with public gestures. She also knew he would have footed the bill for all the booze.

Anna kissed Janine and exclaimed over the flowers, admiring the white roses nestled against deep purple lisianthus, lilies, and freesias, set off with glossy green foliage and finished with lilac tissue tied up with raffia. "They're beautiful," she said, swallowing again.

And then suddenly there was Nick coming towards her with Simon, holding between them a silver board with a big square pink and white cake on it, with what seemed an impossible number of candles. Simon was hamming it up, pretending to be only just short of dropping the whole thing, while Nick was steadying it.

Anna was looking at the ring of smiling faces, watching their expressions. Ellie was beaming, looking from Anna back to the cake with a huge, indulgent smile on her face, almost like a proud mother as the cake was borne closer to her. And then, in a split moment, Anna realised Ellie hadn't been looking at the cake at all. Anna had the strangest sensation of everything slowing down and her face fixing into a smile that held her rigid. She was suddenly watching a film unfold.

They stop in front of her and she obediently blows at the candles but there are too many to do all at once and Nick, laughing, blows some too, his face close to hers as they lean across the icing, him wanting her to have a good time, his eyes full of warmth and affection for her...

But not alight like they were when he was looking at Simon...

"I wanted to tell you," he says, holding her hand. "I felt a bit silly, but I know I would never have had the courage to own to my feelings without you."

"Isn't it wonderful?" cries Ellie. "I am so happy for you both," she says, looking from them to Anna. "I love a happy ending."

And Anna is trying to nod and smile too, though she feels as if the entire centre of her has been sucked out. Her mind clicks a dozen tiny fragments into place and she sees Simon drape an arm round Nick's shoulders in that easy way that Nick has so often embraced her.

She tries to say that she is happy too, but the candles and the crowd and the dozens of babbling voices are too much and she really needs to sit down. She moves towards the back of the room. Nick is there immediately, hugging her, leading her to a chair. Ellie is topping up her glass. One of Nick's fingers wipes a tear from Anna's cheek and he is laughing again as he pulls her against him. "Oh Anna, oh darling, I didn't know you were such a romantic..."

There was no sound when she let herself into her house. Usually the TV was on and Jeremy would be watching an evening news programme. She kicked her shoes off, called out hello, and began to carry her flowers down the long hallway towards the kitchen. The sitting room door was open but there was nobody in there as she passed. She felt a moment's unease as she called out again.

"In here." Jeremy's voice reached her from the other side of the breakfast-room door. As she pushed it open, she caught the scent of an aftershave he hadn't worn for a long time and her senses were assaulted with memories. He was wearing a proper shirt too – the soft grey linen one she'd always liked. Behind him on the table, two flames flickered from the old silver candlesticks they'd bought in an antique shop when they'd first moved here. A jug was filled with red roses. She saw him look at the blooms in her arms. "From the staff," she said. Her voice sounded odd.

"You're later than I thought you'd be." He sounded sad rather than reproachful.

"They put on a drinks party for me."

"That was kind."

He pulled out a chair, steadying himself with one hand still on his Zimmer, breathing heavily as he indicated she should sit down. His arms looked thin. The shirt hung from his bony shoulders. "It's all in the oven. I ordered a curry and had it delivered. I think I got all your favourites."

She nodded. "Thank you. You smell nice."

"I did it for you." He frowned. "You look upset." She shook her head silently, unable to stop her eyes filling with tears.

"I don't do enough for you," Jeremy said. "But I do still love you."

Her voice shook. "I know you do."

She could feel the tears falling so she walked past the chair to the sink, reaching into the cupboard to find a vase and taking the scissors from their hook to trim the stems of her flowers.

When she turned back, he hadn't moved. "Please come and sit down."

She put the flowers into the water while he watched her. She wished Nigel would come bursting through the cat flap to break the moment but the air lay heavy between them and there was only the sound of the oven humming and the tap dripping and two sets of breathing, as she tried to slow the thumping of her heart.

She sat and he pulled another chair close and sat down next to her. Then he leant in and encircled her in his arms. The smell of his aftershave reminded her of days long ago when he had been tall and strong. She had a sudden image of him picking her up and swinging her onto the bed in a hotel room, and her hanging round his neck, laughing.

Now, he held her for a brief moment and then sat back. "Happy birthday," he said.

She couldn't speak. He was looking intently into her eyes, the way he had that very first evening they'd had dinner together. As if everything in his life depended on what she had to say next. She could see him then, as clearly as ever. He'd taken off his suit jacket and undone the silver and jade cufflinks and tossed them into a pocket with his tie. He'd rolled up his sleeves and sat back and looked at her as if she were an exotic delicacy. She'd looked at the dark hairs on his forearms and known that she had to be with him. That she needed that moment when he removed all the rest of his clothes and crushed him to her as if he would never let her go. She took a deep breath.

"Thank you," she managed.

"Oh, Anna," he said, looking more moved, more real, more like himself than he had for a very long time. "I'm so sorry I'm old."

248

Chapter Twenty-Three

"I used to think," said Josh to Ellie, "that my problems would all be solved if only I was older."

He was sitting on the end of Ellie's childhood bed, while she applied make-up at her dressing table.

"Uh huh," she said, carefully drawing a line beneath her lower lashes.

"You know, when you're sixteen you think, if only I was eighteen, I could go to the pub, and come in when I wanted to instead of having Mum keep texting me—"

"Tell me about it," his sister interrupted. "She did that *way* after I was eighteen. Is she still being all strange? I find her so annoying at the moment. She's so sort of ... I dunno ... *intense*. Dad *offered* to take my car in to be MOT'd because I am working *all* the time, so when could I get to the garage?" Ellie raised her eyebrows as if waiting for Josh to supply the answer. "When I am either teaching for the *whole* day or dragging the students halfway round Kent?"

Ellie shook her head. "Mum goes on about being organised. But like, when was I supposed to do it?"

Josh shrugged. "Sometime before it had actually run out, I guess?"

Ellie scowled at him in the mirror. "They don't send you reminders anymore."

"Anyway," Josh went on deliberately. "And then I thought, if I was twenty-one and out of uni, I'd have a job and could have my own flat…"

"Yeah, like all our friends can afford to do!"

"You know what I mean. I thought I'd be independent."

"I think she's menopausal. Lisa at work said her mother was an absolute bitch for months." Ellie selected a brush and began to layer more colour on her eyelids.

"Mum's not like that. Are you even listening to what I'm saying? Why do you ask me how it's going and then ignore my answer?"

"I'm not ignoring anything. I can think about more than one thing at once."

"I'm still living at home and I can't even see my girlfriend when I want to, and it's not going to get any better, because *her* parents won't stand for her having a flat, however much money we had, unless she's married…"

Ellie turned round and looked at her brother with interest. "Well, would that be so bad?"

"What? We haven't even lived together. All we've done is share a student bedroom – for a night or two." Josh sighed. "And we're too young. I don't want to get married right now. And I don't think she does either. Not really…"

"Maybe she's not the one then."

"How do make that out?"

"I think when it's really right, you just know. It's like a thunderbolt. I hadn't lived with Tom but I knew I wanted to marry him."

Josh shook his head. "The same person for the next sixty years? Mum and Dad have only done twenty-six and she's completely fed up with him…"

"No, she isn't. She's just grumpy. I said, it's her age. And I don't think about it like that."

"Do you think about the rest of your life at all? I mean, past you getting the princess dress and having the party?"

Ellie glared as she pulled the top off a lipstick. "Oh, shut up, Josh. What do you know about any of it?"

Ellie ran the tongs through her hair crossly. She didn't think about the future much. Why should she? She often day-dreamed about the wedding and thought about the dress she might get, yes, of course she did, and where they might do it. Mauritius looked amazing. But no, she didn't dwell on the next sixty years like her laugh-a-minute brother. She couldn't imagine Tom any other way from how he was now. If she did think about it, she assumed Tom would age wonderfully and be fit and well – like her father was. Her dad still knew how to enjoy himself and her parents had a good marriage, even if her mum was being more than usually awkward right now.

Tom had been a bit grouchy and preoccupied lately too. But it was because he was an incredible businessman and had won some huge new contract with a building company and was thinking about expansion. He was intent on buying a plot of land to have his own recycling plant and he had to move quickly, he said, if he was to get a loan in place before the land he really wanted came up for auction.

The slightly annoying thing was that the first she knew about it was when she'd overheard him telling her mother on the phone.

"Why hadn't you told me?" she'd asked, when he'd eventually ended the call.

"I didn't think you'd be very interested." He had sounded almost dismissive so she had wound her arms around him and kissed his neck until he had smiled at her, his lovely warm, deep smile that went with his come-to-bed eyes. And then she'd laughed and said, "I'm not really." And she'd begun to trail her fingernails gently across his chest in the way she knew really got him going. "Because I can think of better things to be interested in…"

Afterwards, she had felt she'd better prove she'd only been joking. "Of course I want to know what you're doing," she'd said. "I want to be supportive and help you. Tell me about the land." But he was already tapping away at his laptop and he'd just run a hand down her leg beside him in the bed and said, "No, you're right, it is quite boring. Get some clothes on and let's try that new rooftop bar up by Dreamland…"

Which, she had to admit, did sound a better option than discussing hard core.

Now, Ellie felt a flutter of unease as she looked at her watch. She beamed at Josh.

"There are no cabs for half an hour. Can you drive me back in my car?"

Josh didn't look up. "No way. You've just said it's got no MOT."

"Dad's getting it one in the morning."

"But right now, you're not supposed to be driving it. So the insurance won't be valid and I could get points. I need a clean licence if I'm applying for jobs. I'd probably lose the one I've got."

Ellie gave an enormous sigh. "I'm going to be really late and Tom—"

"Must be used to it by now!"

"Has booked tickets for some play his friend's in... He's going to be annoyed if I'm not there." Ellie suddenly sounded anxious.

Josh looked up "Why have you spent an hour sitting about here then?"

"I wanted to catch up with you. Have a chat..."

"You wanted to nag me about the music for the party of the year. And I'd already told you I'll do it!"

Ellie looked at her phone. "It's Tom, wanting to know why I'm not back yet. Oh, go on, Joshie, please."

Josh raised his eyebrows as they heard a key turn in the front door. "If that's Mum back, I'll take you in hers." He looked at Ellie. "But you owe me."

Ellie gave him a glowing smile as she jumped out of Clare's car outside Margate's Theatre Royal. Tom was standing just inside the doors in the tiny foyer. "Phew, made it! Thanks, bro."

Josh raised his hand and waved at his sister's boyfriend. Tom returned his greeting with a nod and what looked like a brief, tight grimace. Josh watched as Ellie kissed him extravagantly and tucked her arm through his. She was talking and explaining. He saw her gesture to the car, shrug, and laugh. Tom, he noted, was not even smiling.

"When did you go the extra mile to make sure a task was completed on time?" said Josh, as he walked back into the kitchen.

Clare was chopping an onion. She smiled at him. "I hope she said thank you."

"Yeah, she did. Tom didn't look too pleased."

"I don't suppose he did if the play had already started. She needs to buck up a bit. Have you eaten?"

Josh shook his head.

"I'm doing a stir-fry. Dad's meeting up with George from the office so it's just us."

"Great."

"There're some bamboo shoots in the freezer in the top of the booze fridge – can you get them? Get us a couple of beers too, if you like."

Clare felt a moment of relief as he nodded and went into the utility room. She hadn't had any time with Josh on her own for ages. It would be good to talk to him without Rupe making unhelpful comments.

She heard the door of the fridge open and the chink of beer bottles. Then a thud and Josh saying "oh fuck", without any particular emotion.

He returned with two beers and a frozen bag of veg.

"Some idiot put a bag of peas back without closing it properly," he said. "They are now all over the floor."

"You know where the dustpan is."

"When did an assignment you'd been briefed on not go according to plan?" said Josh, reaching into the drawer for the bottle opener and flipping both lids off. "Or, when did you use your initiative and creativity to complete a project that went against the usual methods used by your colleagues?" Josh grinned at her. "I shall hoover them instead!"

He picked up the stick Dyson on charge in the corner and went back into the adjoining room. She heard him switch it on.

She waited till he'd come back, poured her beer into a glass, and was leaning against the work surface, swigging his own from the neck of the bottle.

"I spoke to Nikhita's mother today," she said. She felt his tension.

"And?"

"She was charming."

Josh took another sip of beer. "Go on…"

"I emailed her first," said Clare, "explaining that we were having a family party and would love Nikhita to stay here for the weekend. Said we had a very comfortable en suite guest bedroom" – Clare looked meaningfully at Josh – "so she would have privacy and her own facilities and we hoped this was OK with her parents as I was looking forward to meeting her. I gave my phone number and about half an hour later she phoned me."

"And she was friendly?"

"Apologetic. Said Nikhita always says she fusses too much but that she can't help worrying about her children. Said if it was to stay with the family – there was a slight emphasis on that – she would be happy for Nikhita to come. Thanked me for being polite and asking her. So, it was the right thing to do."

"Nikhita will feel embarrassed."

"She doesn't need to be. I said I worried about my children too and that I quite understood her concern when we were strangers."

"Yeah, like you knew where Ellie was after the age of fifteen."

"Not for want of trying, I can assure you," Clare said sharply. "For your information, I've always liked it best when you're both safely under my roof, asleep in your own beds!"

Josh grinned. "Even now?"

"Even now."

"So you're not so accepting of Tom after all."

"Of course I am. Ellie's a grown woman – I didn't mean that. I just meant you don't stop worrying." Clare laid down the knife and took a mouthful of beer. "Any more jobs on the horizon?"

"I've given up talking about it. I'll tell you if I ever actually get an offer."

"You will."

"Did she say anything about me only being a delivery driver?"

"Of course not. And I would have given her short shrift if she had."

"That would have really helped."

"You know what I mean. You have a decent, responsible job, earning money and providing a good service. It's nothing to be ashamed of. And in time you'll find something you really want to do."

Josh pulled a face. "If I go banging on doors and demand to be heard, like Dad would."

"Don't take any notice of your father – he's only trying to help."

Clare lit a ring on the hob and poured a little oil into the wok. "Shall we have prawns with this?"

"Sure. I meant to remind you not to mention that we eat beef."

"I didn't get into menus!"

"Nikhita loves nothing better than a good burger. But she would never upset them by admitting it. She's really good about the customs and traditions. She says if it's important to them…"

"She's right. And her brother?"

"He goes along with it too, but only at home. He's even less interested than Nikhita."

"I am looking forward to meeting her. I'm sure she is really lovely."

"Yeah, yeah, she is…"

There was a pause. Clare split open a bag of brightly coloured vegetables while Josh turned his beer bottle in his hands. "Can you tell Dad not to be…" He pulled a face.

"Crass?" said Clare, matter-of-factly.

Josh nodded.

"I can try…"

Chapter Twenty-Four

"I thought I'd just try."

Ellie stood on the doorstep with a bunch of vivid gerbera and a hesitant expression. "I was going to leave these on the doorstep and ring you, but I thought I'd try the doorbell and see if you felt up to…" She looked anxiously at Anna. "Are you better?"

Anna nodded. "Oh yes, just a summer cold."

"I've never known you have time off before."

"I was really streaming – didn't want to give it to anyone else."

Ellie peered at her. "Your eyes still look a bit pink."

"Come in!" Anna flung her front door open wider. "Sorry! Didn't mean to leave you standing there. What are you doing in Whitstable?"

"Activities trip, isn't it? Wednesday afternoon! They're all at the castle. But they've got free time now and the group leaders are there so I said I'd meet them at the coach."

"Well it's lovely to see you." Anna took the flowers from

her. "These are so pretty. I've been very lucky with my blooms lately."

She led Ellie down the hall into the kitchen, past the sitting room where the staff bouquet was on the low table in front of the window, and through the breakfast room, where Jeremy's roses sat in their jug. "Thank you so much." She smiled at Ellie. "I think you definitely can be too thin and too rich but you can never have too many flowers…"

The back door was open. Beyond them, Jeremy was sitting in the middle of the small lawn in a slatted wooden garden chair, his feet up on a matching footstool, reading a book. A small table was beside him, with a glass of water.

"Would you like some tea?"

Ellie nodded. She looked towards Jeremy. "Shall I go and say hello?"

"Um, yes, sure." Anna went out with her.

"Jeremy, this is Ellie from school."

He put his book down, and held out his hand, giving Ellie his old, engaging smile. "I've heard all about you."

Ellie sat down in the second chair. "All good, I hope," she said. "So now I need to hear about you…"

Anna heard Jeremy laugh as she went back in to put the kettle on. When she'd made three mugs of Earl Grey, they were still talking. She carried only one outside.

"Are you the one who's buying the flat?" Jeremy was saying.

Ellie shook her head. "No, I live with my boyfriend," she said. Anna breathed out. She hadn't mentioned Nick.

"I've left ours in the kitchen," she said to Ellie. "I

thought you might want to bring me up to date with what's happening at school." Ellie jumped up.

"Lovely to chat to you," she said to Jeremy. "Hope to see you again."

"He's funny, isn't he?" she said to Anna when she was sitting at the table indoors. "He reminds me of my grandad. "He's dead now," she added. Then she clapped her hand to her mouth. "Sorry, that came out wrong. I didn't mean—"

"It's fine."

"Anyway, he was really cool and Jeremy reminds me..." Ellie laughed. "I remember once I was skiving off school because there was a geography test I hadn't revised for and the teacher was terrifying if you didn't know it. And Mum called Grandad round to sit with me cos she had to go into work. She'd completely believed me that I was ill and I was sitting on the sofa under a blanket. But as soon as she'd gone, he said, 'You don't look very sick to me', and he took me on this great long walk along the beach. Told me all about the formation of rocks in the cliffs, like what the different layers in the cliffs meant, and he kept picking up bits of old fossil and telling me how old they were. And then he said, 'Are you being bullied?' And when I said no, he said, 'You get back to school tomorrow then.'" Ellie laughed. "By the time Mum got home I was back on the sofa but I was knackered because he'd walked me so far and she said to him, 'She's clearly not right; she's never this tired usually.'"

Anna laughed too. "Did you ever tell her?"

"Yes – after the funeral. And she said she knew because she'd wondered why my shoes were sandy. And Grandad had said, "Well, she learnt a lot more today than she would have done." She looked at Anna. "Are you coming back to work tomorrow?"

"Yes." Anna sipped at her tea. She had been hoping for another day before she had to face them all again. But now Ellie had been here ... had seen there was nothing wrong with her...

"You seemed a bit..." Ellie paused. "On Friday, when you went home...?"

"Just a bit emotional," Anna said quickly. "Just so touched by the trouble you all went to."

That's what she'd said to Nick, eventually – when she couldn't leave his texts unanswered any more. "It was really lovely of you all. I had such a great time."

"And with your family?"

"Oh yes – that was lovely too."

It felt like a dream now. The twenty-four hours she'd glided through, smiling and eating and drinking and nodding and thanking, holding Tay, listening to Fen, watching Stevie taking his father's arm, guiding him firmly to the restaurant table, while she repeated over and over to herself: *Nothing has happened. Nobody knows. Nothing went on outside your head.*

"How is Tom?" Anna asked now.

"Oh yes, he's great. Very busy, you know," said Ellie vaguely. "Well, we both are. I'm head-banging for the next two weeks because Blake is short of a teacher for this latest group, so I'm on double shifts and that will be me gone for more than twelve hours a day and he spends evenings on his laptop..."

She gave a short, unconvincing laugh. "And you know how knackering it all is at this time of year. I'll be going to bed early…"

"Not long now," said Anna. "Three weeks and it will all calm down again."

"It's so great about Nick and Simon, isn't it?" Was Ellie probing or just making conversation? "I know Si gives it all that, but I think, really, he's been lonely for a long time, and they're so good together. I picked up the vibe before they did. I said it to Tom… And to Janine. I think she had hopes early on, but you could see that was never going to happen…"

Ellie was only chatting. Anna had never shown anything. She had kept her dignity. She'd got everything wrong but nobody knew that.

"He said it was talking to you that made him realise." Ellie was looking at her more intently now. "He does adore you."

"I'm very fond of him too. And yes" – Anna had to say it – "it is wonderful news that they've found each other."

And she had Jeremy, who had made a big effort for her birthday and who had surprised her by taking her hand under the table on Saturday night and giving it a brief, reassuring squeeze. Just for a moment, when Fen was asking how work was going…

There was a time when he'd always picked up on her mood. She'd forgotten.

Ellie was still burbling on, but Anna wasn't sure what about. She fixed on the bright, interested look she used when she'd accidentally zoned out in meetings with Aaron, and concentrated hard to catch up.

"...So Mum said yes, our family is always better well-diluted, so I thought I'd see if you and Nick and Simon and Janine wanted to come too. Safety in numbers – I was teaching the students that expression earlier. In other words, nobody will kick off if we've got friends there too..."

Ellie had finished her tea and was standing up. "Though actually, that never puts Auntie Ange off."

"And when is it again?" asked Anna cautiously, wondering whether Ellie had announced her wedding date and she'd somehow missed it.

"The nineteenth of September. Saturday. We're going to start in the afternoon with a barbecue. His actual birthday is the next day but we thought what with people going to work on Monday et cetera." Ellie rolled her eyes. "Dad's birthdays are always awash with booze. You might want to come on the train..."

———————

Clare had suggested the train to Meg too. "Or you could always get a taxi," she added. "Or drive over, get a cab home, and Josh will pick you up the next day to collect the car."

"Or I could have one drink only to toast his Lordship and then make myself a nice pot of tea." Meg raised her eyebrows. "Unlike the rest of you, I don't need to drink myself into a stupor to have a good time."

"Only making a suggestion," said Clare. "Just wanting you to be able to relax."

"I'm perfectly at ease, thank you. You're the one who looks wound up from where I'm sitting. If this party's getting too much for you, make that daughter of yours help."

Clare pulled a face. "It's her assistance I could do without. She's intent on over-complicating everything. What with her and Angie and the constant saga about her bloody boss..."

"Well, if it wasn't that, it would be something else," said Meg comfortably. "That's Angela for you. Felicity had the beauty, you've got the brains, being awkward is what she does."

"Thanks, Mum."

"Oh, stop looking as if you've had an arm chopped off. Are you making me this cuppa or not?"

Clare put a teabag in a china mug. "Sorry!"

"So you're doing this job for Tom?" Her mother suddenly took on a beady look. "What does Ellie think of that?"

Clare frowned. "I think she's glad I'm helping him out so he's not too stressed."

"She told me she's working all God's hours at that school."

"They're always flat out in August."

"And you're enjoying yourself?"

"Yes, I am." Clare wondered where her mother was heading. Probably about to launch into a lecture about not neglecting the sainted Rupe.

"And his Lordship doesn't mind?"

"Of course not."

"What are you all moony about then?" Meg's voice took on a triumphant note. "With all you've got? That's what you have to remember about your eldest sister. You two have had a lot more good fortune too. She sees Rupe and Don and she thinks…"

"She wouldn't want either of them. Angie likes them younger…"

"Better to be born lucky than rich."

"What?" Clare flicked the teabag into the bin under the sink and poured milk. Meg had an endless fund of homilies she employed in place of getting into anything too deeply. Clare wondered what her mother would say if she spilled out what exactly was chasing around her head…

"Count your blessings," Meg finished now. "Do you want me to make cheese straws?"

Chapter Twenty-Five

C lare looked at Ellie in exasperation. She'd not only turned up early for the first time in her entire life, and interrupted the meeting with Tom before Clare had got as far as discussing the second fixings for flat one, but had now commandeered Clare's clipboard and was being very bossy about canapés.

"I don't think so," said Clare for the third time. "Let's keep it simple. Let people help themselves."

"I'm talking small nibbly bits to have with drinks when they arrive."

"And you're going to hand them round?"

"If I have to. Or Josh and Nikhita can."

"We're not putting the poor girl to work – she's a guest."

"Well whatever, let's get some stuff ordered from Waitrose or M&S, and did you get hold of some of his old friends?"

Clare kept her voice even. "I've invited who I could think of. Some are coming from the office."

"But wouldn't it be great if there were some surprises?"

Clare thought about Polly. She had sounded surprised to be invited. Clare wondered if Rupe would be. Ellie was still talking. "Like people keep walking in that he hasn't seen for years?"

"This is your life," said Tom.

Clare rolled her eyes in mock horror. "I'll knock up a big red book."

"What?" Ellie frowned impatiently.

"It's an old TV show."

"My mother loved it," Tom said. "I think she had a crush on Michael Aspel. Staple viewing in our house when I was at school."

"I can remember when it was the other bloke," said Clare. "That's who we had to watch."

"Eamonn Andrews?"

"Very good!"

Tom grinned. "My mother remembered him as well."

"Trivia question!" said Clare. "Who was the youngest person ever to be surprised?"

"Dunno."

"Twiggy! She was nineteen. *My* mother guessed that one right when we did a quiz at Christmas…"

Ellie gave an exaggerated yawn. "*And*," she said, "I've got Josh to do the music."

Clare raised her eyebrows. "Wouldn't it be better to have music your father actually likes?"

"We will do stuff he likes." Ellie ticked it off on her fingers. "Elton John, Bruce Springsteen, Dire Straits, Johnny

Cash... The Beatles, Joe Cocker, The Beach Boys... Diana Ross, Nina Simone..."

Tom nodded. "Quite eclectic then."

"Some Sex Pistols for me," said Clare.

"You're kidding. Really?"

"Second time around – yeah. But mostly I'm into the Sixties and Seventies sounds too. Rupe's music became mine. And I like a lot of the stuff Ellie plays too. What's his name, that guy I like?"

Ellie shook her head. "George Ezra. Stop acting all old and dipsy."

"I am old," said Clare.

"That makes me old minus eight," said Tom. "And I refuse to age yet!" They both laughed.

"You sound like a couple of pensioners," said Ellie, irritably. "Now come on, Mum, focus. Shall I order party food from Waitrose or M&S?"

Angie wanted her to focus too. On the fact, as she put it, that her sister's entire job was on the line.

Clare had largely glazed over during Angie's account of meeting her boss's boss who had had the temerity to take the line manager's side and use the word "insubordination" ("Does he think he's in the army?") but she was now being called on to properly concentrate on Angie's next move, as well as unpacking the shopping. Angie had pitched up just seconds after Clare had let herself in with four Waitrose carrier bags and an urgent need for a large cup of tea, followed, quite possibly, by a small lie-down, and her sister wasn't showing any signs of disappearing again.

"I really don't know what I can contribute," Clare said, after Angie had finished her rundown of the bigger boss's shortcomings and was demanding input. "You've already involved the union."

"You can agree they're being unreasonable," said Angie firmly. She held up a half-empty bottle of red wine with a cork stuck in it. "Can I have some of this or will he moan?"

"Yes you can, and probably," said Clare shortly, stacking cheese and ham into the fridge. "I don't know who's being unreasonable, Ange. I don't know enough about it. If you're deliberately breaking the rules then I guess you have to take the consequences."

She began to pile apples into the fruit bowl, as Angie hissed her annoyance. "They can't sack me after only one warning. The bloke from the union was very clear on that!"

"Can't you just say you won't do it again?"

Angie took a swallow of the wine she'd poured. "Well, yes, of course I can, but it will still be on my record and then I'm admitting I was in the wrong."

Clare put two lemons in with the apples and turned and faced her sister. "Well, you were, weren't you? If taking the right lunch hours is part of your contract," she added, as Angie's eyes flashed.

"I've worked there for nearly thirty years—"

"And that's a bloody wonder in itself," Clare exploded. "Look, Ange, you're lucky to have a job. Especially round here. Which reminds me, I wanted to ask you," she went on, in a tone designed to mollify, "as you know a lot about these things, is it right that you can't get benefits without a fixed address?"

She gave her sister a brief lowdown on Tony's situation. "Can he really not get on some sort of housing list? He says social services won't help."

Angie shook her head. "Single man? He's got no chance. They might help a mother with children, but if he's got no issues to make him vulnerable then he's on his own."

"It's awful."

"That's why there're so many people on the streets," said Angie matter-of-factly. "Especially young men who've been kicked out by the girlfriend. He could use a care-of address. He could use this one!" she added challengingly.

"That's a thought," said Clare steadily. "I've given him my phone number in case I can help. And I'll suggest that next time I see him."

She took advantage of her sister's stunned silence to try to bring the encounter to a close. "Anyway, I'm really tired and I need to go and have a bath."

"We haven't finished talking about my problem!"

"We have because I really can't help you. Ask one of your friends. Or why don't you give Figs a ring for a change? See what she has to say?"

Clare stuffed the empty shopping bags into the bottom of a cupboard and stood up. "I'm going upstairs."

"Huh!" Angie banged her glass back onto the tiles and swung her handbag over her shoulder. "I'll go then," she said, pausing for a moment so that Clare could say she should stay, and then sweeping out in high dudgeon when

Clare remained silent. "And I don't ever bother asking Figs anything. All she cares about is herself!"

"So you've played a blinder there," Clare said two days later, as she stood in the doorway of Figs's garage, watching her sister wrestle with a frankly phallic-shaped lump of wet clay. "Oh, for Ange not to bother with me either."

Figs stopped the wheel, pulling a face as the phallic object collapsed sideways. "It was wrong from the start," she said, wiping her hands on a cloth. "Want a drink or something?"

"I'm not staying." Clare held up a gift bag. "I just brought this round for Tilda – a little congratulations present from all of us. I'm so pleased she did so well."

"God, yes, such a relief. It seems they were getting in some studying after all. Ryan did really well too – got exactly what he needed for Bristol. So they're very happy, the pair of them. I just need her to keep it up now so she gets the right grades next summer."

"I'm sure she will." There was a little silence while Clare scrutinised her sister. "How are you?" she asked eventually. "Did you go to that lunch thing?"

"Er, no. It's next week."

There was something about the way Figs said it. And the way she was busying herself scooping up wet clay instead of looking at Clare.

Clare moved a bit closer. "Have you seen him already?"

Figs kept her eyes on the job in hand. "No. Well, not in person. We Facetime, you know."

"A lot?"

"Quite a lot."

"Well, I guess if you're only talking…"

"We've been doing a bit more than that."

"What do you mean?"

"Oh, come on, Clare, use your imagination!"

"Figs!" Clare stared at her sister, who was now looking directly at her with something like defiance in her eyes. "Figs, don't meet him then. In case it leads to you really—"

"Which it inevitably would."

"Oh Figs, please!" Clare knew she sounded emotional. "I keep having a feeling that something bad is going to happen to one of us and I really don't want it to be you. Don't go to London if you think you're going to get involved." She stepped closer and gave her sister's arm a small shake.

"Just don't!"

"I don't have to," Ellie twisted her hair into a knot on top of her head and fastened it with a glittery clip. "I can pull out if you—"

"I don't mind at all," Tom interrupted her. He smiled. "I'll get some work done for a change. I was only wondering…"

"Well, it won't be *that* late. They're all getting old and boring now. Cassie's got a kid! We won't be partying till dawn like we did when we were in the sixth form." Ellie laughed. "Mum used to do her nut!" She gave a small twirl in front of the mirror, swinging her short dress. "But don't wait up if you're tired." She grinned at him as she picked up her tiny silver backpack and dropped her phone and keys into it. "I can always wake you up to say goodnight…"

She knew Tom probably would be in bed when she got back, even it was before midnight. She was getting up pretty early for work at the moment, but he was on the go even earlier. They hadn't been out in the evening all week, and Ellie was looking forward to seeing her old schoolfriends. The evening was warm and the seafront busy, as she strode past the clock tower to The Mechanical Elephant where they were starting off – a venue that Tom was sniffy about but which her friends, appreciating the cheapness and buzzy warmth of the Wetherspoons, always gravitated to as a meeting place.

Cassie, Gemma, and Tiff were already at a table with brightly-coloured drinks in front of them when she walked in. After the usual hugs and squeals, Tiffany waved a menu card at her. "They're doing two jugs of cocktails for a tenner. Seemed rude not to?" She pushed an empty glass towards Ellie. "You've got catching up to do, girlfriend."

"Photo!" Gemma leaned in close to Ellie and put an arm out to gather in Cassie as she held her phone at arm's length in front of her. "Get in, Tiff!"

She sat and tapped for a moment, as Ellie took a mouthful of what was apparently a pornstar martini.

"There!" said Gemma. "I've put our table number on

Instagram. Just in case anyone, seeing how gorgeous we all are, wants to buy us the next one on the app."

Tiff laughed. "You'll probably get another Fruit Shoot from Kurt." Gemma rolled her eyes. "I still haven't forgiven him for that. He sent a yoghurt lolly from the children's menu when I was out with my sister, the bastard."

Ellie laughed too and took another swig of her drink. The last time she'd met up with them, she'd been the only one without a proper relationship. Cassie was married with a two-year-old, and both Gemma and Tiffany lived with their boyfriends. Now she was part of the club too. She held out her hand. "Who wants to see my ring…"

More jugs came and went. Ellie held her stomach muscles. "Oh guys, I haven't laughed like this for ages," she said, when Cassie had finished a tale about dealing with the wife of a drunk with a broken toe in A&E, where she was a nurse, and Tiff had been very funny about her fiancé Pete's attempts to make a paella. "It's so good to see you!"

"What the fuck?" Gemma looked up as a waiter approached with a tray of shot glasses. "Kurt's upped his game!"

"Good old Kurt," said Tiffany, shooting out an arm. "Do you think you could get him to send some chips next? I'm bloody ravenous."

"No, it isn't him." Gemma was prodding at her phone again. "You're never going to believe this. I've got a message on Instagram – it's from someone called Bobby98. Says do we remember Andy Chambers?"

"I do!" Cassie was slurring slightly. "He was in my Geography group. You know him too. Very tall, bad skin."

"You're not selling him," said Tiffany.

"Well, he's here," said Gemma. "With this Bobby and someone called Jack. They're saying hello to you, Ellie. Have tagged you in."

"Tell them to come over," instructed Tiffany. "Let's have a look."

"I think I'm going to have to go soon," said Cassie. "I'm drunk. Can't take it anymore on no sleep and Ruby wakes up at five."

"It's only— Bloody hell! It's nearly midnight!" said Tiffany looking at her own phone.

"Jack who?" said Ellie, wondering if it could possibly be.

"Yes!" said Gemma, nodding at her. "I think it is…"

Later, Ellie couldn't remember whose idea it had been to go on to Crackpots – a newly opened nightclub near the station. But by the time they'd put Cassie in a cab and waved goodbye to a slightly weaving Gemma, whom a grinning Kurt had come to collect, she and Tiffany had decided it was the best plan ever.

Now, settled into a red velvet booth with Andy – whose acne had cleared nicely – Tiff, and Jack, Ellie had got her second wind. Every now and again she got a snatch of Tiff advising Andy on how best to deal with a girlfriend who monitored his Facebook messages and then cried a lot, but the noise was such that Jack was pressed up close so she could hear him.

"I was gutted when you dumped me," he said. "I thought you were the one, Ellie."

"You were so not," she said. "And I didn't dump you. It just fizzled out. Particularly after you started seeing that Carly."

"I was trying to mend my broken heart." He gave her a winning smile. "We should give it another go," Jack shouted over the din. "Seriously. You're special. Let's go out soon."

"I've told you. I'm living with someone."

"Your granddad!"

"Tom. Who I love, thank you."

"Aw, come on. He's going to be getting his pension soon. We could have some fun!"

Ellie shook her head. "Not going to happen."

Jack was gorgeous – there was no doubt about that. He'd been the one all the girls wanted when they were all eighteen, and he'd only improved in the years since. Brown wavy hair swept back, soulful brown eyes, very good teeth, and clearly, from the look of his biceps in that tight white T-shirt, he worked out endlessly...

But she was with Tom. She raised her glass to Jack and smiled.

"Nice to see you again though."

Jack grinned back. "Dance won't hurt?"

She was already moving to the music as she got to her feet.

"Come on then."

"I need to be up again in four hours," Ellie said, as the four of them walked back along the seafront, her arm in arm with Tiffany, and Andy and Jack on either side of them.

"Me too," Tiff yawned. "It was fun though."

"You going to be OK, walking back?" Ellie was suddenly tired and glad Tom's flat was nearby.

"We'll go too." Jack strode easily along beside her.

Tiffany laughed. "You can sod off when we get to the corner. Don't want Pete looking out of the window and thinking I've been up to no good."

"Tell him we're the hired heavies," said Andy. Ellie giggled. Andy looked more like a very gangly accountant than any sort of bouncer.

"Thanks for looking out for her," she said to the boys, kissing Tiffany and fumbling for her keys as they all stopped outside the double doors to Tom's building. "And for the drinks."

"Don't forget where I am," said Jack, "when the geriatric's had to move into sheltered accommodation…"

"In your dreams," called Ellie happily, blowing them all a kiss and dropping her bag as she tripped up the step.

She woke with a pounding head to the sound of Radio 2 coming quite loudly from the kitchen. The bedroom was filled with the scent of Tom's aftershave. Usually, she liked it, but this morning it was too sweet and cloying and brought on a wave of nausea. She put a hand out for the glass of water she usually took to bed but there was none there.

Ellie groaned and rolled over. She couldn't actually remember coming to bed. She recalled being *in* it – and trying to get Tom to put his arms around her. She had a dim memory of him being annoyed, and complaining that she had made too much noise...

Sitting up, she looked at the clock and groaned again. She needed to get up right now if she wasn't going to be late for work. She also needed fluids urgently – and painkillers. Urgghh. Why had she drunk so much?

Tom appeared in the doorway, already immaculate in chinos and a Ralph Lauren polo shirt. He looked fresh-faced and healthy. She felt like utter shite.

"I've got an eight o'clock," he said shortly. "There's some coffee, if you want it." He scrutinised her. "Looks like you need something."

"Sorry if I woke you last night." She smiled weakly at him.

He didn't smile back. "Just a bit."

"I've got such a hangover."

"I expect you have. What did you do it for? You knew it was a work night."

"Oh, you know how it is, we were having a laugh. You tell yourself it will be fine, don't you?"

"I don't know," he said stiffly. "Anyway, I need to go. You'd better get moving as well."

He turned and left the room, leaving Ellie pulling a face behind him. Even her dad would have been more sympathetic.

Gingerly, she put her feet on the carpet. She still had on her underwear from the night before. Her dress was a crumpled heap in the corner. She stood up and another wave of nausea rolled through her, as she heard the door to the flat clunk firmly shut.

_____

Chapter Twenty-Six

C lare ducked her head and shoved her trolley out through the glass doors into the driving rain. Her car was over at the far side of the Waitrose car park and by the time she reached it her shoulders were soaked and her hair was flattened against her head. Usually she liked to see a good summer downpour – and God knows the garden needed it – but it would have been helpful if it had held off till she got home and could watch it through the open kitchen door, a much-needed glass of wine in hand.

She held onto this image as she wiped the water from her face and stacked the carrier bags into her boot, feeling the droplets trickle down her neck, before breaking into a run to the nearest trolley point.

She started the engine, turning the hot air blowers to full blast, despite it being August, and putting the wipers on full.

As she pulled into Queen Street, and joined the queue of traffic crawling past the front of the store, she looked across to the doorways opposite and spotted Tony sitting back against the entrance to one of the closed-down shops, the dog still beside him. Both looked bedraggled. Tony seemed pale. Clare felt a pang thinking of the food and booze stashed behind her. She waved and saw him recognise her. He immediately started gesticulating, pointing urgently at the dog, putting his hands up as if he didn't know what to do.

Clare pulled in, half on the pavement, earning herself a honk and a raised finger from the young man who had to pull round her. Head down, she crossed the road.

"You're drenched," she said in concern. "Have you still got nowhere to live?"

"I can go to the shelter place but they won't take Belter." Tony looked close to tears. "I've got no food for him. Nobody's given me anything all day. Please, I'm sorry to ask but could you…"

Clare nodded. "I can get you some dog food, but what are we going to do about you? Where are your shoes?"

Tony looked at his sodden socks. "They got nicked from the beach."

"What size are you?"

"Ten."

"So you could wear an eleven with extra thick socks?"

He nodded hard.

"I'll be back as soon as I can – forty minutes tops."

"You'll get dog food?" Tony stroked Belter's head. "He's really hungry – he keeps whining."

Clare looked at where her car still straddled the pavement. "Would he eat a pork chop?"

Grabbing as many bags as she could manage, Clare hurried into the house, glad for a change that Rupe would almost certainly be there. She dumped the shopping, dripping, onto the kitchen floor.

Her husband, looking relaxed in a short-sleeved shirt and shorts, was just opening a bottle of rioja. "Ah, perfect timing!" he said, smiling broadly at her. "You look a bit damp. Do you want a shower first?"

Clare shook her head, sprinkling droplets across the floor. "I'm going back out. Have you got an old pair of trainers I can have? Or any sort of footwear?" She told him about Tony. "I think there's a couple of sweatshirts of Josh's in the bottom of the airing cupboard he's not worn for years. I'm going to pack those up too."

Rupe took a small mouthful of the wine he'd poured and then put the glass down. "I've got loads of clothes I never wear. I'll go find you some now."

By the time Clare had dumped the rest of the shopping indoors, she was wetter than ever and Rupe had filled a black sack. Lying on the top was the jumper she'd given him two Christmases ago. "I've put in socks, and two pairs of trousers," he said. "And he can have that raincoat you got me in the sale."

Clare looked at him in surprise. "You've barely worn it!"

"Shows I don't need it then. What else?"

"Shoes?"

"Pair of trainers and a pair of lace-ups. My old office shoes. They're almost new too."

Clare looked at him gratefully. "Thank you. Let's just give him the essentials for now though. He won't be able to store all this – it will just be more for him to have to drag about. She decanted one set of clothes and the trainers into a carrier bag.

"I'll come with you."

Clare smiled and nodded at the glass that was back in his hand.

"I'll drive."

The rain had eased off a bit as they pulled up next to Tony once more. He and Belter were as far back in the doorway as they could get. The packet of minced beef she'd left him for the dog – safer for him than pork, Tony had told her – was empty and he was lying beside Tony with his head on his paws. There was a plastic ice-cream tub full of water beside him. Tony, she noticed, was shivering. "Call this August?" said Rupe heartily, swinging the bag of clothes out from the back seat.

"I wish you'd go to the shelter," said Clare. "Would they let you leave Belter outside somewhere safe?"

"I can't do that." Tony put a protective hand on Belter's head. "He needs me."

"Would your friends on the beach have him?"

Tony shook his head. "It's sort of broken up down there." He hesitated. "It got a bit shady, you know?" He took the coat Rupe was handing him. "Thanks, boss, this means a lot."

Rupe pushed the bag back, out of the drizzle. "Shoes in there," he said.

Tony gave a weak smile. "Well appreciate it."

"You need to get warm and dry," said Clare. "I know you're attached to Belter, but I really think you need to think of yourself. Suppose I could find a rescue centre for him?"

Tony was shaking his head as Rupe turned to Clare. "What about your nutty sister? She's always banging on about saving the animals."

Clare stared at him. "That, actually, might be a brilliant idea…"

———————

Angie opened the door and cried out at the sight of Belter. "Oh, you poor chap." She threw a beam at Tony who was hovering doubtfully on the top step up to her narrow terraced house, clutching the dog's lead. "I can give him a bath. Do you want to have one too?"

"Well," began Clare, as Angie ushered Tony indoors. "Tony's going to stay at the shelter and—"

"I know, you told me," said Angie briskly. "Up near the Sally Army." She addressed Tony. "It's a five-minute walk away. I'll look after him tonight and you can come fetch him in the morning. Why don't you have a hot bath here first and put on some of these new clothes? She turned to Clare. "Did you buy the dog food? And the flea drops, just in case?"

Clare held out a carrier bag. Angie looked in it. "We'll

get the proper stuff from the vet tomorrow," she said. Clare saw Tony look anxious.

"He's still going to be mine, right?"

"Of course he is! I'm night-time foster care only." Angie looked directly at Tony. "He'll be all right with me. And you can collect him as early as you like."

Tony nodded, apparently dumbstruck. "Means a lot to me," he mumbled eventually.

"OK, come on, let's get going." Angie pointed down the short hallway behind her. "Bathroom's along there. Bottom of the stairs. I'll give you a call later," she said to Clare, clearly dismissing her. "I've got this."

"Ange, are you sure you—?" Clare said hesitantly, as Tony and Belter ambled towards the back of the house. She lowered her voice. "I just meant you to take the dog…"

"Yes, well," said Angie, a note of triumph in her voice. "You're not the only one who can play Florence Nightingale."

"Is this a good idea?" Clare said anxiously, as they sat in the car outside Angie's firmly closed front door. "Should he be having a bath there?"

"I don't see why not." Rupe grinned. "Which one of them are you worried about?" He gave a loud guffaw. "If you think she's going to ravage him once he's fragrant again, he might be damn grateful. Any port in a storm et cetera…"

"Oh for God's sake," Clare said crossly. "I just meant—"

She stopped. What did she mean? She felt instinctively that Tony would feel nothing but gratitude and Ange was doing a wonderful, generous thing. Was it just that she felt strangely pushed out? But she didn't want to look after the dog, which had smelled pretty ripe on the drive here. She'd had to open all the windows. She wouldn't know how to anyway. Angie loved animals more than people. Still, Clare felt uneasy.

"Good for your sister, I say," Rupe continued. "She's bloody annoying but she's come up trumps this time. Perhaps she'll find him somewhere to live through her office."

"No." Clare told him about the conversation she'd had with Angie before. "He needs an address to get any financial help. And then he'll need a deposit, so he needs a job. His labouring work finished just before his relationship did. That was one of the factors apparently. I wonder if any of the blokes working on Tom's place need anyone...? Where are you going?"

Rupe was opening the car door. "To have a quick word. You stay here." He was gone before she could protest.

Clare watched him lope back up the steps. Angie was doing a terrific thing – Tony would hopefully be warm and dry tonight and Ange would lavish attention on Belter. Clare had forgotten how giving and helpful Rupe could be too, when the chips were down. She just hoped he was not now going to wind her sister up. She saw the front door open and Rupe step inside.

Clare watched the door close again. The rain seemed to have stopped for a while but the sky was still grey. She looked through her phone while she waited. There was a WhatsApp from Josh, who was surprised to find an empty house full of abandoned shopping and checking she was OK. She tapped out an answer, seeing that Ellie had been in touch also – with a picture of blinis with sour cream and caviar. "You can make them!" Clare said aloud, while sending a couple of smilies and an emoticon that was rolling its eyes.

She knew Rupe wouldn't much care what party food they had, as long as the atmosphere was convivial and the wine kept flowing, but she would make an effort with it all if that was what Ellie wanted. Clare still felt there was something precarious about her relationship with her daughter that she wished were different. They'd been much closer before Tom – before Ellie became prickly and defensive. Or Clare – to quote her daughter in one of their spats – had become "critical and joyless". Clare looked across the road through the film of fine rain that had started up again. She didn't want to be like that but she recognised the seeds of truth in Ellie's words. She needed to take a deep breath and talk to Rupe…

At that moment the front door opened and Rupe bounded down the steps and across the road. He got in beside her and sighed with satisfaction.

"Sorted!" he said. "Now let's get home and have a bloody drink."

Clare started the engine. "What have you done?"

"Angie is going to speak to some letting agent she knows and some charity that helps find lodgings. I offered to pay the deposit if he needed one."

As Clare turned to look at him, hand still on the brake, he went on, "You don't mind, do you? It can be my birthday present. I figured if I'd told you I wanted to spend money on a few days away, you'd have agreed straightaway so…" he shrugged. "Come on, drive, woman! Why are you staring at me like that?"

Clare released the handbrake and indicated to pull out. "Because," she said, grinning at him, "you still never fail to surprise me."

Chapter Twenty-Seven

"**S**urprise me…"

Dave's voice was low and warm from the end of the bed, where Figs had her phone set up on a tripod she'd bought from Amazon.

She laughed, smoothing down the silky red negligee she'd rediscovered stuffed at the back of her knicker drawer. She hadn't felt this sexy for years.

Figs picked up her flute of prosecco and raised it at the screen.

Tilda had gone out for the evening with Ryan. Alex had been taken paintballing with his friend Connor and wouldn't be home for at least another hour. Figs had been in a lather of anticipation all day, swinging wildly between excitement and guilt. It wasn't real infidelity, she told herself, because she was here on her own. It wasn't like she was having physical sex with him in person. They still hadn't met. But if she did go to London next week, she was no longer in any doubt about what would happen…

The thought thrilled and terrified her in equal measure.

It was sort of like porn, she'd convinced herself. And Don liked a bit of that, occasionally. They'd watched it together. Who knew what he got up to in his apartment in Dubai, after all?

As Dave made appreciative noises, Figs draped herself across the bed, gazing into the camera provocatively. "Oh," she murmured, "I can be full of surprises…"

"Yoghurt?" she giggled, a few minutes later. "I don't think so!" She laughed. "But you're not here to lick it off… Amaze me with something that's not a dairy product…"

He had a pretty vivid imagination involving all sorts of things, Figs soon found. She was hovering in an almost dreamlike state, floating on a haze of pleasure, when suddenly she heard the front door open and feet thunder up the stairs towards her. Figs gasped, shock waves roaring through her whole body.

"Jesus!" She leapt off the bed, shutting off the video call, and grabbing her towelling robe, fumbling as she tried to get her arms into the sleeves – it was somehow inside out – the rush of adrenalin and fear making her shake violently. She could say she was talking to Don, that the phone was on a tripod fixed to the bed frame because she was painting her toenails at the same time. She looked wildly about her for varnish and grabbed a bottle of red from her dressing table, her breath coming hard and fast in her panic.

But the footsteps did not come to her. They pounded across the landing and what sounded like Tilda's door slammed shut. Figs waited until she was breathing normally again and tiptoed cautiously from her bedroom. She could hear the sobbing already.

Tilda was lying face down on her bed, her arms around her pillow, her shoulders heaving. As Figs lowered herself down beside her daughter, the crying only intensified.

"Oh darling, what's happened?" Figs stroked her daughter's back, as Tilda's whole body shuddered. "Is it Ryan?"

At this, Tilda gave a sort of howl and Figs leant forward and took her in a half-hug. "It's OK. Everything's going to be fine."

Tilda's words in reply were lost in a fresh torrent of sobs. Figs caught "no" and "never", and continued stroking.

It was some minutes before Tilda made any real sense. Her face, when she finally turned to Figs, was streaked with make-up. Figs felt in her pocket for a tissue. "What's happened?" she said again.

"He's broken up with me," Tilda wailed. "He says we've got to have a break because he's going to uni." She scrubbed at her face which was awash with tears. "Before, he said we'd live together."

"Oh darling." Figs managed to get her arms right round her daughter, expecting Tilda to push her away, but instead she collapsed against her mother in another fit of weeping.

Figs held her tight. What could she say? She couldn't verbalise any of the thoughts chasing through her head. That they were very young, and that she'd always known this would happen. That she was sort of grateful that at least Ryan had done it now. If he'd announced this halfway through the A Level year, it could have devastated Tilda's studies. But her heart twisted for her daughter; she felt Tilda's desolation as keenly as if it had happened to her. "I'm so sorry," she murmured, hugging her hard.

"I can't live feeling like this," Tilda cried. "I can't bear it. He said…" The rest was lost in another convulsion. "I want to die," she stuttered eventually.

"No, you don't," said Figs firmly. "You can be sad, you can be angry, and you can weep and wail, but you don't talk like that. You are young and beautiful and I am going to promise you something. Are you listening?"

Tilda was making a hiccupping, gulping noise. Figs waited. "I know how painful this is right now," she said, "but there will come a day when you don't feel like this, when you feel completely happy. When you don't even—"

"No!" Tilda's voice was shrill with anguish. "You don't understand."

"I do," said Figs. "It won't happen straightaway, but you will get better. When I was sixteen," she went on, before Tilda could interrupt, "I was crazy about this boy. I loved him, really, from when I was fourteen. We were at school together and I used to look at him all the time and long for him to ask me out, and when he did, after nearly two years, I was so, so happy. And we went out for a few months when I was sixteen and then he just dumped me, overnight, and went off with someone else."

Tilda had stopped sobbing, though tears still streamed from her eyes as she watched her mother. "And I cried and cried and cried," said Figs. "And I couldn't sleep or eat, and your gran was really worried about me – and furious with him," she added. "She said she wanted to kill him."

For a second Tilda gave a ghost of a smile.

"I wouldn't have rated his chances," said Figs, hoping to build on it, "if she'd seen him." But Tilda was already crying again.

"The point is," continued Figs, "that gradually, the pain is not so deep and the grief passes, and one day you suddenly realise you haven't thought about him at all. Just for an hour at first and then for a few hours and later for a whole day. And later, when I met Dad, I hadn't given him a thought for years. I had thought he was the love of my life and yet I could barely remember his name." She stopped abruptly, realising that it was true. She felt a wash of shame at the thought of what she had been doing when Tilda had burst through the front door.

"And I knew then," Figs went on resolutely, as her daughter wiped at her eyes, "what real love was like, and oh my goodness, I am so glad that he dumped me otherwise I might not have married Dad and had you and Alex."

"What was his name?" said Tilda, sniffing.

"Dave," said Figs. "And do you know what? I saw him on Facebook recently in some silly school reunion group and he's all old and fat and bald. So a lucky escape, eh?"

She smoothed the hair back from Tilda's hot, damp face. "I'm going to get you some more tissues." She stood up. "Then you have a bath and put your pyjamas on and I'll make you some hot chocolate and we'll watch a film. OK?"

"I don't want—"

"Yes, that's what we're going to do," said Figs. "And

don't text him," she added, as Tilda reached out and looked hopelessly at her phone screen.

"I expect he's feeling awful too," Figs added. "So let him!"

"He might change his mind."

"And if he did, it would only happen again later," said Figs. "Or he'd meet someone in that first year at university."

She had a sudden memory of her and Don, entwined in bed in his flat in London, sharing stories of their teenage loves. She'd told him how Dave had dumped Carly eventually too, and then a succession of other girls, and Don had told her about a girl called Chloe he'd been besotted with in a way that was singularly unrequited, and they'd both agreed how very lucky they were that they now had each other instead.

Figs suddenly wished Don was here now. She wanted to be dressing sexily for him, not some illusion on a phone screen. She tightened the cord of her robe. She would go and change into sensible pyjamas too.

"Come on," she said to Tilda. "I'll start running the water." She stepped onto the landing and stopped, startled. "Oh! I didn't hear you come in."

Alex was standing in the doorway of her bedroom, a strange expression on his face. "What's going on?" he said.

"Tilda—" Figs began, and then saw the phone in his hand. It was hers. Her heart hammered. She was sure she had turned the video off. Christ, had Dave phoned again? Had Alex been through her recent calls, wondering why she'd been filming? Figs was cold with fear. How ironic if she'd been discovered just when she'd seen the light about how stupid she was being, how much she was risking for someone who had only ever treated her badly. She'd have to beg Alex not to tell Don. Or she'd say they were just talking. But was Alex looking at her like that because he already knew or had drawn his own conclusions from the fact that she was dressed in a bathrobe? Her mind was racing so fast she barely heard what Alex was saying.

"It was ringing so I answered it," said Alex. "It was Dad. I said I could hear Tilda crying so I'd better not come in, but I said you'd call him back."

"Oh, thank you." Figs felt weak with relief. "I was just going to Facetime him when Tilda came home." She gave a strange, high laugh, which sounded deeply weird even to herself. "I was going to try out my new tripod. I bought it so I could talk to him when I was cooking – or painting my nails. Or we could set it up and all sit on the sofa together to talk to him." She knew she was babbling.

Alex gave her the sort of frown that suggested she'd always been peculiar but was now losing the last of her marbles.

"Yeah, sure." He shrugged as if he'd already lost interest. "Whatever."

Chapter Twenty-Eight

C lare picked up the long double string of freshwater pearls Rupe had bought her at Pier 39 in San Francisco when she was just pregnant with Ellie.

She remembered how happy she'd been, how tightly she'd held his hand as they walked from their hotel in Union Square to get the tram. How delighted Rupe had been, when the chap selling the pearls had engaged in a protracted and good-natured haggle that had gone on for at least half an hour, while Clare sat smiling at the bustle around her, holding the single pearl that had come out of the oyster Rupe had bought her earlier from the grinning guy on the stall that guaranteed a pearl every time.

She put the pearls around her neck and looked at herself critically in the mirror. She'd scrubbed up OK. She was pleased with her newly-cut hair – short and choppy with fresh blonde streaks. Her make-up had gone on smoothly; her lipstick was a good shade. She was wearing a long, dark-green silk shirt that Rupe said brought out the colour of her eyes, over a pair of black palazzo trousers she'd got in a sale from Jigsaw, which achieved, she hoped, her aim of looking stylish and as if she'd made an effort, without going over the top. It always felt odd to put on a dress and heels in your own home. She'd found a pair of beaded mules that would be easy to kick off once everyone was there.

She was suddenly glad they were going to celebrate. She wanted Rupe to have a good time. She'd hugged him tightly this morning and he'd looked almost startled. But he'd put his arms around her and squeezed her too. Perhaps they were on their way to things getting back to how they should be.

And the weather had held. It wasn't actually sunny but it wasn't cold either. All their garden chairs were out on the patio. The barbecue was ready to light. Ellie had arranged plates of mini savoury pastries, blinis, and vol au vents around the kitchen and dining room, with wasabi nuts and olives and breadsticks. The salads were all on the dining-room table with focaccia and cheeses and cold meats. There was enough booze to knock out half of Thanet. Clare was ready. But still her stomach was churning…

"Hey, Granny!" Ellie stood back to let Meg into the hall. Her grandmother was holding a large plastic-wrapped package with leaves sticking out of the top. "Where is he? I've bought him a bare-root rose tree. And I need your brother to get the pot. Gordon from next door lifted it into the boot. It's too heavy for me." She held out car keys.

"I'll get it." As Ellie went out of the house, Clare walked slowly from the kitchen. Her mother was always early and always brought Rupe a present that required input – the more labour-intensive the better.

Meg had on a bright-red trouser suit that Clare hadn't seen before, with a navy tunic beneath the jacket and big blue glass beads. Clare lent down and kissed her. "He's in the garden," she said.

"Good!" Meg walked past Clare into the kitchen towards the back door, talking over her shoulder. "I need to give him the instructions for this. It's a patio rose. I'll have a smoke while I'm out there to help me get over the journey."

Clare shook her head at her mother's retreating back. Her mother's bungalow in Birchington was less than eight miles away but Meg always made a big deal of the distance. Ellie came back in with a large, colourful terracotta planter in her arms. "There's a whole smelly stilton in her boot, too," she said. "Shall I get that in as well?"

"Better check first!" She turned as the doorbell rang. "That's going to be Ange now, isn't it?" she said, as Ellie went into the garden and Clare headed across the hall.

But it was Tom, coming in on a cloud of expensive aftershave, all dark glasses and designer stubble. "You look nice," he said.

"And you look a bit cleaner than last time!" They grinned at each other. They'd spent yesterday crawling about in the loft of the house they were converting, digging about amongst an astonishing number of objects left behind by the previous owner. Tom had wanted to put it all in one of his skips that was standing on the small patch of concrete at the front of the house, but Clare had pointed out that much of it might have a resale value. "Vintage kitchenalia," she'd said, holding up a large copper bowl. "Very popular on eBay."

"Sounds time-consuming," Tom had replied as they'd carried the lot downstairs to the basement. "But if you want to do it…"

"I've got a clearance bloke coming," she told him now. "He'll give us a job-lot price on Monday."

"Did you keep the vintage jam pots?"

She smiled. "I did."

"You sound like an old married couple," said Figs, coming through the open door behind them. She was wearing a flame-coloured halterneck dress, her tan deeper than ever. She'd put her hair up and was wearing large gold hoop earrings. She looked, Clare thought, with her dark curls piled high and full red lips, like a picture-book Gypsy Queen.

"Great dress," said Tom, while Clare, irritated by her sister's comment, muttered, "Don't be ridiculous," before turning to hug her nephew. "No Tilda?" she asked.

"We couldn't persuade her," said Figs, looking rueful. "She said she might come along later if she feels up to it…"

She and Clare exchanged glances. "Josh is out there somewhere," Clare said to Alex, continuing to Figs as he wandered off. "Is she still bad?"

Figs sighed. "At least she's not crying the whole time now."

Suddenly the kitchen had filled up. Rupe was popping champagne corks, Josh was snapping the tops from beers, and Ellie and Nikhita were handing round the canapés over which Ellie had won the day.

"Thank you," said Clare, as Nikhita swung past her with a tray of spinach and feta puffs, still warm from the oven. Clare had somehow pictured her son's girlfriend as quiet and shy with a gentle manner – or, as Ellie put it, "You are so stuck in your stereotypes, Mum!"

Instead, Niki, as she'd asked to be called, was a bouncy, glossy beauty with a huge smile and a raucous laugh. Everything so far had been "cool" and she had thrown herself into the party spirit, taking the box of hired glasses from Clare's arms within ten minutes of arriving, and setting to them with a tea towel. When Josh looked at her, it was as if he couldn't believe his luck.

A sentiment his father, of course, with a hoot of laughter, had to put into words. "What are you with doing with *him*?" he'd enquired, grinning. And Nikhita had looked directly back at him and said firmly: "I love him," which had put even Rupe off his stride. Clare had wanted to hug her.

"There are chairs outside," Clare called, winding her way through the bodies. She'd left the front door open and there were more guests to welcome in the hall. She smiled at the two men. "Hello?"

"We're Simon and Nick. Ellie invited us?" said one, striking a pose. "Of course!" Clare waved them through to the garden. "Ellie!"

Three of Rupe's old employees arrived next. "Help

yourselves when you want some more," said Clare, dispensing drinks and waving an arm at the ice-filled buckets containing wine and beer that were outside the back door and the array of red wine and soft drinks on the counter.

An hour later, the sun had come out and people had gravitated outside. Rupe was now holding court on the patio. Clare could hear laughter and the boom of his voice shouting out to the new arrivals. Ange had swept through the kitchen earlier in electric blue with Chrissy in tow, but hadn't stopped to converse, for which Clare was thankful.

Angie had been in the house for three hours the day before, updating them on the house-share she'd found for Tony and Belter with an elderly woman who used to work in Asda and who loved animals and needed a lodger who would also help with the garden. Clare had been awash with gratitude but was also Angied-out. She knew her sister well enough to know she would make it clear they were in her debt for some months to come and there would be sessions enough of listening to the latest dramas.

She could see them both through the kitchen window, standing together next to a tub of bright geraniums talking to Alex, who in turn looked as if he'd rather be playing a video game. Smoke was rising from the barbecue. Someone had brought Rupe a tall paper chef's hat. He was waving the tongs, and clearly telling some sort of story.

"Clare!" A voice yelled from behind her. "I couldn't get a taxi from the damn station but I am here at last. Give me a bloody drink!"

Clare swung round. Rupe's first wife had developed an

American twang since setting up home with a New Yorker and appeared to be modelling herself both in voice and delivery on a younger Shirley MacLaine. Even the hair now, Clare thought, as a bobbed and highlighted Claudia dropped her handbag onto the floor and flung out her arms. Then she stood back dramatically, her hands on Clare's shoulders to appraise her. "You look absolutely marvellous, sweets. You're still surviving the old bastard?"

Clare smiled. "I am and you look pretty good too. Here." She put a full glass of champagne in Claudia's hands. "He's outside."

Claudia made no move to go out. She shrugged off her jacket and draped it on the back of a kitchen chair before taking a big swallow of her drink and then leaning on the sink to look through the window. "You'll have to tell me who all these people are," she said. "I was going to get you flowers at the station but I always forget what a backwater this is. I'll send some."

"You really don't need to. It's just great that you've come," said Clare, adding as an afterthought and blatant untruth, "Rupe's really looking forward to seeing you."

Claudia gave a wry smile. "I don't doubt. Oh, my Lord, look at this handsome boy," she cried, as Josh came into the kitchen with Anna. "There's some mineral water over there," he said, as he was enveloped by Claudia.

"Still or sparkling?" Clare asked Anna, as she reached for the bottles and Figs joined them to be exclaimed over.

"Everybody looks so healthy!" Claudia cried. "Now tell me all the latest gossip. Have you got a gorgeous girlfriend now, Joshua? And how's that other sister of yours?"

While Figs gave Claudia a whistle-stop who's-who of party guests and current relationships, Clare handed Anna a glass of water and exchanged smiles. She had liked Anna immediately. She was as refined and elegant as Ellie had described, but with a warm face and steadfast manner – the sort of woman you could talk to and depend on in a crisis. Clare noticed that she had not gone into a huddle with her colleagues, apart from a brief chat with Ellie's friend Janine, but had spent time chatting to Clare in the kitchen, had introduced herself to Meg, and busied herself quietly picking up abandoned glasses and leaving them beside the sink.

Claudia had put her empty flute there too. "Joshua, sweetie, where does your father keep the gin?" She looked at Clare. "Have you got tonic?"

Clare nodded at the fruit bowl. "And a lemon!"

Claudia put out a hand and cupped Josh's cheek. "Would you like to make me a G&T, sweetheart?"

Before he could answer, Ellie put her head round the back door. "Dad says can you watch the sausages for five minutes?"

Josh put up his hands in a gesture of helplessness and grinned at Clare. "When have you had to prioritise in a high-stress environment? Sorry, Claudia, can't let the food burn. I'm sure my sister will make you one..."

"I've just come in for the pork balls." Ellie removed a tray from the oven and swung back outside, blowing Claudia a kiss. "Back in a mo!"

"I always think Joshua is mine," Claudia said. "He looks so like Daniel. You'd never think those boys had different mothers. But Ellie – she takes after you," she told Clare.

"And she gets more and more beautiful," said Anna. "She looks like a model."

"I know," said Clare, with a smile. "Oh, for that figure…"

"Don't be bitter," said Claudia, ploughing on while Clare's mouth flapped open in protest. "She is gorgeous for sure, and so is Daniel's Mia – that girl's legs go on for ever too – and it would be easy to resent it but you know, I don't know whether it's living with a much younger man"—here she paused and appeared to preen for a moment—"but I've had a bit of a sea-change with that one…"

Clare noticed Anna watching Claudia with interest. Figs had her eyebrows raised, listening too, and Claudia was clearly enjoying having the floor. "I used to look at the young and be consumed with unspeakable envy," she declared. "All that smooth skin, those uplifted butt cheeks…"

Anna's eyebrows now rose a fraction too.

"But these days I just tell myself that in youth you know nothing. I have experience. And some people die before they ever get any. I'm still here and I know better." Claudia looked at them all victorious.

"I don't think I do," said Figs. "I just wish I'd appreciated how attractive I was at the time. I've been looking at photos of myself when I was sixteen. I felt so dull but I looked pretty good, I can tell you…"

"You look pretty damn good now, sweetie! Ah Rupe, will you make me a gin?"

Rupe came forward and kissed Claudia. "Trust you to want something different." He went into the dining room and returned with a bottle of Hendricks, handing it to her. "There's ice in the freezer."

Claudia sighed and picked up a tall tumbler from the tray of glasses. Ellie, who'd come in with her father, took it from her. "I'll do it."

Rupe poured himself a glass of red wine. "You haven't brought that bloke of yours then?"

"Jerome had to stay with Ziggy. We've got this adorable puppy," she announced to the kitchen at large. "And we are both besotted but you can't leave her alone for a moment. Jerome's trying to train her but honestly, I can't say there's much evidence of any comprehension yet."

"He's still not working then?" said Rupe.

"You know very well Jerome works from home. He's an artist," she told Anna. "He's working on a new collection."

Rupe gave a deliberately loud guffaw. "The sort of artist that begins with a P," he said.

"I want to go and talk to this girl with Angela," said Claudia, ignoring him. "She might be able to help with the puppy – how we can stop her chewing everything."

"She's a cat shrink," said Rupe. "The clue's in the name."

"Jerome sends me pictures of the latest casualties," Claudia said, without looking at Rupe. "Whenever one of us goes out the other is on WhatsApp the whole time. It's like having a baby together." She shot a smile at her ex-husband. "Or what I imagine it would be like if there were two of you doing the parenting," she added sweetly.

"Where is my son?" Rupe looked around.

"He'll be here soon. He and Mia were about to leave when I spoke to them this morning."

"I can't wait to see him." Ellie put an ice-filled glass back into Claudia's hand. "Hope that's strong enough."

Claudia laughed. "So do I, sweetie. That's why I came on the train…"

"You all get on then?" said Anna to Clare when Claudia had drifted outside.

"Oh yes. She's a character but she's family. I get on with her better than Rupe does. Do you have stepchildren?"

Ellie had given Clare a potted biography. She knew Anna also had a much older husband, with whom Ellie had been very taken.

Anna shook her head. "Jeremy came baggage-free, I am pleased to say." She threw her head back and laughed. "Gosh, I didn't mean that the way it sounded… I wasn't meaning to suggest Claudia…"

Clare laughed too. "Rupe would think that hilarious." She held up the bottle she was clutching in invitation. "He's had all sorts of names for her in the past. But they shake along OK these days. We only really see her at weddings and funerals. And big birthdays," she added, pouring a drink for Anna. "I think the last time was Danny's thirtieth. And—" She paused as a loud shriek of delight came from Ellie in the hallway. "I think he has arrived."

Chapter Twenty-Nine

E verybody she'd expected was now there, Clare thought, looking around the garden. She'd asked Mrs P from next door but she'd said she'd be quite happy to listen from a distance. Josh had handed a glass of champagne and a plate of Ellie's canapés over the fence, and there was now plenty to hear.

Josh had put his boom box on the edge of a raised flower bed and it was belting out Shirley Bassey. Clare guessed Meg had been putting in requests from the Spotify playlists. Their friends were laughing and talking in groups or sprawled on sunloungers or in folding chairs. Claudia was sitting next to Tom, talking intently; Nikhita was with Chrissy and Ange – no doubt being cross-examined. Rupe was in the middle of a group of their one-time employees. Polly stood closest to him. Clare hadn't spoken to her yet, other than to wave a self-conscious hello. She would find an opportunity before too long.

She felt peculiarly removed from the action, slightly

light-headed. She'd had two glasses of vintage cava. She probably needed to eat now. The air was full of the scent of burgers but Rupe appeared to have given up cooking and a man called Stuart that he'd once played tennis with was wielding the tongs. Clare went across to the barbecue and the platter beside it and put a cooked sausage on a bamboo plate.

As she looked across at her husband, Polly met her eyes, her face straight, expression unreadable. Clare tried to throw out a smile but could feel her lips, despite her best efforts, twist with the undertones of a snarl.

In the dining room, it looked as if the locusts had been. Clare picked up a bread roll and began to break it open, stopping as Polly walked in. She looked hesitantly at Clare, who waved an arm at the table. "What would you like? There's more cooked chicken and burgers outside too…"

"I was just going to get some salad."

Clare moved the bowl towards her. "I'm so glad you could come," she said pleasantly. "I thought it would be nice for Rupe to see some old faces." Rupe had looked bemused to see his one-time PA there, neatly dressed as always in a fitted black skirt and short-sleeved blouse. For a split second, to Clare's intense relief, he hadn't known who it was – Clare could see that. Polly's hair was shorter and she'd allowed the grey to come through. Then he'd recovered and swept Polly into a hug, blustering about the good old days – how she'd always kept him on the straight and narrow.

Polly took the wooden servers. "I was very surprised,"

she said, her eyes downwards as she picked up leaves. "I wouldn't have expected you to include me."

"Why ever not?" Clare kept her voice even. "You were a part of our company and I knew Rupe would love to see everyone again."

"Oh. I wondered whose idea it was."

"It was mine. I don't think Rupe would know how to get hold of you these days." Clare's voice held a slight question to it that she hadn't intended.

"No, he probably wouldn't." There was a small pause. "I've been waiting to see if you would speak to me." Polly scooped up onion and tomato and looked directly at Clare.

"Sorry, I've been—"

"Nothing ever happened, you know," said Polly conversationally. "I know you thought it did, and I suppose I sort of wanted you to. I had a bit of a crush on him." She gave a short, brittle laugh. "That old falling-in-love-with-your-boss chestnut. But he didn't see me like that. He liked me – I was good old Polly. Polly Whatever-would-I-do-without-you? But that was all."

Clare looked back. She could feel her heart beating.

"And he'd take me for a drink after work sometimes – but only to talk about work. Or you."

So she'd not imagined it all. Clare knew she hadn't ever been told about these drinks. If Rupe had mentioned going to the pub, he would have made it sound as if it were a group of them.

"Really?" she asked tightly.

"Yes – you were never long out of the conversation. It

was always Clare thinks this, and Clare says that … and eventually, Clare can do your job instead…"

"It wasn't like that."

"It was and that's OK. Why wouldn't he want his wife running everything with him?"

"Presumably because he chose to go to the pub with another woman rather than coming home to her!" Oh God, why had she said that so sharply? It was years and years ago. But she had been right. She had *known*… "I'm sorry," she began. "I didn't mean… I had two young children," she finished. "It was a difficult time…"

Polly was nodding. "Well, thank you for having me," she said. "I must say my goodbyes." She left her salad on the table.

As she walked away through the kitchen, Ellie appeared in the doorway from the hallway. She was looking at Clare in disbelief.

"Mum! What the fuck are you playing at?"

"Nothing. We were just talking."

"You were accusing her. Is that why you invited her? Because you thought she had an affair with Dad?"

"No, no." Clare was shaking her head. How long had Ellie been hovering out there?

"Mum, I heard you!"

"She brought it up, not me."

Ellie's eyes narrowed. "Don't you ruin this."

Clare stared into the mirror in her en suite. Her heart was still thumping. Even if Rupe had been having an affair, Ellie would probably take his side, find a way to make it her mother's fault.

Her daughter's words about ruining things still stung. Clare had done everything she could to make today go well and everybody was enjoying themselves. A few more people had left but there was still a small crowd in the garden. She could hear their voices and laughter floating up from here. She remembered that Ellie had got a cake. She'd go back down and speak to her about it. They could light the candles together and maybe Ellie would smile at her again. Clare would get out more fizz. Figs would help hand it round and Nikhita would too. Clare would propose a toast. Say some nice words about Rupe. She would show Ellie she loved him and that she wouldn't have said a word about the past if Polly hadn't...

The early evening sun beat in through the bathroom window. Clare took off her shirt and changed into a linen vest top, adjusting her pearls. She put on more lipstick and fluffed up her hair, spraying herself with perfume. She went downstairs in her bare feet, breathing deeply. As she reached the hall, Chrissy came out of the downstairs loo. "Great party!" she said. "Lovely food."

Clare rearranged some of the platters on the table, clearing away empty ones, making what was left look less decimated. Through the open kitchen door, she could hear Rupe's voice and gales of laughter. She should go outside and join in. She threw some bamboo plates in a paper sack in the kitchen and picked up a clean glass. The buckets outside the door needed replenishing. Figs came over to her. "Where have you been?"

"Oh, I was just clearing up a bit." Dire Straits was playing. Josh sat on the low wall, his arm around Nikhita's shoulders. Ellie was leaning against Tom. Rupe was listening to Meg, with a large glass of wine in his hand – his face was red, but he looked happy. The two men from Ellie's school, Nick and Simon, were sitting nearby smiling at whatever Meg was saying. Anna was at the far end of the patio, talking to Claudia.

"That can wait till later," Figs was frowning at her. "Are you all right?"

"I spoke to Polly," Clare said in a low voice. "Nothing ever happened."

Figs shook her head. "Well, of course it didn't! I told you that. So now relax. Sit down and have a drink."

Clare looked at the bottle bucket. "I wanted some cava…"

"I'll get it."

Clare nodded. She sat in the chair Figs had vacated. Tom smiled across at her. He mouthed, "You OK?" Ellie looked at her, expressionless. Clare beckoned her over.

"What?"

"When do you want to do the cake?"

"Oh!" Ellie looked around. "Soon?"

"I'll go and see how much fizz we've got left. Do you want to get it out on a plate? There are some candles in the top cupboard…"

"I'll wait a minute," Ellie said in a softer tone. "Dad's just gone in."

Clare got up feeling lighter. The Polly exchange was unfortunate – especially Ellie earwigging half of it – but she'd gone now and they wouldn't see her again. Soon they'd be singing 'Happy Birthday' and raising their glasses to Rupe. She'd make sure to mention all the work Ellie had put into the party…

Clare walked into the kitchen. Rupe wasn't there. The door to the utility room was slightly open. Clare pushed it wider and went in. Figs was standing at the big fridge; the door was open, she had a bottle under one arm, and was reaching inside. Rupe was behind her. Clare stood stock still, mouth open, as she watched her husband's hand close in a familiar gesture around her sister's left buttock.

Chapter Thirty

C lare stared, not breathing, waiting for Figs to swing round, to shout, to slap him maybe, to tell Rupe to keep his fucking hands to himself.

But Figs barely moved. Her free hand came back, waving vaguely into thin air. Clare heard her say calmly, "Behave," and Rupe give a throaty chuckle.

She heard herself make a strange shrill noise in her own throat and then they both swung round. Rupe looked as if he'd been shot.

"What the hell are you doing?"

Rupe said "Nothing" at the same time as Figs rolled her eyes and said, "He's just pissed."

"Oh!" Clare's voice rose. "Is that what you always do when you've had a few drinks? Grope my sister?"

"I wasn't—"

"You were. I saw you!"

"Does he?" she demanded, staring at Figs. "Does he always try it on when he's drunk?"

"Clare, Rupe was not trying it on." Figs sounded as if she were addressing a child. "He was just being..." she stopped. Rupe continued to gape at Clare – looking almost comically aghast, as if it were she who had done something unthinkable.

"He was just messing around," Figs finished. "He's had too much to drink."

"We all have – but we're not all fondling each other!" Clare glared. "Or is there more to this? Is there something going on between you? Is that it?"

"Clare!" Figs looked angry now. "Do not be ridiculous."

Rupe looked horrified. "No, no, darling."

"Do not call me that!" Clare was shouting now.

"This would explain everything!" she shrieked, as suddenly Angie was in the doorway. "You don't want to sleep with me, but you're happy to put your hands all over my sister's arse! Well, don't let me stop you. Have a go at the other one, too. Angie, do you want to be touched up as well? Get in line and Rupe will no doubt oblige!"

"What is going on here?" Angie looked around the small room. "Figs, what have you done?"

"Bloody hell, Ange. Why does it have to be me?" Figs shook her head. "Rupe put his hand on me while I was leaning into the fridge. For a joke! And Clare—"

"A joke?" Clare screeched.

"Look, he's always done it, haven't you?" Figs scowled at Rupe. "When he's pissed, he pats my bum. It doesn't mean a thing and usually I slap him one but I had my hands full."

"I was watching," said Clare furiously. "You didn't move."

"Probably because it barely registers and it doesn't matter."

"It does to me! Now I know why you encouraged me to leave him! Why you wanted me to move into your flat in London."

"What?" Rupe was staring in disbelief from Clare to Figs. "When was this?"

"Stop!" Figs yelled. "Now you really are being fucking stupid. I offered you that so you could calm down. Because I wanted to *save* your marriage. Anyone can see you're made for each other."

"I didn't even know about this!" Rupe was sounding affronted.

"It was fucking years ago," said Figs. "The kids were small. You were being a twat."

"Shagging Polly probably," put in Clare. Rupe's eyes widened.

"Mum!" Ellie had pushed her way into the tiny room too. "What is wrong with you? People can hear you shouting. Are you going mad?" Her voice was thick with fury. "Why are you obsessed with that Polly? She's already driven her out," Ellie said to Angie. "Is she having some sort of breakdown?"

Clare felt the rage swell inside her chest. "It is not me!" she snarled at Ellie. "Ask *them* what they've been doing!" She jabbed a finger at Figs and Rupe, who still stood frozen in front of the open fridge. Then she shoved past Angie back into the kitchen. Anna was looking at her in concern.

"What's happened?" she said, as Tom and Chrissy appeared behind her. Through the window Clare could see the remainder of the guests looking towards the house.

"I'm having a fucking breakdown apparently," she said loudly. "According to my daughter. Because no matter how badly anybody else behaves, it is *all down to me*." She yanked open the door of the kitchen fridge and pulled a bottle of white wine out, holding it up to see what was left. Then she sloshed the remainder of it into a tall glass and took a big swallow.

"What's the matter?" Tom asked. "What's Ellie said?"

"I've said she's bang out of order," Ellie was at his side. "And she is."

Clare was trembling. "I've done nothing wrong." She pulled open the dishwasher, needing something to do, and began putting the empty plates she'd cleared into it, dropping cutlery into the rack with a clatter.

"You never wanted this party." Ellie's voice was low and angry. "And you were obviously determined to spoil it. You had a go at that poor woman and now you're screaming at Auntie Figs. Dad's really upset…"

"*I'm* really upset," said Clare, her voice breaking. "Doesn't that matter at all?"

"Not really! Because you caused it."

Clare's eyes filled at the injustice. She straightened up, keeping her back to Ellie so she wouldn't see. "You don't even know what happened. Why do you always think the worst of me?"

"Oh great! So you're going to be the martyr now, are you?"

"Stop it," Tom said. "This is not helping."

"Don't take her side," said Ellie. "Don't let her fool you."

Clare swung across the kitchen and collected more dirty glasses from the island, gathering several to her. "Go away, Ellie," she said. "I don't know why you are being so nasty but—"

"Probably because you're drunk." Ellie was standing in front of her now.

"I bet I've had less to drink than any of you," Clare said hotly. As she went to side step around her daughter, a glass slipped from her grasp, and shattered on the terracotta tiles.

"Fuck!" she said, as Ellie snapped, "Looks like it!"

Clare saw Anna spring forward towards the debris. "It's OK, I'll do it," Anna said. Clare bent forwards at the same time and they almost collided. Clare stood up again quickly, catching her necklace on the knob of a drawer. As she pulled away from it, the string snapped and a shower of pearls bounced across the kitchen in all directions.

"Oh fuck, fuck, fuck!" Clare leaned her hands on the work counter and burst into tears.

She felt arms go around her and then Tom was speaking calmly into her hair. "It's OK. You're OK..."

Dimly she heard Anna asking where she could find a dustpan and Ellie saying, "She's ruined everything. I knew she would."

"Stop it, Ellie," Tom said again, and then Clare was sobbing into his shoulder, while Ellie was saying crossly. "Don't do that. Leave her to it."

And Tom was still holding Clare tightly as he said, startling her with his quiet rage. "For Christ's sake, Ellie!

You're the one causing a scene here. Stop going on right now. And grow up!"

Angie shut the door of the utility room and leant against the inside of it.

Rupe groaned.

"What are you two playing at?" Angie said, looking from Rupe to Figs. "As if I need ask."

"Nothing at all," said Figs. "As you very well know. Rupe was doing his Benny Hill routine and Clare walked in."

"Idiot," said Angie. "And why do you let him?"

"I don't," said Figs. "Or I don't even notice."

"You've always been a scrubber."

"Ange!"

"I was just being—" said Rupe, looking stricken. "I didn't mean…"

"I know," said Figs, wearily. "I'll go and talk to Clare."

"Leave her alone," said Angie. "Tom's got it. You get out there and get rid of everyone else. I'll deal with this. Go on!" she said, as Figs hesitated. "I'll sort it." She opened the door just enough for Figs to get through it and then leant on it again.

"Not you," said Rupe.

"Me," said Angie. "Tough."

"Don't have a go at me."

"Why ever not?" Angie shook her head. "Tell me what's going on."

"Nothing. You know me and Figs – we're mates."

"Hmmm. So what did Clare mean? About you not sleeping with her?"

"I don't um... I can't discuss it with..."

Angie addressed him sternly. "Tell me, Rupe. Right now."

Figs had hoovered up the last fragments of glass but Anna was still on her hands and knees, filling a freezer bag with the final stray pearls.

Clare sat at the dining table staring at the remains of a cheeseboard, as Josh and Nikhita cleared up silently around her. Tom put a coffee in front of her and sat down opposite. Ellie had disappeared. "What can I do?" he said softly.

She shook her head. "I don't know," she said brokenly. "I just want to crawl into a hole."

He leant across the table and squeezed her arm briefly. "It will all seem better tomorrow."

"I'm so embarrassed. Everyone will think I'm mad."

"Nobody thought anything," Tom said. "They'd all had a really good afternoon. Your mother has ensured total confusion by telling everyone something different and they were all so smashed they won't remember tomorrow anyway."

Clare gave a weak smile. "What did she say?"

"Oh, that you'd had bad news, Rupe had food poisoning, Figs had an injury, there was a life-threatening gas leak... Believe me, nobody will have a clue what went on when they wake up tomorrow. They'll just remember the amazing food…"

"That poisoned someone!"

"There are still some of those brilliant burgers outside. Shall I get you one?"

Clare shook her head. "No, thank you."

Anna came through from the kitchen. "I can restring these. I used to make jewellery as a hobby."

"I don't want them," said Clare. "Thank you for picking them up but you can throw them away now. Or have them yourself. They'll always remind me of this bloody disaster of a day. And—" Her voice broke and she swallowed hard.

"No reason to waste a perfectly good necklace!" Meg appeared in the doorway. "Heavens, if I'd thrown away every trinket I'd been wearing whenever your father was being tricky, I wouldn't have anything left." She waggled her wrists, jangling her many bracelets as if to illustrate the point. "What's his Lordship done anyway? You were all making such a racket I couldn't get to the bottom of it."

"Nothing worth bothering with, Mum." Figs came in behind her. "It was all a misunderstanding. Just the drink taken."

"Well, you all drink so much!" Meg pushed out her lips in disapproval. "It makes you cranky. I still remember your fortieth. That all ended in tears."

Figs frowned. "No, it didn't! That was just Ange sounding off as usual. She had a row with our neighbour about beef production," she added to Tom. "He made the mistake of saying vegans always looked very pale, and what they needed was a nice juicy steak. Ange gave him

326

both barrels. Animal exports, welfare standards, effects of methane on the environment, you name it. She had him pinned against the wall in our kitchen with her hands practically around his throat. We had to separate them in the end."

Meg gave a loud cackle. "Don was trying to get everyone to shut up so he could make a nice speech, and that man shouted, 'Are you seriously trying to tell me the world's going to end because cows fart?'"

She looked at Tom. "There's always commotion in this family," she said. "You'd better get used to it."

Meg swung her gaze onto Clare. "And so should you. You must know what he's like by now. No point coming over all sensitive after all these years."

"Well, it's over now," said Figs briskly, as Clare shook her head in disbelief.

"Where's Claudia and Danny and Mia?" she asked.

"Down the garden," said Figs. "They're waiting to say goodbye. Danny's going to run Claudia to the station."

Clare took a deep breath. "I'll go and see them." She hesitated. "And Rupe? Is he there?"

"No. Ange hasn't let him out yet."

———

Angie looked calmly at her brother-in-law. "I'm not surprised you can't get it up," she said, "with the amount you drink. If you cut that down, you might not even need the pills. Didn't the doctor say that? Didn't Clare?"

"She doesn't know."

look over her shoulder. "She's still very attractive you know, plenty of men..." She gave him another meaningful look. "So you get your act together. You're not ninety. Use it or lose it, Rupe. And if you can't use it," she finished sharply, "at least buy her a vibrator."

———

Half an hour later, Angie stood in the doorway of Ellie's bedroom, surveying her niece. Ellie was under her duvet. She'd been crying.

"I hate them both," she said, her voice muffled. "Tom was so horrible. And Mum is being completely—"

"So you leave them all to sort themselves out and you come home with me," said Angie. "Chrissy and I are leaving in a moment. Pack an overnight bag and come home and we'll drink tea with brandy in it and watch some shit on television. You can stay in my spare room."

"But Tom—"

"Shouldn't have spoken to you like that, so you take control. Come downstairs and straight out of the house without speaking to him. Chrissy's only had one drink. She'll drive." Angie grasped the corner of the duvet and shook it. "Send him a text from the car. Say, 'I've grown up all right, pal. It's over.'"

Ellie gasped.

"I know you all take the piss because I've made a career from falling out with people," said Angie. "But I've learnt a few things along the way. He'll be round here grovelling by morning, and you, my lovely niece, will be elsewhere."

Clare looked at the table in the hall covered in Rupe's presents. Nearly everybody had bought him booze. There was whisky and red wine and champagne in various coloured bottle-bags. A box of chocolates was a lone non-alcoholic gift.

"You know he gets cuddly when he's had a few," Figs had said, pushing her way into Clare's bedroom, when Clare had fled upstairs. "You've seen it."

Clare surveyed her ravaged face in the bathroom mirror. "Yes, he hugs you or puts an arm round you. I didn't know he felt you up."

"He doesn't really. It's just a ... jokey gesture. Really." Figs had looked at her appealingly. "Rupe adores you. He's terrified now of losing you. He wouldn't last five minutes if you left him."

"He's got an odd way of showing it." Clare turned and looked at Figs. "He hasn't wanted sex with me for months. So imagine how I felt when I saw him touching you." She felt her eyes fill with tears again, and grabbed angrily at a tissue.

Figs frowned. "Are you sure? You said he was driving you mad being here all the time. Maybe he thinks *you* don't..."

"Of course I'm fucking sure! He avoids it like the plague." She gave a short, sharp laugh. "And there's nothing like not having it on offer to make one want..."

"Tell me about it," said Figs. "That's why I went a bit

crazy over Dave. I was that close to—" She held her finger and thumb a few millimetres apart.

"But you aren't going to now?"

"No. I said I wouldn't, didn't I? I phoned Don instead. Told him to get his arse home next weekend..."

Nikhita lay on the top of Josh's quilt with her head on his shoulder. He had one arm around her and was holding her hand with the other.

"You can see how mad and dysfunctional they all are now," he said.

"Best afternoon I've had all year."

Josh sighed. "What would your mother have said?

Nikhita twisted round and smiled at him. "My parents have their moments, believe me. My mother threw a huge wooden pepper grinder at my father's head once when he was annoying her. He ducked and it smashed into a shelf and broke a load of china. And he had to clear it up!"

"Talking of believing," said Josh diffidently. "Did you mean what you said to my dad?"

"What, about loving you?"

"Mm."

Nikhita lay back again and looked at the ceiling. "No, I was lying through my teeth."

As he exhaled, she burst into one of her riotous bouts of laughter. "Josh! Are you crazy? Of course I did!"

Chapter Thirty-One

"I'm so glad you called." Tom stood in the doorway of the downstairs kitchen of the semi-converted house and looked searchingly at Clare. She leant against the newly installed units that were still covered in a fine film of plaster dust, and breathed deeply.

"Of course I did. I needed to see you."

"And I—"

"To give you this." She picked up a folder from the pile of tiles on the work surface and handed it to him. "Everything's in there to show you exactly where I'm up to with the project because obviously … I cannot work for you anymore."

He looked at her gravely. "I thought you might feel like that, but I wish…"

Clare shook her head. "Oh, Tom, why did you have to do that? Ellie didn't mean what she said. It was my sister with her big mouth."

"But I did." Tom's voice was quiet but resolute. "When I

got the phone message saying it was over, I felt a bit sad. I felt bad it had come to that, bad that Ellie was upset. But most of all I just felt … relief."

"Why?" Clare burst out. "You've only been together a few months. If you didn't mean it, why did you buy her a ring?"

"Because she so wanted one."

Clare stared at him. "She thinks this is all my fault."

"Well, it is in a way."

"What?"

Tom looked around the room. "Getting to know you has made me realise … Ellie is bright and beautiful and sweet and fun but increasingly she has felt, well, young. I've become aware I do need someone my own age. I need to have the sort of conversations I have with you." He'd stopped surveying the various building materials and was watching her steadily. "And over the weeks of talking to you and being with you, I have begun to feel—"

"No!" Clare's voice was sharp.

"You must have felt us drawing closer."

"No," she said again. "Don't say it. Don't even think it. Do not let any sort of thought about us enter any corner of your mind." She was shaking. "We've been friendly because you are – were – the boyfriend of my daughter and I have been working for you, which has now ended. There was nothing more. What sort of monster mother do you think I am?"

"Of course you're not. You're—"

"Don't you say any of this to Ellie."

"No, no, I won't." Tom shook his head. "I just said I

thought the age gap was too much and that I didn't think it would work long-term. She's coming round in a day or two to get her stuff and I said we would talk then and I'd explain more."

"You do this properly," said Clare emotionally. "You get it right. You don't break my daughter's heart any more than you have already."

"I'll do my best. Clare, can't we still be friends? Can't you…?" He indicated the folder.

"No. We can't. My daughter won't speak to me because of you and I can never see you again."

Tom looked at her sadly. "I feel a greater sense of loss hearing you say that than I do breaking up with—" He put his hands up defensively as Clare hissed with annoyance. "I'm sorry," he went on, "but it's true. I've loved getting to know you. And Rupe too, of course. And Josh. But you, you're funny and sharp and so clever and … I've really begun to look forward to seeing you and I think you have too."

"No," said Clare again. "All I know is that my sister tells me that my daughter was sobbing her heart out and I was not the person she wanted to see to comfort her. She won't return my texts. She holds me entirely responsible. I need you to make sure she knows this has *nothing* to do with me."

"I will make sure," said Tom. "But it won't be true."

"Make it true," Clare insisted. "Tell her that if Saturday hadn't happened, you would still have been having misgivings about the future. That you were already feeling the age difference."

"Well, I was. But when I put my arms around you..."

Clare looked around the kitchen she would not see finished. Downstairs, she heard the plumber that she would not banter with again coming through the front door, calling out to his mate.

"I'm going now," she said.

———————————

Clare sat in her car, trembling, her mind swinging from visions of Tom's dark eyes looking sadly at her and the thought of her daughter crying into Angie's pillow. There was a time when she'd have been lying on Clare's bed, weeping. When Clare was her first port of call for any anxiety or worry that wouldn't go away.

And even when she was out of her teens, when she'd got a job and her new friends, Clare always knew what was going on. When Janine was being annoying, when the students wouldn't listen, when Ellie was too tired to do another weekend trip and felt hard done by. She had sent Clare strings of WhatsApps with the minutiae of her day. Had sat on a kitchen stool and shared her irritations and small joys. Before Tom.

Clare felt sick as she remembered how she had felt when Tom had taken her into his arms, and talked soothingly to her. Had sat with her, talking quietly, assuring her everything would be OK. She remembered them laughing in the attic together, only days earlier, arguing over what to do with the junk. She had seen then the warmth in his eyes.

She hoped their paths would never cross again. She

336

would stay away from this part of Ramsgate, would not go to Margate Old Town. She could never, ever see him again.

Clare pulled her phone from her handbag and searched for the number of the school, willing her voice to remain steady as she waited to be put through. "Oh, Anna," she said in a rush when the extension was answered. "Please, please can you help me?"

Chapter Thirty-Two

There are times when I wake first and look at him sleeping, his face turned towards the morning light, and I almost feel afraid because how can joy like this last? We have promised each other that nothing will ever break us apart, that ours is an unshakable bond that will last for ever. But sometimes fear strikes me in the pit of my stomach and I imagine how, if it were all to suddenly crumble, I could possibly survive without him. They always say life goes on, but I don't know how I could even put one foot in front of the other, if he should ever leave me...

Ellie looked very young and very wretched. Anna wanted to hug her.

"You are strong," she said. "You will be OK."

Ellie scrubbed at her face with a ball of damp tissue. "I just can't believe he's done this to me," she said for the third or fourth time.

"But better now," said Anna gently. "If he didn't have confidence it would work long-term, it was right to end it now."

"He said we could get married!" Ellie broke into fresh tears. "Why would he say that and then finish with me?"

"I'm sure he meant it at the time."

"I don't understand how he could change so quickly."

Ever since she'd persuaded Ellie to come and stay with her for a few days – not a difficult task as she was clearly not overly comfortable at her aunt's – Anna had had the same conversation several times, and was not progressing very well with her promise to Clare to try to get Ellie to see reason about returning home.

"People do change," said Anna now. "They feel one thing at the start, when it's all heady and exciting, and then when it all settles down, that's the real test."

Anna was aware of Jeremy coming into the room as she said it. She heard the wheels of his Zimmer, his breath laboured from the exertion. She kept her eyes on Ellie. "One day," she said, "you will see it was the right thing."

"But now," Ellie sobbed. "What do I do now? Suppose I see him out? Suppose he's with somebody else. I can't bear it. I need him to move away so I can't ever see him again."

"Well, I guess he's got his business to run," said Anna reasonably. "And you probably won't see him. Think of all those years he was in Margate before you met him. You hadn't ever bumped into him before."

"It's not that long. He's only been here a few—"

"Well, I expect he'll think of you and keep away from places he thinks you'll be."

"But I will know he's there," said Ellie, her voice rising to a wail. "I'll be always worrying about seeing him. Why can't he go to Australia or China?"

Jeremy had pulled out a chair and was lowering himself down on to it, breathing hard. He cleared his throat and spoke to Ellie. "Why don't you go instead?"

Ellie, sniffing, stared at him.

"You were telling me you wished you'd done more travelling. You've got a teaching qualification. Go and get a job somewhere abroad! You can't change what he does, but you can take control yourself." Jeremy shrugged. "And I'll still go and give him a good hiding if you want me to."

Ellie gave him a watery smile.

Anna smiled too. Although it was sad to see Ellie so upset, they were both enjoying having her there. Jeremy, in particular, seemed brighter and more interested in life with Ellie around. And Ellie seemed to recover a little when she and Jeremy played scrabble or watched old films together. She was crying again now but last night when they'd put on *Crocodile Dundee* – one of Jeremy's absolute favourites – she had actually laughed.

"Thank you," she said now. "Thank you both for looking after me."

"We like it," said Jeremy. "Anna's relieved to have someone else to cook for. I don't eat enough."

"Nobody's eating enough!" said Anna. "Shall we have some of my cake?"

She'd been baking ever since Ellie arrived, always asking Ellie to help her, more in a desperate attempt to distract her young friend than because she and Jeremy needed a tray of flapjacks, two carrot cakes, and a chocolate and coconut sponge.

"And it's time we started that drama Marcus said we should watch," said Jeremy. "Now I'm a fully-fledged operator of Netflix" – here he winked at Ellie – "I shall go and locate *Ozark* and await my refreshments." He beamed at Anna. "Can we have tea too?"

He levered himself out of the chair. Ellie waited until he had pushed his Zimmer along the hallway, its wheels rattling slightly as it clonked off the long mat and onto the polished wood.

"He is so lovely," she said emotionally, getting up to fill the kettle as Anna opened a large square patterned tin. "He always makes me feel better."

Anna remembered how she used to say the same. How, when she got stressed with the kids, or work, or her mother when she was still alive, Jeremy would always put everything back into proportion. "It doesn't *matter*," he would say, or "Who cares really?" He would talk about something else, make her laugh, suggest an outing; tell her to forget it, to dismiss it, or occasionally a heartfelt "Fuck that for a game of soldiers" would be the end of the matter.

"You know," said Ellie, "that first night when I told everyone about marrying Tom, and you said…"

Anna nodded. "I still feel shame when I think of that."

"Don't do it?" finished Ellie. "Well, I haven't done it obviously and I can see now that it was too soon and it was all a bit of a fantasy, but you … married Jeremy. Were you just having a bad day when you said that? You're not really sorry you did it?"

Anna paused before answering. Tried to keep her voice level and calm. "I found my old diary recently," she said. "I wrote in it every day in the first years of my relationship with Jeremy. I couldn't believe my luck. He was everything I wanted and I was so in love with him. I honestly believed I would never regret a moment of it."

She stopped again and lowered her voice. "And although there have been times when it has been challenging" – Anna looked away, out of the window – "and I've had regrets about the way things have altered over the years, I still would not change a thing." She spoke more firmly. "I loved him then and I love him still, and age doesn't actually matter a jot. Things are testing now sometimes because of his physical health but not because of the age gap." She looked back at Ellie. "And you are not with Tom now because he wasn't the one, but you will find someone who is and it won't matter how the hell old he is."

"I think," said Ellie hesitantly, "he actually fancied my mum."

"No, no," said Anna briskly. "He just wanted someone very capable – as Clare is – to run his business." She smiled at the younger woman. "Ellie, you will meet someone wonderful who will be absolutely right for you. Tom wasn't that person. Don't blame your mother for any of it."

She watched Ellie pouring hot water onto teabags and thought how Jeremy would have loved a daughter. She'd always wanted boys, but it was good to have Ellie around the place – someone youthful. Even if she did keep bursting into tears. But now Ellie was smiling back at her as Anna handed her a large plate containing a selection of sweet stuff. "I'll bring the tea."

Ellie took the big plate, picked up the three small ones Anna had put on the table, and walked ahead of Anna. Anna put the mugs on a tray and followed.

She heard Ellie's scream bounce down the hallway.

Her voice when it came was shrill with terror.

"ANNAAAAAAA!"

Chapter Thirty-Three

"**P**lease don't keep trying to blame me," said Clare tightly.

"I'm not," said Rupe. "I am only trying to explain. You're angry and I'm trying to get you to listen to me so you understand and then perhaps we can stop walking around each other and you can stop scowling at me and we can get back to normal."

"Huh!" Clare glared at him. "I don't even know what that is. Do you mean that normal where it's OK to grope my sister?"

Rupe shook his head. "I don't fancy your sister. You *know* I don't. She's family; she's a mate. We mess around. I probably shouldn't touch her – I don't know why I do – but honestly, it's like clapping her on the back. It's not sexual."

"Of course it is! Everything between men and women is." She felt a flash of shame and guilt. Had it been between her and Tom?

Rupe was still talking – fast, urgently. "It really isn't. She told you that. And I will never, ever, do it again. Ever." Rupe looked downcast. "I love you. Not Figs. And certainly not that Polly – I never for one moment entertained... I don't know how you could think that. Clare, I am telling you the most honest truth here. I have never, ever, thought for a single moment about any other woman but you for twenty-six years. You are all I want. Don't upset our whole marriage over me being an idiot. Figs is just..." He shrugged hopelessly.

"This isn't even about Figs," said Clare. "It's about you lying to me."

"I did not lie to you," said Rupe immediately. "I just didn't tell you. In fact, I did tell you. You knew I was going to the Well Man Clinic and I said—"

"You said everything was fine."

"Well, it was fine. They said, overall, I was in pretty good shape."

"With high blood pressure. That's the sort of thing you tell your wife, Rupe." She glared again. "And you particularly tell her you're impotent."

She saw Rupe wince. "I wasn't sure," he said, "but it seemed—"

"And you don't let her think that you're just not interested in her anymore," continued Clare over the top of him. "Because I was getting to the point when I wasn't even sure I cared. Do you know why I invited Polly to your party? Because I wanted to see if it would make me jealous seeing you together. If I could rekindle those feelings of your being mine, the man I loved for life and for whom I'd fight anyone to the bitter end."

She stared at him, breathing hard.

"And did it?" he asked with interest.

"No! You've carried on being the bloody annoying bloke who never goes out anywhere, and drives me mad hanging round the kitchen, and who I don't even get the compensation of sex with!"

"I told you I've cut the dose down and I think it might be a bit better now. I said we could…"

"*I don't want to now!*" she shouted.

Rupe looked at her for a long moment and then he suddenly grinned. Bizarrely, she felt her own mouth twitch.

"Oh darling," Rupe tried to put his arms around her. "I do love you. What shall I do then?"

Clare burst into noisy tears as Rupe hugged her clumsily. Her voice, when it came, was a wail. "Tell me what to do about Ellie!"

The paramedics were calm and reassuring. They said Anna could go in the ambulance. Ellie would follow in the car.

Anna sat back on the small fold-down seat, feeling the bounce of the ambulance, listening to the wave of the siren, looking from Jeremy's grey face to the concentration of Antoni bending over him.

"Will he be OK?" she asked again. *Please don't die, not now…*

"He is stable," the kind Polish paramedic replied. "Soon we will be at the hospital."

Anna stared at her husband lying so still. Jeremy had

come round again by the time the ambulance arrived but he hadn't been able to say anything much. There was a trickle of blood on his forehead where he had banged his head on the fireplace.

Anna's long-ago nursing training had deserted her as she'd stood there frozen. It was Ellie who'd dialled 999 and put him into the recovery position.

At the hospital, she was at Anna's side minutes after the curtains had been drawn around Jeremy's cubicle and Anna had been directed to a row of plastic chairs. "What's happening?"

"They're doing an ECG."

Ellie gripped Anna's hand. "He'll be OK, won't he?"

"I don't know."

"I've been praying all the way here."

"That's nice." Anna looked at her. "I didn't know you—"

"I'm not. But as my gran says, you don't get many atheists on a sinking ship." Ellie clapped her hand to her mouth. "Oh my God, I'm sorry. That wasn't good, was it? He's not sinking – he's going to be all right." She took Anna's hand again, as Anna's eyes filled with tears. "What did they say?"

They hadn't said much. Just told Anna to wait and someone would come to see her soon.

Ellie found them coffee that didn't taste of much, from a machine in the waiting room outside, and then they lapsed into silence. Anna's phone was still at home; Ellie's had little signal. "Do you want me to go outside and call anyone?" she asked.

Anna shook her head. "There's no point until we know what to say." It was something she imagined from time to time – having to phone her sons to tell them their father was dead. Stevie would be quiet, shocked, asking a few clipped questions in a flat voice – it always took him a long time to process his feelings. Marcus would be more emotional. He would ask if she was OK, would talk fast and fire questions at her, wanting all the details, perhaps breaking down, telling her he would fly home as soon as he could find a flight. She'd probably have to send him the money for the ticket.

Ellie was sitting close to her. Anna could feel her warmth through the thin cotton of her shirt.

"Mrs Ward?" A man in scrubs stood in front of them, introducing himself. Anna, leaping to her feet, realised she hadn't taken in his name. He was explaining he had carried out an echocardiogram on Jeremy. His voice was almost melodic as he spoke of a faint systolic murmur, a narrowing, and a tight aortic valve. Anna looked at him in silent panic and was grateful for Ellie's hand on her arm and the younger woman's calm questions when Anna found herself unable to speak.

"A couple of days at the most." The doctor smiled for the first time. "Maybe even the next day. We will have to see how things go."

"Thank you," said Anna, finding her voice in a sudden burst. "Thank you so much." She turned to Ellie as he walked away. "Did you get all that?"

"They're going to do a valve replacement on the end of a catheter through the femoral artery in his groin. He says they do them all the time. Sounds scary but it's very straightforward."

"Sounds terrifying," said Anna faintly.

"They're going to do it tomorrow because it's so tight they don't want him to go home like that. But he said he should be fine."

"Only 'should' be?"

"It's just how they speak."

"Oh my God, Ellie."

"I know." Ellie hugged her. "But we can go and see him. You can go and see him," she corrected herself.

"No, come on – we're both going."

Ellie hadn't wanted to go to work but Anna had insisted. It was time, she said, for Ellie to get back to some sort of normality and Anna would text her the moment there was news.

"That school can't manage without both of us!" she'd said briskly, knowing that this time she had to go through the fear on her own. They'd told her that the procedure would take an hour and a half to two hours and that Anna would be able to see Jeremy in the evening when it was all over.

He could be home in a couple of days, all being well.

The surgeon, Professor Weston, was a round, charismatic man in his fifties. He knew who Jeremy was; he told Anna they'd been chatting about their training and Jeremy had been telling him about his days at Charing

Cross Hospital. Professor Weston had trained at Imperial College.

"He knows what he's doing," Jeremy had said to Anna the evening before. "Don't worry."

Anna didn't know how she felt. She was worried, yes, but there was more than that. Her mind was a kaleidoscope of memories – things she hadn't thought about for years. Her and Jeremy up in the middle of the night when Stevie had a fever, walking on the beach in Barbados, drinking in a crowded bar one freezing cold New Year's Eve in Venice, him crying out joyfully that it was a boy when she gave birth to Marcus, even though she knew he'd been secretly hoping for a girl, holding her face in his hands when he asked her to marry him...

I don't know how I could even put one foot in front of the other, if he should ever leave me...

She had fetched her old diary again and marvelled at her younger, rounded writing, so full of passion and love and wonder at her own good fortune. Her certainty that they would be together forever, her fears of losing him...

She'd also brought down her old jewellery-making box – a small wooden chest – that Jeremy had bought her at an auction.

Nigel jumped onto the table, sniffing with interest as she opened each small drawer. As she spread Clare's pearls carefully on a cloth in front of her, he stretched out a paw and batted one to the floor.

Anna laughed. "You couldn't resist that, could you?" The cat arched his back and pushed his head into her hand to be stroked. Jeremy hadn't particularly wanted a cat but had agreed to one because she did. It was she who'd chosen the tiny black kitten from the rescue centre – the runt of the litter – and set up the bed and the toys and the litter tray, had coaxed him to eat minute amounts of the porridge-like sludge she'd got from the vet to build him up.

Jeremy had said he looked like a Nigel – which seemed a daft name for such a teeny scrap, but it had stuck.

She remembered coming in from the garden one day and hearing Jeremy talking to someone in the front room. From his conversational tone, she'd assumed a neighbour had popped in, but there he was with Nigel curled up on the arm of his chair, chatting to him in a perfectly ordinary voice about the lunchtime news. After that, Nigel would always take his naps wherever Jeremy was, and although her husband continued to refer to him as "your cat" she knew he was equally devoted.

Anna's eyes filled with tears at the thought of never seeing them together again. She hastily opened another drawer of the chest and pulled out some French wire. She needed to keep busy...

———————————

Ellie arrived home from work in record time. She hugged Anna, still sitting at the table in the breakfast room. "Still nothing? I got back as quickly as I could. I left the moment lessons were over."

Anna shook her head. "It got put back again – he was the end of the list. He didn't go down till half four. Probably still in there."

Ellie went through into the kitchen. "I'll put the kettle on."

Anna looked at the clock. "I probably won't see him tonight now. He'll be in recovery and then he'll be woozy after the anaesthetic. He won't want me peering at him. I'll go in the morning."

If he's pulled through, she added silently to herself.

"Remember what the surgeon said about how many of these he does?" said Ellie, as if reading her mind.

"Yes, but are they all eighty-six?"

They looked bleakly at one another.

"I'll make you some tea," said Ellie.

"What have you been doing?" she asked, when she put the mug next to Anna. She looked at the wooden box on the table. "That's nice."

"I got all my jewellery stuff out. I've been mending your mum's pearls."

"Oh." Ellie frowned. "I thought Mum said she didn't want them."

"It was something to do. And they're beautiful. I thought I'd do them in a new design for her. And if she still doesn't want them…" Anna shrugged. "I had a load of old beads upstairs – from the old days." She opened the box. "Look!"

She held out the necklace. It was three entwined strands of pearls – the original creamy pearls from Clare's, mixed with more coloured freshwater pearls, interspaced with beads fashioned from turquoise and moonstone, small glass baubles, tiny crystals, and decorative wire balls, finished with an ornate clasp that looked antique.

"God," breathed Ellie, taking it. "That's gorgeous. How did you learn to do that?"

"Evening classes, then practice. I used to make presents for family and friends. One of the mothers from the boys' school was a silversmith who did the craft fairs. She used to sell a few of my pieces."

Ellie was turning the necklace over in her hands. "It's amazing…"

Anna smiled. "I always enjoyed it when friends gave me bags of broken jewellery and I turned them into something new."

Ellie sat down opposite her.

"Anna, I don't want to overstay my welcome – once Jeremy is home, shall I go?"

"No, we love having you here. Jeremy loves you. And I…" Anna hesitated. "Please stay. I need you right now." As she lifted her tea, she realised she was trembling. "Oh, I don't know, maybe I should go to the hospital anyway? Just to be there if – when – he wakes up. In case I can see him, in case I can just look through the door?"

"If you—" Ellie began. Then she clapped a hand to her mouth. "Oh!" They looked at each other in expectation and alarm as on the table between them, Anna's phone began to ring.

Chapter Thirty-Four

Jeremy, the nurses said, was remarkable.

Anna had seen how he had charmed them all. Even the fierce-looking sister beamed at Anna as she came through the ward with a bag of clothes for Jeremy to come home in, and the tin of chocolates he had asked her to bring in for the staff.

As she looked at him now, settled into his chair with Nigel on his lap, she could see the fatigue on his face. But he was a good colour and his breathing was mercifully normal again.

"You must have realised you were getting breathless," she said. "You must have known what it could mean. I only really noticed just before you collapsed. I wish I'd made you go to the doctor for a check-up Why didn't you—?"

Jeremy put up a hand. "It's done now," he said. "And I'm still here."

"Yes," she smiled at him. "And I am so bloody grateful." She bent and kissed him. "I'll make you some tea."

"Wait," he said.

She turned back and looked at him, struck by the tone in his voice.

"Sit down and talk to me for a minute."

Anna sat on the sofa opposite.

"I don't know whether I really want to know the answer to this," Jeremy said. "But it will eat me up if I don't ask."

Anna's heart began to beat more heavily.

"Anna, did you have an affair?"

"No!" There was a flicker of relief across his face and then she saw the look in his eyes and added: "Well, only a small one. Entirely in my head."

He breathed out and nodded. "I'm so glad you didn't deny it because I knew. I saw you go off each day and I saw the clothes and the make-up and the way you couldn't quite look at me."

Anna was suffused with shame. "Were you angry?"

"Worried. I thought, Oh bloody hell, I hope she doesn't leave me."

She moved over to him, sat on the arm of his chair, and gripped his hand. "I would never, never do that."

"I couldn't blame you. You are beautiful and tall and strong and vivacious and ... I am... Look at me. Shrivelled! Fresh out of a hospital bed."

Anna squeezed his hand more tightly. "I love you."

"Do you remember what you said when you were pregnant with Stevie, and I said by the time he goes to school everyone in the playground will think I'm his granddad?"

She nodded. "I said by the time Stevie is at school,

having two parents who love each other and who will be together for ever will be a novelty; people will be looking at that, not how old you are."

He gave a chuckle that became a cough. "And nobody ever did think that. They knew I was his dad."

"Because you looked so young and were so fit and had all your hair."

He gave a wry smile. "She said, all in the past tense..."

"You've still got your hair!" She touched his steel-grey crop. "We were good parents and we loved each other and we still do."

"And what happened to the affair you had in your head?"

"I came to my senses."

"You seemed to be upset."

She pulled a face, embarrassed. "And he turned out to be gay!"

"Oh. Awkward." Jeremy's face broke into a slow grin.

She started to laugh despite herself. "No, I'm glad."

"So am I."

Jeremy had had some toast and gone early to bed with Nigel in attendance. Ellie had opened the bottle of wine she'd brought.

"I'm a bit of a shit cook, but I could make you some pasta or something?" she told Anna.

"It's OK. There's a Chinese five minutes away. Shall we do that for a change?"

"Top comfort food!" Ellie grinned. "I'll go and buy it…"

"Thanks, but just before you do, I went to see your mum today."

"Oh!"

"I took the necklace, and we had a chat. She's really so upset not to be in touch with you. She loves you so much." Anna left Ellie to digest that and swept on. "And I went to see Aaron too. To give in my notice."

Ellie raised her eyebrows. "What did Aaron say?"

"He was shocked. But I'm going to be there three days a week until the end of the year. And I'm going to find my own replacement. Nobody is indispensable." She paused. "In fact, I have thought of just the right person already."

Ellie's hand went to her mouth. She looked as if she might cry.

"Not Mum. Oh Anna, please, not her."

"Janine."

Ellie looked startled, then smiled. "OK, great idea."

"She's kind and good with people, and I think the extra responsibility will really give her a boost – and the extra money will help her. You know, with her mother and everything." Anna smiled back. "I'll enjoy showing her the ropes and it's so much better to have someone who knows the school already."

As Ellie nodded, Anna said quietly: "Although Clare does come into my future plans. We're going to start an online jewellery shop together. Don't look so horrified," Anna went on. "Your mum is going to set up the website and do the admin, and I'm going to make the stuff. We're going to advertise making new pieces out of old as well as

buying up broken vintage jewellery and revamping it."
Anna tried to speak calmly but knew her voice sounded
eager and enthused. "I want to do this," she said. "This feels
very good for me and very right. I can work here – I can be
with Jeremy. Him being ill has been a wake-up call," she
said honestly. "And we all need those sometimes."

Ellie was sitting very still, her shoulders slumped. Anna
had always seen her as fit and strong. Now she looked
fragile.

"Clare hasn't done anything wrong," Anna said quietly.
"She's a good person."

"She's been quite vile to Dad."

"You don't know what goes on inside a marriage unless
you're in it," said Anna firmly. "All relationships have their
ups and downs. "You might get on better with your father
but—"

"Because he's nicer to me!"

"And what has Clare done that isn't 'nice'?"

"Made all that fuss in the beginning being against me
and Tom and then—" Ellie stopped then carried on in a
burst, "And yet later when I heard them talking on the
phone, Tom was talking to her like…" She stopped again.
"Gradually it became as if I was his girlfriend but Mum was
his real *friend*."

"Maybe that shows how it wasn't right between you and
Tom?" Anna said. "You do need to be friends as well.
Because that's what lasts when all that first passion has
calmed down." She went on thoughtfully, "I said age
doesn't make a difference when you asked me the other
day, but that isn't strictly true." She gave Ellie a small smile.

"I could see it clearly, rereading my journals. Jeremy and I worked because he stayed young for a long time and I grew up fast. I didn't do all those things that other girls in their twenties did. I gave that up so we could meet in the middle."

She took a sip of the wine Ellie had poured her and went on. "You told me Tom was annoyed when you stayed out late and got a hangover. Said when you had work the next day, you should be more responsible?"

Ellie nodded.

"A partner your own age might have laughed instead, because he'd done exactly the same thing when it was his turn to get smashed with the boys? Some differences only become more marked. You might have had to give up quite a lot to keep things compatible…"

"Well, I'll never know now." Ellie's voice was flat.

"I think I know," said Anna. "When I did meet my friends, I always felt older than them – as if I was from a different place. I didn't mind," she added quickly. "I loved my life with Jeremy. But it could have been an issue. And from all you've told me, I think it would have been for you."

Ellie sighed. "Jack, a guy I went to school with, keeps texting me after that night I got drunk. Asking me if I've left 'the pensioner' yet." She rolled her eyes. "Wants me to go for a drink."

"Well, perhaps you should," said Anna. "Take your mind off things. You never know," she smiled, "you might enjoy yourself. But," she continued firmly, "the fact that Tom became aware of the gap, that he felt comfortable with your mother because she was nearer his own age, that isn't Clare's fault. Nor is it her fault that she knew that Tom wasn't the one for you."

Ellie looked doubtful. "I thought she was fine with it for a while – when he'd been for a couple of meals…"

"She wanted it to work because she wanted you to be happy," said Anna kindly. "It's all she still wants." As Ellie stayed silent, Anna swept on.

"I'm going back to see her on Saturday. We're going to talk about our plans for the business." As she said it, she was shot through with excitement and pride. "Why don't you come too?" she suggested to Ellie. "Just to break the ice?"

Rupe bent the ice tray back and shot ice cubes across the work surface. He scooped them into two glasses. "I'm going to make you the G&T to end all G&Ts," he said, "and we will toast our long and happy marriage. And then we will go upstairs and I will give you the massage to end all massages." He met her eyes so she could be sure of what he was saying. "And tomorrow I will stop drinking and confine it to the weekends. And I will make an appointment with the GP to discuss my health and medication properly, as I was so eloquently instructed to do by your dear older sister."

Clare nodded.

"In return," Rupe said, "would you please come back to me?"

"I never left."

"Not physically." He sliced into a lemon. "But I need you to be my friend."

"I am your friend," said Clare wearily. "But I need things to change."

"I know."

"I'm going to start this venture with Anna, and I want it to work. I'm going to work at it 24/7 and I need you to support me. I don't want you hanging around the whole time, waiting for me to entertain you. You could do the shopping instead, or put a frozen something in the oven, or go and play tennis again, or join the golf club, for God's sake."

"And maybe I could help you," said Rupe. "You know what a good salesman I am. I'll get your pieces into the big stores…"

"Maybe, later, yes," said Clare. She grinned. "And if you really want to help, you can search the auctions and eBay for materials. And answer the phone. And make me coffee." She stopped and spoke seriously. "But I'll be the boss this time."

Rupe sloshed gin over ice and squeezed in lemon juice with a flourish. He looked at Clare and shook his head in wonder, as if she had misunderstood something fundamental. "You always were."

Chapter Thirty-Five

Anna could hear Jeremy and Ellie laughing as soon as she opened the front door. She walked down the hallway towards the kitchen, stopping at the sight of the breakfast-room table. "Hey, what's this?"

"A bottle of champagne!" said Ellie unnecessarily, indicating the ice bucket. "And I've bought us all sorts of lovely things from M&S. Party food and nibbles."

"I thought you shot off quickly. What are we celebrating?"

"I got the job!"

"Oh wow!" Anna hugged Ellie tight.

"I fly out in January."

"That's fantastic."

"And we've got your birthday present," said Jeremy.

"Oh gosh, that's ages ago now. I wasn't expecting—"

"It's all sorted."

Anna sat down and allowed a glass of champagne to be put in her hands. Ellie brought in two different sorts of pâté,

363

and some houmous and crackers. "The hot stuff has just gone in the oven," she said. She looked at Jeremy. "Go on!"

He was grinning, Anna thought, like a boy, and looked healthier than he had for a long time. His Zimmer wasn't even in the room. "You look very happy," she said curiously. He leant over and opened the drawer of the pine cupboard that housed his whisky. "This is for you."

She opened the envelope. "Oh my goodness."

"First class," said Jeremy proudly. "And I'll get you a car to the airport."

Anna swallowed, turning over the flight confirmation to Vancouver as her eyes filled. "But what about—?"

"Everything's arranged," said Ellie. "You're leaving work at the end of November. There'll be hardly any students left by then and Janine will be ready to take over. I'm going to stay here to look after—" She caught Jeremy's expression and laughed. "Look after *Nigel* and keep Jeremy company," she said deliberately, "while you have three wonderful weeks with Marcus and Rudi and come home in time for Christmas."

"But will you be—?"

"I will be fine," said Jeremy. "I'm too old to go all that way but you can go for both of us. I'll stay here and keep an eye on Ellie!" He grinned. "We can do that Facetime thing. And tell Marcus we'll send him and Rudi tickets to come here in the summer if they can get the time off."

The tears ran down Anna's face. "I don't know what to say."

Jeremy leant over and put a hand on her shoulder. "It was Ellie's idea. A bloody good one, eh?"

"Mum!"

"Up here!"

Josh came up the stairs onto the landing and stopped in surprise in front of his parents' open bedroom door.

"Mum? Oh!"

Josh's eyes darted from Clare in her towelling robe to Rupe still sitting up in bed.

"Um, sorry, I—" he said, looking at the floor, embarrassed.

Clare smiled at him calmly. "Afternoon nap," she said.

"Oh, right. I've got something to tell you," Josh said, leaning in the doorway.

"You're moving out," said Rupe.

"I'm working towards that, yes."

"Oh, shut up, Rupe! You don't have to go anywhere," said Clare. "We love having you at home. Don't listen to your father."

"Well, I will be finding a flat or something at some point, because…" Josh stopped and smiled self-consciously. "I've got a job!"

Clare shrieked. "Oh, darling!" She swept him into a hug. "What is it?"

"Car PR in Ashford. You remember that job I almost got? Where I was down to the last four and they said they'd keep me on file, and we thought it was just something they said? Well, they phoned me up and I had to do another Skype interview and today I went into the office to meet everyone and—"

The words spilled out fast. Clare could not remember when she'd last seen her son look so excited and joyful.

"—And I've got it. I start next month."

"Oh, darling," said Clare again, feeling the tears behind her eyes. "That is just the best news."

"Well done!" Rupe was out of bed, clapping Josh on the shoulder. "I'm going straight downstairs to open the Bolly. Still got a bottle left in the fridge from the party. "Excellent, son, really excellent."

Clare smiled at Josh's expression as he fixed his eyes at a point over Rupe's shoulder.

"Maybe some clothes on first?" she said.

"There's something else," Josh announced, when the three of them were sitting around the breakfast bar in the kitchen, glasses in hand. "I'm getting married."

"What?" Clare tried not to splutter, and failed. "That's sudden."

"It's the only way," said Josh. "Niki and I need to be together and we can't get a flat unless we're all above board and legal. Her parents would be too ashamed." He smiled. "So I'm going up to see her parents this weekend and do the whole ask-her-father bit. Even though she's said yes already," he added happily. "She says they'll be relieved," he explained. "They think she's in danger of being left on the shelf now she's twenty-four."

"An older woman!" said Rupe.

"It's just lovely," said Clare emotionally.

She and Rupe looked at each other as there was a ring on the doorbell.

Josh got up. "That will be Ellie."

Clare's stomach flipped over. "Why isn't she using her key?"

Josh shrugged.

Clare jumped off her stool and hurried past him to the front door.

Ellie's hair was loose and she was wearing jeans and a jacket that Clare hadn't seen before. Clare felt a stab of anguish go through her as Ellie seemed to shrink into it, her eyes wary.

Clare held out her arms. "Oh, darling, I've missed you so much."

"I'm here for Josh. Has he told you?"

"Yes, isn't it wonderful?"

"And he's not too young?" asked Ellie, stiffly.

"He's not too young." Clare paused. "I've thought about it a great deal," she went on in a rush. "It wasn't about the age gap. How could it be?" She made a gesture of pointing at herself. "I think I just felt instinctively, deep down, that Tom wasn't the right thing for you. Call it mother's intuition. I don't know." She stopped and looked appealingly at Ellie.

"I don't know either. Have you seen him?" Ellie looked anxious despite her cold tone.

"No, of course not. Well, only once. To give him all the work stuff back."

Ellie nodded.

"Anyway," said Clare. "I'm very happy for Josh. And I

will be very happy for you too. When it happens."

"I'm going to Peru."

Clare's guts turned in on themselves. "Whoa. What an adventure. Come and tell us all about it." She hugged Ellie again. "I've missed you."

This time she felt her daughter unbend a little.

"I'm sorry I handled it badly," Clare said urgently. "It's been a funny old time. But I love you and I only want you to be happy. You know that, don't you?"

Ellie nodded.

"Come on then. Your father has a bottle of bubbly open…" She smiled. "Of course!"

As they walked through to the kitchen, Clare saw Rupe's face light up. "Poppet!"

"Hello, sis." Josh grinned at her. "Come and have a drink before Dad guzzles it all."

"You all know me so well." Rupe stood up and pulled Ellie into his arms. Ellie wound hers around his neck and hugged him back hard.

And I, thought Clare, standing back and surveying the three of them with a startling rush of joy, *now know us better…*

Acknowledgments

I always aim to write "what I know" but as usual, have depended on kind friends and colleagues to help me out with what I don't.

I am immensely grateful, therefore, to the following kind souls who generously answered my questions for *Old Enough to Know Better*. Thank you so much to Professor Stephen Westaby FRCS (a compelling author himself), all at the Oasis charity shop, Nistha Bhattarai, Judith Haire, Amanda George, Lesley Gleeson, Aneta Idczak, Sharla Lammin and Catherine Pool.

I would also like to thank my wonderful writing friends in our Friday Afternoon Zoom Club – a highlight of this funny old year of Lockdowns – namely Judy Astley, Katie Fforde, Milly Johnson, Catherine Jones, Bernardine Kennedy, Jill Mansell, Janie Millman, AJ Pearce and Jo Thomas for a weekly dose of sanity and laughs, while I was working on this. Janice Biggs for all you do for me. And my son Tom for much hilarity, and being offspring-extraordinaire in so many ways.

Finally, thank you to the brilliant team that is One More Chapter at HarperCollins – especially Kate Bradley my super-skilled editor, Publishing Director Charlotte Ledger and Assistant Editor Bethan Morgan. Never forgetting my inimitable agent, Teresa Chris, for her fearsomeness and unwavering support. Love to you all x

YOUR NUMBER ONE STOP

ONE MORE CHAPTER

FOR PAGETURNING BOOKS

One More Chapter is an
award-winning global
division of HarperCollins.

Sign up to our newsletter to get our
latest eBook deals and stay up to date
with our weekly Book Club!
<u>Subscribe here.</u>

Meet the team at
<u>www.onemorechapter.com</u>

Follow us!
🐦 <u>@OneMoreChapter_</u>
🅕 <u>@OneMoreChapter</u>
📷 <u>@onemorechapterhc</u>

Do you write unputdownable fiction?
We love to hear from new voices.
Find out how to submit your novel at
<u>www.onemorechapter.com/submissions</u>